The Regalus Chronicles:
RISING TIDE

By J.B. JOHNSON

For my wife, who is my partner and my biggest fan. Thank You!
Also, to everyone who helped make this possible. It's been an
interesting journey.

CHAPTER ONE
Zanna

<u>Seven Spires Space Station: Chalpin Star System</u>

Zanna Yuturi had been in this place countless times before in her dreams. She'd walked down this very corridor and had seen the masses of unrecognizable, yet strangely familiar, faces in the crowd. They would stare intently at her, following her every move, willing her forward.

Her body would tremble, and her throat would tighten, but she was never quite sure *why* she was afraid. Despite the fear, an intense resolve always coursed through her veins, steeling her against the overwhelming instinct to turn and run away.

In the dreams, she forced herself to search the faces for her mother and brother, to find something familiar to calm her frayed nerves. She never could find them though, and the fear would persist and eventually give way to outright panic before she inevitably woke, screaming and drenched in sweat. Her mother or father, or sometimes both, would rush to her side to soothe her, and she'd stare up at them with her violet eyes and tell them everything she remembered.

This moment, however, was not a dream. It was undoubtedly real. Her footfalls on the cold metallic floor echoed through the eerie silence. She looked out over the faces in the crowd and they seemed to be staring right through her as if she were merely an apparition. A thought occurred to her. Maybe it was never she that was dreaming. Maybe she'd somehow found her way into the collective dream of the mob. Perhaps she was nothing more than a mental projection of all of their hopes and fears.

Her heart quickened in her chest, and she willed herself to break free of their slumbering thoughts. Deep down she knew the attempt was futile. No one was dreaming.

This is real, she thought. *I'm really doing this.*

She'd trained for this practically her entire life, but she often pondered how much anyone could prepare to be jettisoned into an anomalous hole in space.

How will it feel, and what will I find in there? she wondered.

The three slender fingers on her right hand twitched uncontrollably, and she could feel the tiny bumps forming on her tongue like they always did when her nerves were on edge. She sighed in disappointment. All the training she'd done to enhance her ability to control her emotions seemed for naught. The weight of this monumental moment threatened to crush her.

I'm really doing this, she thought again.

As she walked down the dimly lit corridor, she scanned the crowd again. Her mother and brother were still nowhere to be found. Despair tugged at the fringes of her mind as the realization set in that she may never see them again.

She pictured her mother's broad smile that brought with it a gentle warmth. Hyperthymesia is a feature of the advanced Cortaran brain structure, so Zanna could vividly remember the day she was born. She recalled gazing into her mother's oval-shaped, purple-tinted eyes as she cradled her in the comfort of her bosom, and though she did not yet possess the ability to comprehend their bond, she'd found immense solace in the embrace. Now, as she searched the sea of faces, she couldn't find that smile or those eyes anywhere.

She glanced over her shoulder to peer at the other five youths being escorted behind her. Her eyes met Zarath's, and he offered a shy smile. The Cortaran boy reminded her a lot of her brother Dayvyn, so curious and introspective. She smiled back at him, then craned her neck to look over his head. She couldn't see the others, but she knew they were there. There were always six.

They must be as nervous as I am, she thought.

Her father's voice broke her reverie. "I am so very proud of you," he said.

He'd been escorting her in silence, walking with his arm intertwined with hers. She stared up at him for a long time, wondering if it would be the last time she would lay eyes upon him. He gazed back at her with a pair of close-set, dark-green eyes flecked with purple, and a thought occurred to her.

Why am I never searching for him in my dreams? It's as if I knew he was always right next to me.

The brows below his bulbous, three-lobed cranium furrowed and he asked, "Are you okay?"

"Yes, father," she managed.

She never doubted that he was pleased with her and Dayvyn's accomplishments, but she couldn't remember ever hearing him say he was proud. Her thin lips quivered, and she wanted to say something that could adequately express her gratitude, but no words came to her. The moment of opportunity passed, and he was looking straight ahead again, his face an expressionless mask.

She followed his gaze down the wide corridor lined with curious observers. The curved walls were coated with a thin sheen of moisture, giving it an organic quality, like the esophagus of an enormous beast. Her flesh tingled and fine hairs rose on her smooth blue-green skin.

I'm being swallowed whole, she thought.

She forced the image from her mind and concentrated on her breathing. She counted each step as she walked, one of the techniques she learned at the Potentials Academy as a way to calm herself in stressful situations. The Academy had prepared thousands of youths for the Great Journey, and she could recall each of their names engraved on the wall honoring them.

After today, my name will be among them, she thought.

Up ahead, the corridor opened up into a large hangar, crowded with more spectators. Her father's grip on her left arm tightened slightly; it was firm but not rough and his skin felt clammy against hers.

Several fighter ships were arrayed near the walls on either side of the hangar. They all bore the emblem of the Regalus Guard, which showed two staff weapons crossing each other to form an "X" upon the face of a dark green shield. Fully clad Regalus Guard soldiers formed two columns to create a path for the procession. Their gleaming green and gold armor reflected the bright lights of the hangar as they stood holding their staff weapons out at an angle.

As she was ushered along the line of Guardians, she spied a broad ramp ascending toward a large hexagonal platform. Atop the platform sat six metallic capsules emblazoned with the emblem of the Chalpin League, three silver crescent moons overlaid on a dark blue circle. Each silver moon was engraved with a crest representing one of the binary star system's three main governing authorities.

The Cortaran crest depicted a brilliant light hovering over the palm of an open hand. The Dumian crest displayed a glowing figure hovering above the outstretched arms of a crowd. The Gorgan crest portrayed a solitary figure bowing before a distant light in an otherwise starless night sky.

Zanna's father led her to the base of the ramp and paused. She looked up to find that he was staring down at her again and she noticed that his normally matte skin was now glistening with a fine sheen of tears. The sight sent a shiver down her spine as she'd never seen her father cry. To see him, the dispassionate Mazrack Yuturi, in public with tears freely flowing from his skin was almost more than she could fathom. She felt her feeble emotional barriers start to crumble, but she resolved to contain herself, even as he succumbed to the moment.

After all the sacrifices he's made for Dayvyn and me, she thought, *he deserves to let this moment wash over him. There is no shame in it.*

Mazrack didn't speak a word when he unhitched his arm from Zanna's. He simply offered a quick nod, turned, and briskly walked away. She felt more alone with each step he took. She watched as the crowd absorbed him, then she ascended the ramp with the other Potentials close behind.

As she stepped onto the platform, she saw two figures standing near a podium that was situated at the center of the metallic pods. A gruff-looking Gorgan, with unusually kind eyes and immaculately kept fur, stood to the left of the podium. Adorned in the full regalia of the Regalus Guard, she recognized him as Bolvaanar, the Regalus Guard Commander who'd protected the Potentials

Academy during her time there and for many years before. She had never personally witnessed it, but she'd heard the tales of Bolvaanar's prowess in battle.

If even half of the stories are true, I pity anyone foolish enough to endanger anyone under Bolvaanar's charge, she thought.

Previn Cal stood directly behind the podium. As the Victros of the Regalus Conclave, he was the ultimate religious authority within the Chalpin League, and he held more influence over the citizenry than even the Chalpin Commission.

Zanna and the other Potentials spread out and walked to the center of the platform where they knelt facing the podium. Zarath's shallow ragged breathing confirmed for her that she was not the only one of them feeling anxious about what they were about to do.

Previn's bright eyes studied the crowd, and he spread his robed arms out to his sides. "Behold, fellow devoted Helianists," he began in a booming voice that belied his slight stature. "We have once more been granted the opportunity to serve the will of the Helia as we gather to offer up our brightest to Regalus. In so doing, we willingly sacrifice our selfish desires that we may fulfill the Great Prophecy which foretells that, one day, one of our brave children will return to rescue the galaxy from an unspeakable evil, an evil so vile that it will spell the doom of everything we hold sacred." He grasped the edges of the podium and leaned forward as he continued. "We understand there will always be those who do not believe, who do not accept the Great Prophecy as truth. They deride us for our devotion and accuse us of murdering our children by sending them into Regalus. They enjoy pointing out the fact that none who have entered Regalus have ever returned." He pointed a finger at his chest and bellowed, "But I say, in the midst of doubt, we must remain vigilant. In the midst of ridicule, we must remain faithful. And in the midst of persecution, we must remain steadfast in our faith. Because there will come a day when the entire spiral arm will look to us for salvation as the galaxy burns, and we must stand ready to answer the call."

Zanna studied Previn's eccentric mannerisms as he spoke. His hands waved in the air, accentuating his words with precision. His eyes darted over the assembled faces as if he were etching his message into their minds. The passion seemed to erupt from his body like a solar flare.

He fixed his gaze on the children kneeling before him. "Before us today are the six Potentials destined to make the next Sacred Journey into Regalus. They shall join with those sent before them, and they will commune with the Gods to absorb the knowledge and wisdom they have to offer." He pointed a gnarled finger at each child in turn. "By the will of the Helia, there will come a day when it may be one of you who returns to rescue us from the clutches of the unspeakable. May your journey be safe, and your communion fruitful."

With a flourish of his dark green robes, he stepped from behind the podium and lifted his arms high into the air. "Let us begin."

Zanna flinched at the hissing noise from the tops of the six capsules as they began to slide open. She stepped into her designated pod and lowered herself into a seated position as the other Potentials did the same. Previn walked around and touched each child's forehead as he uttered a silent prayer for fortitude.

Her attention was drawn to the rear of the hangar as a large hatch began to open. There was a faint flicker in the containment barrier as it activated. Then, she drew a sharp breath as it came into view… Regalus! Its center was a dark hole in space, rimmed with a brilliant white light situated at the center of a swirling orange and yellow vortex that shone brightly against the absolute black void of space. It shimmered like an immortal beacon beckoning the faithful to come forth. She'd seen the sight before, of course, but never from this vantage, and never with the anticipation of it being her immediate destination.

A bolt of panic surged through her, and with an effort, she managed to tear her gaze away from the sight. She stood and frantically searched the masses once more in a failed attempt to find her family. The fear bubbled up inside of her as she fought against the urge to leap from the pod and disappear into the crowd. She took a steadying breath and lowered herself back down into the capsule. She laid back as the lid slid closed above her with a soft hiss, and the capsule rotated and began to move toward the open hatch.

She folded her arms over her chest and whispered, "I am a

Potential, and my Sacred Journey begins now. I will be the first to ever return from Regalus."

She closed her eyes.

CHAPTER TWO

Altar

<u>Dullestoon Space Station: Tyros Star System</u>

Altar Unis had been dreading the conversation he was currently having with his wife. He'd known for five days he would need to have it, but that wasn't enough time to prepare himself. A millennium wouldn't have been enough.

"Are you listening to me Altar?" Alara asked over the holographic communicator.

"I'm sorry my dear, I zoned out for a moment.

"I was saying that Danlon planned a surprise party for your homecoming. I know you hate surprises, and parties, but you need to at least pretend to be excited, okay?"

He was hard-pressed to think of anything he detested more than having to fake jubilance.

"Listen, Alara, about that…" he began before losing his nerve.

Her face sagged. "You're not coming home," she said more as a statement than a question.

"No, no, I am coming. I just won't be able to stay for as long as I'd hoped."

"What do you mean as long as you hoped? You were to be permanently reassigned to Birgh."

"And that will still happen, but I was informed that my services would be needed on the station for a while longer. For now, I've only been approved for seven days of leave."

"I see," she said with disappointment dripping from her words.

"You do realize that we haven't seen you in over a year?"

"I know, I know. Trust me, I did all I could to change their minds, but High Command wouldn't budge."

"You apparently didn't try hard enough. How much longer are they going to keep you on that forsaken station?"

"It's in pretty bad shape, and with the problems on Caristo—"

"How long Altar?" she asked again, cutting him off.

"Two more years."

The words seemed to visibly wound her.

"Two more years!"

"It's a lot to ask, I know, but please be patient darling. It will be over soon, I promise."

"Two more years," she said again, seemingly to herself.

"I've been thinking," he said with a cautioned tone, "what if you and Halmon came to stay with me?"

"Leave our home and come to the Tyros system? Where would we stay? You yourself said Dullestoon station is practically falling apart, and everyone knows the Dark Hand operates freely on Caristo. There's a reason so few Forrack live on that planet. So, tell me, where would we live?"

"Yorinar," he offered with a hint of hope in his voice. "It's not so bad there. The Dark Hand's presence is minimal there, and Averan-Ginest station is much nicer than Dullestoon."

She shook her head. "No, Altar. You've promised time and time again that you would retire from military service and come back home, but you always find a reason not to. We hardly ever see you anymore. Your own son barely knows you. No, I won't uproot our lives in order to help you break another promise."

He sighed deeply at the truth she spoke. He'd been promising to leave the Forrack military for years now, but there was always the next project to complete or the next critical mission that only he could accomplish.

As if she were reading his mind, she said, "Your work seems to be the only thing you care about, and one of these days it may be the only thing you have left."

His shoulders slumped as the will to debate the issue drained from him. For all his strategic cunning, he knew this was one fight he had no hope of winning.

"I'm sorry Alara."

"I am too," she said.

His wrist communicator chimed, and a voice said, "Commander Unis, Chief Copand requests your presence in his office."

"Tell him I'm on the way," Altar responded. He looked at Alara and said, "I have to go. Tell Halmon I love him and I will see him soon. I love you too."

"I'll tell him," she said, then she disconnected the link.

He sat for a few moments staring at the empty space above the holographic communication pad where Alara's face had been. He didn't know how much longer he could expect her to tolerate his tenuous balancing act, but something told him she was reaching her limit. He desperately needed to find a way to keep both his family and his career.

Maybe I can think of a solution before I see her in two weeks, he thought as he rubbed at his temples. *Or maybe she'll come up with a solution of her own.*

That idea turned his insides into gelatin.

The nondescript maintenance ship joined the queue of vessels bound for the hulking station. Its scarred and dented hull was unremarkable among the dozens of other ships ferrying workers and parts from the planet below.

The weapons officer turned from his station and asked, "What are your orders Durmok?"

Orrick Klemo was studying the scene through the forward window. His slitted eyes narrowed as his forked tongue flicked in and out of his mouth.

"My orders haven't changed since the last two times you asked. We will maintain our course and you'll establish a target lock on my command."

Chastened, the weapons officer turned back around. "Yes Durmok," he said meekly.

Orrick sensed the officer's tension; he could feel it too. The next few minutes would be the culmination of centuries of patience and years of planning. He understood that the consequences of failure were severe, but he wasn't the failing type, no one who'd attained the rank of 'Durmok' was.

He watched through the window as Dullestoon station loomed larger and larger. A considerable area of the station's olive-green exterior was worn and discolored, and spots of rust were accumulating around the massive structural bolts holding it together. Scorch marks and dents marred the hull and told the story of terroristic attacks and the occasional raids carried out by the Dark Hand.

He sneered approvingly at his source's accurate description of the station's state of disrepair.

The Norvekian does not disappoint, he thought.

"Approaching the station's security checkpoint," the pilot reported.

Orrick spied the oval-shaped multi-spectral scanning checkpoint that each vessel had to pass through before gaining docking clearance for the station. The scanner would flood his ship with infrared and electromagnetic waves, and neutrinos that could detect the presence of hazardous materials and life signs on board. It would surely alert the station's security force to the dozens of heavily armed shock troops occupying the cargo hold.

He slithered closer to the pilot's station and said, "Keep on our current heading and stay within the convoy. Do nothing to arouse their suspicions. We're simply a maintenance crew reporting to do repairs. Don't give them a reason to suspect otherwise."

The pilot nodded his understanding and said, "Yes Durmok."

The exterior of the ship appeared just like any other AUG-75 model Forrack maintenance vessel, but the interior was retrofitted especially for this mission. The cargo hold had been stripped down to allow for troop transportation, and four photon turrets and two focused energy beam ports were hidden behind false plating along the exterior on the port and starboard sides. The modifications wouldn't make the ship a match for the station's defenses, but if the Norvekian did as he promised, most of the station's security force would join in Orrick's surprise attack and sabotage the station from within.

That will be more than enough to take the station, he thought.

His second-in-command, Ongbo Dutt, slithered next to him at

the front of the ship. The thick scales of his tail on the metal floor made a soft scraping noise as he moved.

"Durmok, what's the backup plan if the Norvekian fails to hold up his end?" he asked.

Orrick considered the question for a moment before responding. "He's a zealot Ongbo; nothing will deter him from his cause. I've provided him with an irresistible opportunity to strike a blow at his oppressors. He'll come through."

Ongbo seemed skeptical. "Yes, but he's still only an individual. What if he can't get the others to join the attack?"

Orrick pulled his eyes from the window. His vertical black pupils restricted as he stared at Ongbo. "Your lack of faith in my plan is becoming worrisome."

Ongbo bowed his head slightly as a show of subordination. "You misunderstand me Durmok. My lack of faith isn't in you or your strategy. I simply don't trust this Norvekian. Our entire plan, all that we've set in place, rests on his success. If he fails, we have no hope of taking the station."

"We've never been slaves to hope," Orrick said. "Hope didn't restore our previous might to us. It didn't forge us into the warriors we are today. Disgrace and hatred did that. The hatred that these Norvekians hold for the Forrack will allow us to succeed where our ancestors failed. They have endured a great shame at the hands of the Forrack, and they have never forgotten it. We'll be the weapon of their revenge."

"Weapons are put away once they are no longer needed," Ongbo said.

"That's only true of weapons that are controlled. The Norvekians won't control us. All they want is what the Forrack stole from them, their lands, their autonomy, their dignity. We'll restore those things to them, and once they have them, they'll come to realize they'll need us to keep them."

"They might view that as simply replacing one master with another," Ongbo said.

Orrick's glistening tongue flicked out of his mouth and back in. "Not all masters are created equal. Never underestimate what one will sacrifice for security."

An alert sounded from the communications station behind

Orrick.

"The station is attempting to contact us Durmok," the communications officer reported. "How should I respond."

Orrick turned back toward the window where the scanning ring now dominated the view. "Open a frequency, but don't respond." He slithered next to the weapons officer. "Lock weapons on the station and fire on my order."

The weapons officer offered a menacing grin.

The communications officer tapped at his station, making clicking noises as his claws struck the glass top.

A computerized voice sounded through the ship's audio relay. "Maintenance vessel N-J-6-9-0-4, provide docking clearance code before proceeding through the checkpoint." After a few seconds without a response, the voice repeated, "Maintenance vessel N-J-6-9-0-4, provide—"

"Now!" Orrick shouted.

Droplets of spittle landed on Altar's right thumb as he sat with his hands clasped on the desk. The rotund station chief, Sul Copand, was leaning toward Altar with his palms flat on the desk.

"Completely unacceptable!" Sul shouted as more saliva flew from his mouth.

Altar removed his hands from the desk and rested them on his lap. He couldn't decide if Sul was leaning over the desk as an intimidation tactic, or if he was simply trying to support his ample weight.

"I'm afraid there's no other alternative Sul."

"There is always an alternative to throwing credits out the window," Sul shot back. "You're already costing me dearly with these delays in getting shipments and workers on and off my station. Now my fleet is at a standstill because of all these unnecessary security protocols you keep implementing. And as if all that weren't enough, now you want to suspend all operations indefinitely. Out of the question!"

Altar massaged his temples as he focused on maintaining his composure.

His station. His fleet. He wouldn't so much as change the wall color without permission from his superiors, he thought.

Sul's jowls shook vigorously, and his cheeks flushed a dark shade of violet as he continued his tantrum. This wasn't the first time Altar endured one of Sul's tirades, and he was certain it wouldn't be the last. The Station Chief's temper was legendary, but his squat stature and soft rounded features failed to complement it.

Altar leaned back in his chair. "You are the chief of this station, but I'm responsible for its security. You have the luxury of measuring your success by profits and productivity, but I must measure my success by ensuring the safety of the thousands of souls who call this station home."

"I live and work here too," Sul countered, pointing at his chest.

"My point exactly," Altar said. "I must even ensure the safety of someone like you."

Sul glowered at him.

Altar employed a more conciliatory tone to his voice. "Look Sul, I want nothing more than to keep your pockets fat and this station's productivity at peak levels, but Dullestoon is literally coming apart at the seams. Security equipment is malfunctioning, dormitory facilities are in poor condition. There's even literal tape holding together some of the wiring in the maintenance panels. Tape Sul! The mechanics can't keep slapping on glue and tape to hold this place together. It creates vulnerabilities in our security. We need to shut down all nonessential functions and do a complete overhaul of this place."

"Absolutely not. Our security is just fine. We haven't had an incident with those terrorist scum in months."

"That's what concerns me," Altar said, attempting to maintain his even tone. "Things have been too quiet lately. Also, I'm getting reports of suspicious transmissions originating from the station."

"We're orbiting Caristo for goodness' sake. There're hundreds of thousands of transmissions from the station every day."

"I know that, but we've flagged several highly encrypted and unlocalized communications recently, ones whose specific origins we haven't been able to trace. Why anyone would go through all that trouble unless they were hiding something?"

"Maybe they don't want the military rummaging through their personal messages. Have you considered that?"

Altar rolled his eyes. "We don't have the luxury of considering privacy concerns here. We're constantly under imminent threat of terror attacks by separatist groups, or have you already forgotten the promenade incident last cycle?"

Sul grunted. "A lot of good your prying did there."

"The point is, we can't properly analyze and decode the transmissions because the meta-data processors aren't functioning properly. We need to shut everything down so the maintenance team can make the proper repairs. We can get everything back online in three days max."

"The answer is still no. My station, my call. I will not disrupt my entire operation because you want to snoop through holo-vids of some politician's wife pleasuring herself."

"Gimme a break Sul, you know that's not it. Something more is happening—"

His words were cut short by a loud explosion, accompanied by the sound of the station's emergency alarms. Two more explosions followed in quick succession.

"What... what's happening?" Sul stammered.

Altar ignored him and spoke into his wrist communicator. "Status report Damu."

Damu's static-laden voice replied, "The station is under attack."

"By whom?"

"Unknown sir."

"Take a response team to central command. I'll meet you there."

"Yes sir, moving out now."

Altar turned to Sul and said, "You should get to the bridge and commence lockdown procedures."

Sul nodded his head vigorously and waddled from the room.

Altar pulled his Hartec energy pistol from the holster on his hip. He needed to secure the central command station.

What the hell is going on? he wondered.

Fermal Lindar started moving the instant he felt the first blast rock the station. That was his cue. He'd been waiting for this moment for the better part of a week, and dark circles ringed his eyes from his lack of sleep as of late. He picked up his tool bag before exiting the storage closet. He glanced down at his hands, which were steady and dry. He thought he'd be more nervous.

As he hurried down the hallway toward the central command station, he took note of the startled faces moving past him in the opposite direction. A stream of civilians and maintenance technicians rushed toward their designated evacuation sites. Panic hadn't yet taken hold of them, but they chattered nervously amongst themselves as they walked briskly down the corridor.

"Is this another Dark Hand attack?" one of the passersby asked a nearby security officer.

The confusion spreading through the crowd was palpable. Fermal also wore a look of confusion on his face, but his was only a mask. He knew all too well what was happening.

And I'm the one who made it possible, he thought pridefully.

The feeling was intoxicating, and he felt his fingers and toes tingling as he walked.

A familiar voice in the crowd yelled, "You're going the wrong way Fermal."

It was Brustol, one of his fellow station mechanics. He was caught up in the flow of foot traffic heading for the emergency exit.

Fermal didn't respond. He had a mission to complete. For years, he'd been proselytizing to anyone who would listen to his musings. He'd even gained a small following who regularly tuned into his anonymous holo-vids on the hub. His message was simple: Caristo and Yorinar were Norvekian planets, and the Forrack swooped in and stole them away. Worst of all, they took them without firing a shot. They came disguised as liberators, but all they really wanted was territory. While most of the Norvekian populace had resigned themselves to Forrack subjugation, Fermal's message was one of hope that, one day, Norvekian honor would be restored. His mother preached the same message, but no one listened to her, and her failures taught Fermal a valuable lesson. Words, powerful as they might be, could always be dismissed. Action, on the other hand, could not be ignored.

Fermal reached into his bag for the third time, feeling around for the device as if it might somehow disappear from existence. He'd received it three days ago, and it arrived with clear operating instructions. He was to place it on a wall near the main shield generator. The device would then self-activate, evidenced by an orange blinking light, and override the shield generator's relay signal. After a few seconds, the blinking orange light would turn solid blue and the device would disrupt all command functions from the relay, thus preventing power to be redirected to the shields. Afterward, he would remove the device. The signal disruption would last for several minutes, allowing Orrick's ship plenty of time to dock with the station and board with his troops. If all went according to plan, he could place the device, allow it to perform its function, then remove it before anyone was the wiser.

Simple, he thought.

He wasn't so naive as to believe that helping Orrick take the station would instantly restore to the Norvekians that which was rightfully theirs, but he hoped loyalty would count for something.

We'll be partners in their quest for empire, and if all goes well, we'll partake of the spoils. Maybe we'll even end up with a small empire of our own, he mused.

He walked into the command station holding his tool bag and pretending to be just another mechanic performing emergency repairs during an attack on the station. He approached the shield generator relay and removed the device from his tool bag. The Forrack technician next to him didn't even glance in his direction.

They don't even bother themselves to notice us anymore, he thought with disdain. *We'll no longer give them a choice. After today, they'll be the ones bowing and scraping at our feet.*

He glanced around before discreetly placing the device on the wall near the relay. Being rid of it felt like a weight being lifted from his shoulders. He took a tentative look down to confirm that the orange light was blinking. Confusion bloomed in his chest when, instead of seeing an orange blinking light, he saw two solid red lights.

His insides twisted into knots as he softly tapped the device with his finger.

Something's wrong, he thought. *But how? I followed the instructions precisely.*

If Fermal Lindar had the time to formulate a final thought, he might have used it to bask in the righteousness of his cause. He may have dwelled upon the pride he felt at advancing his mother's vision for a brighter Norvekian future. Maybe he would have even held a grudging respect for what Orrick Klemo had just done to him. But the explosion tore through the central command station at a terrifying speed, and Fermal never had a chance to think at all.

———

"Internal detonation in their command station," Ongbo reported with a grin. "It would seem the Norvekian has succeeded."

"Indeed," Orrick hissed. He turned to the weapons officer and said, "Target their shield generators."

"Target locked," the weapons officer confirmed.

"Fire!"

Orrick gripped the command console tightly as the glowing green disks hurtled toward the station. The first impact was a direct hit to Dullestoon's dorsal shield generator. The view panned to the right as the ship maneuvered into position to get a lock on a second shield generator just below the bridge. Another direct hit produced a shower of orange and white sparks. The lights on the station's bridge flickered briefly.

"Two of the four shield generators have been destroyed," the weapons officer reported.

Dullestoon's shields were crippled, but the modified maintenance ship lacked weapons capable of inflicting substantial damage to the station's hull. Orrick didn't mind, because destroying the station was never the goal, quite the contrary. He wished to preserve Dullestoon as much as possible. Now, with weakened shield coverage, Orrick's ship could couple with one of Dullestoon's docking ports.

Ongbo pointed at the window. "Durmok, docking port A-6 is unshielded."

"Then that is where we go in," Orrick said, touching the ship-wide communication panel on his command station. "Battlegroup, prepare to board the station."

The maintenance vessel approached the exposed port and extended its docking arm toward the exterior door until it formed a vacuum seal. Moments later, a high-pitched whine signaled the opening of the station's inner docking hatch.

Orrick pulled a curved energy blade from its sheath on his back. "Stand ready," he instructed the shock troops who'd assembled behind him at the hatch.

The circular hatch opened to reveal a Norvekian security officer standing on the other side. His four eyes fixed on Orrick and his entourage with nervous anticipation.

"I… I'm Pasco Vernil," he managed.

Orrick sheathed his energy blade and slithered through the opening, followed by his troops. "I take it your security teams have begun sweeping the station."

"Affirmative. They've rounded up the Forrack security officers and placed them into holding chambers alongside the Norvekians who refused to join with us. The station's residents have been placed on lockdown in their quarters."

"Show me to the bridge," Orrick demanded.

"Of course, this way," Pasco said extending a hand toward the nearby lift.

Orrick turned to Ongbo. "Take your men to these holding chambers and execute the prisoners, we have no need for them."

"Yes Durmok," Ongbo said.

A look of shock crept onto Pasco's face.

"Do you have something to say?" Orrick asked.

"I… I did not know there would be executions."

Orrick slithered up to Pasco. "Does your heart bleed for those who took everything from your race? Or for your comrades who were too cowardly to take up arms against them?" He fixed Pasco with a menacing stare as his forked tongue slowly slid in and out of his mouth. "Arrangements can be made for you to join them if that is your desire."

Pasco looked from Orrick to the cadre of Cohannic troopers at his flanks. His face turned ashen, and he looked back to Orrick. "That won't be necessary."

"Excellent," Orrick said. "Now, the bridge."

Altar tried to slow his breathing as the lift descended toward the central command level. His mind raced with the possible theories about what was happening.

Could this be the Dark Hand? he wondered.

The criminal cabal was always the prime suspect for disorder in the Tyros system. The group engaged in smuggling illegal weapons and illicit drugs. It was even known to conduct violent raids on mining and banking vessels.

A full-on attack on a sovereign space station is different, he thought. *They've never been this brazen.*

The lift came to a halt on the command level. As he stepped through the doors with his energy pistol at the ready, an intense blast of heat enveloped him. The shock wave vaulted him into the air and slammed him against the back wall of the lift. He struggled back to his feet, shaking his head to regain his senses. His hearts pounded in his chest.

Have they breached the hull? he wondered.

What remained of the central command station lay in ruin. Showers of sparks cascaded in every direction, and smoke billowed from a gaping hole in the far wall. Twisted metal and severed limbs were strewn along the gangway leading to what remained of the command station.

That blast came from inside the station, he concluded.

With no reason to continue toward central command, he touched the panel for the bridge, but the lift didn't respond. After several more fruitless attempts, he stepped from the lift, found the level access shaft along the wall, and removed the cover. The shaft was narrow, but there was room enough for him to climb inside.

He activated his communicator as he crawled along his belly through the small space. The odor of coolant and fried electrical components penetrated his nostrils and brought on a wave of nausea.

"Damu, what's your status?" he asked.

The distinct sound of energy rifle fire sounded in the background as Damu responded, "The Norvekian security staff is firing on us! Baas and Eggershaw are dead, and Thara is badly injured. I think whoever attacked us in that ship is now on the station."

Altar's mind searched for answers.

What are the Norvekians doing? Are they in league with the Dark

Hand?

"I'm making my way toward the bridge level via the access shafts. Meet me there," Altar said.

A jumble of static answered him. He repeated his message but received no response.

"They're jamming our communications channels," he said to himself.

He couldn't be certain that Damu had received his message, but he had no choice but to keep moving. Up ahead, the shaft forked, and he took the left tunnel. Several feet in, he spied the access tile that allowed access to the bridge level. As he approached the tile, he froze in place at the sound of energy pistol fire coming from below.

This is no simple terrorist attack. There's too much coordination, he thought.

The sound of the firefight proceeded down the hall. He slid the tile away and peered through the opening. The bodies of two Forrack security officers lay face down on the floor directly beneath him. He oriented his body and lowered himself down to the floor of the bridge level. He checked the bodies; both were dead.

He took a cursory look around, then moved toward a large electrical conduit halfway down the corridor. He cautiously peeked down the hall that led to the bridge access doors, and his blood froze in his veins.

Sul was laying on the floor near the door to the bridge. He was on his side facing Altar's direction. He was moving, but only barely. Dark stains streaked the front of his uniform, and he was clutching his throat with his remaining hand. His other hand lay nearby, still gripping an energy pistol.

Two soldiers loomed over Sul. The taller of the two held a curved blue energy blade in his hand. They were clad from the waist up in black and gold battle gear. Visored helmets covered their heads, and their chests were adorned with bulky tactical vests. They wore metallic gauntlets on their forearms, and the three fingers and thumb of each hand were tipped with razor-like claws. The lower half of the soldiers' scaled, snake-like bodies were coiled beneath them. The soldier with the energy blade slowly and methodically slithered around Sul's prone form as if admiring his work. Then, without a word, he decapitated Sul in one quick stroke of the energy blade. Sul's head spun several times before coming to rest, eyes wide open, staring in Altar's direction.

He was a difficult person to like, but he didn't deserve to die this way, he thought, clenching his fist.

He watched helplessly as the soldiers slithered onto the bridge, and he became aware that his mouth was extremely dry. He could almost feel the blood draining from his face. He turned and went back the way he'd come, energy pistol still at the ready, making sure to watch out for any other intruders.

The Station Chief was dead, and the bridge was lost. That meant the entire station was lost. He found the nearest escape hatch and climbed inside the pod.

As he punched in the coordinates for the Forrack base on Caristo, he subconsciously cycled through his next steps.

I need to evacuate the station before the hijackers establish full operational control. Once I reach the surface, I'll request that High Command send a response force to retake the station immediately.

Some part of him wondered if High Command would even believe what he had to report. He wouldn't even have believed it if he'd not seen it with his own four eyes.

After all this time, the Cohannic were back.

CHAPTER THREE

Cassyn

Arcus: Pharus Star System

Cassyn Spreen placed the blue lanteriums at the base of the memorial and took a step back to appraise the view. Tiny rain droplets gently pattered off her umbrella as the holographic image of her smiling father stared back at her from the glass grave marker. The exotic plants were his favorite and she'd taken to putting them at his memorial site every year on his birthday.

"They're beautiful honey," her mother said from behind her.

Cassyn rolled her dark brown eyes but didn't respond.

"Devlin loved those flowers," Pharie continued undeterred. "He used to brag that he was an amateur horticulturist," she chuckled.

"They're plants, not flowers. Not that I'd expect you to know the difference," Cassyn said.

"Oh, plants then. Either way, he loved them. I never understood how he could spend so much time tending to them with all the work he was doing. I remember how thrilled he was when his hobby rubbed off on you."

Cassyn shuffled her feet in the wet grass.

Plants will have to suffice, she thought. *I'm not exactly a pet lover, and settling down to start a family doesn't appear to be in the cards for me.*

"Do you have anything you want to say to him?" Pharie asked.

Without turning around, Cassyn responded, "Not with you here." There was an edge to her voice, and she hoped her mother felt the cut.

Pharie sounded wounded when she spoke again. "Why must you be so hurtful? I loved him too you know."

Cassyn spun around, her caramel-complected cheeks flushed purple. "You sure had a funny way of showing it. He wasn't even gone a year before you moved on to a new life."

"It wasn't like that Cass. We've talked about this."

"No, you talked about it, Cassyn said, pointing a finger at Pharie. I was only fifteen; all I could do was listen and accept your decision. You never asked me how I felt about it. You just ran off and married Tamon, and what, did you think we'd just be a happy family?"

"That's just not fair Cass."

"Fair?" Cassyn blurted, her right eye twitching as it tended to do when her temper flared. "What's not fair is that my dad was murdered, and it's like you just kept moving on with life as if nothing happened. Then you ran off with some guy I hardly knew and forgot all about the man who stood beside you all those years. You still don't care how I feel about it, do you? All you want is my blessing so you can sleep better at night. Well, guess what Mom? You'll *never* get it. I won't give you the satisfaction of erasing Dad from my life like you did from yours!"

Cassyn saw the tears welling up in Pharie's eyes as her words sliced through her. She didn't care. She was fighting back her own tears of anger now.

Pharie gazed at her with a look that was part despair, part defiance. Tears cascaded down her cheeks, and her brown knuckles had gone white as she squeezed the handle of her umbrella.

"I know you're hurt Cass, and I hate that I can't do anything to take that pain away from you. But your father has been gone for over six years now, but we're still here. We're here, and we're still family. You have to find a way to let go of this hatred you're harboring. If you don't, it'll eventually hollow you out. Trust me, I know."

Cassyn turned away and dabbed at her face with a rain-soaked sleeve. "I have to be getting back," she said.

"So soon?"

"The transport back to Ardhamn leaves in an hour. I don't

want to miss it."

Pharie shifted her umbrella to her other hand. "It's not too late you know."

"Too late for what?"

"To change your mind. You know, about this military thing. I know it's not what you truly want Cass. You only joined as a way to escape, maybe even as a way to get back at me and Tamon for—"

"It's always about you," Cassyn said cutting her off. "My life doesn't revolve around you and your new husband." She brushed past Pharie before turning back. "You wanna know why I joined the military? I joined because I'm a damned good pilot. And I'm going to stay out of a sense of loyalty, something you wouldn't know anything about."

Cassyn watched as Pharie cast her eyes upward in a failed effort to stem the tide of fresh tears. Then she stormed away, leaving her mother standing alone at the memorial.

She can move on, but I'll make damned sure she never forgets.

Ardhamn: Pletea Star System

Within hours, Cassyn was back at her barracks in the Pletea system. She lay under the covers in her bunk, staring at the dull brown ceiling. Although the planet, Ardhamn, orbited closely to its red dwarf star, the temperatures stayed perpetually cool. Cassyn hated it, but the climate was ideal for the cultivation of the exotic plants in her small conservatory, so there was that.

She glanced at the small habitat near the window. She smiled knowingly as she reminisced about how her father had tended to his much larger conservatory back on Arcus. He had a rare talent for growing and sustaining exotic plants. She was just getting the hang of it, and it was much more challenging than she realized. She'd directly contributed to the slow deaths of countless hargesses, numolees, and lanteriums, among other flora.

She chuckled to herself as she thought, *I'm a certified plant serial murderer. Cassyn the Destroyer.*

She pushed aside the blankets and rolled out of the bed. She walked over to the plant habitat and lifted the mesh lid. The earthy aroma filled her nostrils. She admired the colorful array of plants as she gently brushed her fingers across the petals and leaves. Her hand hovered above the green and orange-spotted leaves of the hargess plant, one of her favorites. Aside from its beauty, it was also known for its beneficial therapeutic and medicinal uses. She twisted a large leaf from the stalk and held it to her nose with one hand as she replaced the habitat lid with the other. The hargess leaf had a faintly sweet smell, infused with citrus and nutty undertones. The fragrance awakened a desire deep within her bones.

She walked over to the desk and touched a panel that unlocked the bottom drawer. The drawer slid open, and she lifted a small black ceramic container from its hiding place and set it on the desk. She placed the leaf on the desktop and unscrewed the lid of the black container. A pungent odor wafted up from the dark liquid inside. The scent always reminded her of the fact that the crude liquid was a byproduct of the refinement processes of ethnelene fuel, the very fuel that was used in the ships she piloted. The thought never deterred her; neither was she dissuaded by the fact that she could be expelled from military service just for possessing agiomtrinelene, or 'aggie' as it was commonly called.

She ran a finger around the rim of the container as she thought about how the aggie soothed her frayed nerves and quieted the ever-present commotion in her mind. She wouldn't deny that the drug also filled a void within her, providing an escape from her constant emotional anguish. She knew she should stop and she constantly told herself she would.

It would be a simple thing to attribute her addiction to the loss of her father, but it pained her too much to associate such a stain with her pristine image of him. It was much easier to just not think about it at all.

She used a pipette to squeeze three drops of the aggie onto the hargess leaf. Within seconds, the leaf dried up and its vibrant spots turned shades of brown and copper. She picked it up, crumbled it in her hand, and ate the fragments from her palm. Despite the aroma of the leaf and the odor of the aggie, there was no discernible taste to the concoction. The aggie could also be heated, and the gaseous fumes inhaled, but the process was more intricate and she preferred the tactile experience of ingesting the aggie-infused leaf.

She replaced the container and laid back down on the bed to await the drug's effects. She knew sleep wouldn't come easy this night, but she hoped she could at least focus on something other than how much she missed her dad. She stared back up at the drab ceiling and it seemed a little more vibrant now.

She smiled as the warm sensation coursed through her body.

"Happy birthday Dad," she said softly.

Cassyn bolted upright at the sound of the holographic communicator chiming on the nightstand. The flashing message read 'INCOMING TRANSMISSION'. She looked at the time and was amazed to see she'd slept for nearly three hours. Stifling a yawn, she activated the call-response feature on her wristband and the face of Yero Labin materialized in front of her.

"Yero?"

"Hello Cassy," he said with a smile. "I hope I have not disturbed you."

She rubbed at her eyes. "Not at all, I was just looking over some data logs," she lied.

"How are you?" he asked.

She donned her best fake smile and said, "I'm good."

His smile widened. "You are so much like your father. Devlin was never one to let his true emotions flutter about the room either. He kept them tightly caged. He would always joke that he worked around so many of us Cortarans, that he was forgetting how to feel emotions. He said he feared he was slowly turning into one of us."

A genuine smile now broke through on Cassyn's face. "That sounds like him alright. He complained a lot, but I know how much he enjoyed his time at Sagis. I remember how happy he was when you recruited him for, um, whatever it was you guys worked on there. I never really quite understood."

"Well then, count yourself lucky. If he had ever tried to explain it to you, it would have surely put you right to sleep."

They shared a laugh.

Yero's laughter died down and a more serious look clouded his features. "I think of him often you know, especially on his birthday."

"It doesn't ever seem to get any easier," she said. "I mean, I feel like every day that passes should dull the pain a little more, but it doesn't seem to work like that."

Yero's holographic image looked intently at her as he spoke. "I will not patronize you by pretending to know how you feel. The average life expectancy of my race is less than half that of you Humans. I suppose we simply lack the time for grieving during our short lives. What I do know, is that ever since Devlin's life was tragically cut short, I feel an emptiness. It is as if a piece of my life has simply vanished, and I have no want to replace it."

Her tears from earlier in the day threatened to return. "You're kind to say that. Have you spoken to my mother?"

"Indeed I have. And I must say, she seems very concerned about you."

Her eye twitched as her defenses started to go up. "So, she sent you to talk some sense into me about joining the military. Is that what this call is about?"

He shook his bulbous head. "Not at all. In fact, it's quite the opposite. I have a confession."

She raised an eyebrow. "A confession? What about?"

"My call is for selfish reasons. I have a proposal I would like you to consider."

"I'm listening."

He cleared his throat and said, "I apologize for my bluntness, but your duties on Ardhamn are beneath your abilities. You're meant for so much more than simply screening refugees from intergalactic space and safeguarding the exotic wares they bring with them. You're a pilot Cassy, a very talented one at that. Yet there you are, languishing in an outpost star system performing menial tasks. Why?"

Her defenses perked up again, but she decided brutal honesty was the best response.

"I've been told I don't necessarily play well with others, and I'm not exactly the best at following orders either. Soldiers like me aren't meant to be seen or heard from."

He sighed. "You have always had a competitive spirit, and you never were one to blindly follow orders. You are truly Devlin's daughter." He paused for a moment, staring at her. "What if I could help get you assigned somewhere else, somewhere where your abilities could be put to their full use?"

She barely managed to contain her excitement.

"How?"

"I will tell you, but first I need to know that you would be open to the idea of leaving Ardhamn."

She thought about it and couldn't imagine a place she'd less rather be. Escaping the cold and the boredom alone would be a major upgrade. And it wasn't like it would be difficult for the Pharus Confederation military to find someone else to babysit the exotic oils and spices.

"I'm definitely open to the idea," she said.

He smiled and rubbed his hands together. "Okay then. Have you heard of the Sensitive Materials Defense Compact program?"

She rubbed behind her neck as she searched her memory. "That's the agreement our military has with Sagis, isn't it? The one where soldiers are assigned to Sagis escort ships to protect your convoys."

"Precisely," he said.

She shrugged. "What about it?"

"Well, we could use a good pilot for one of our more important shipping routes that runs primarily from the Carmo system to Fenghou station. I am confident I can get you assigned to that convoy detail aboard the Vengeance."

Her chest tightened.

"Carmo?"

He softened his features. "I realize that means you would be making frequent trips to the facility where your father died, so I was unsure how you would feel about my offer. But Cassy, I know that you long for more than what you have on Ardhamn. You can think of this as an opportunity for a fresh start."

She couldn't find the words to respond. It was a great opportunity, and she genuinely appreciated him for offering it to her. But the mere suggestion of going to the Carmo system affected her more than she could have imagined. She hadn't been back there since the one time her father had taken her to the Sagis facility. She remembered how excited he was to show her all the interesting things he did there, even though she didn't understand most of it. She was just glad that he was happy.

He died at that same facility just a few short years later, she recalled painfully.

Apparently sensing her apprehension, Yero said, "You don't have to decide now. Just think about it and let me know your decision when you're ready. Understand that if you do take me up on my offer, it will be a bit more of an unorthodox posting than you are used to. I, for one, think the change of scenery would be good for you."

She nodded her head absently, still struggling to find an appropriate response. "Thank you, Yero," she finally said. "I promise I will let you know."

His holographic image faded out, and she flopped back onto the bed.

Carmo, she thought.

She thought back on her mother's hysterical tears as she attempted to tell her the news of her father's death. Cassyn didn't cry though, at least not right away. She was too stunned by the realization that her hero was gone, and he was never coming back. The tears came the following day, and they didn't stop for weeks. They hadn't really ever stopped.

Almost seven years later and I'm still the same broken young girl.

She was never so naive as to think there was anything she could have done to prevent what happened. She once overheard Tamon say that it was simply a hazard of the job.

What the hell would he know about hazards? He's in his fancy office all day, sitting safely behind a desk, twiddling his finely manicured thumbs.

She lay in bed thinking most of the night. Alternate waves of fear, grief, and excitement contributed to her restlessness. By the time the large, reddish-orange Pletea rose over the horizon, she'd made up her mind. She had no future on Ardhamn; it was her prison. She was meant for more. And if it meant facing the ghost of Devlin Spreen on Sphercal, then that's exactly what she would do.

CHAPTER FOUR
Madrin

Aegus: Flux Star System

Flanked by his personal assistant and his head of security, Madrin Veleko strode toward the large building, feigning a level of confidence that belied his frayed nerves. He halted next to a hover car that was parked in the expansive courtyard and bent to check his reflection in one of the windows. He flashed a wide smile, and his ivory-white teeth shone brightly against his dark complexion. Using his tongue, he dislodged a tiny food particle stuck between his teeth, then he stood and straightened the collar of his silk tunic.

Nhila Gorban stood behind him, scanning the courtyard. "You look fine," she said.

He turned toward her with a grin. "I do, don't I? I will admit, I'm a bit anxious. It's not every day that I get summoned to the Chamber."

The 'Chamber' was how most referred to the Great Council Chamber. The domed structure was situated on a large hill overlooking the Revocin Valley. Soaring skytowers dominated the landscape in all directions, and an absurdly long walkway led to a curved portico supported by six massive columns. The walkway was lined with marble statues of long-dead remnants of the Sukarian Council, and it terminated at a steep stairway that spanned the entire width of the building's front. The Chamber was widely regarded as a marvel of Sukarian architecture, but it reminded Madrin of a titanic herg shell, like the type that dominated the coastal regions of Revocin.

His assistant, Veran Gauld, panted dramatically as they ascended the stairs. "What's the point of so many damned steps?" he griped.

"Opulence Veran. It's always opulence with them," Madrin said. "The Sukarians need always remind us of their place in the natural order of things. They are the first race, and we'd best not forget that." He directed a wink and a smile at Veran.

"Well," Veran said between grunts, "assuming I don't die from exhaustion before reaching the top of these stairs, I'd sure like to know what couldn't wait until tomorrow. Flux has nearly set."

Madrin looked to the horizon to see that Veran was correct. The top of the star glowed blood orange as it gradually dipped below the skytowers that lined the distant horizon.

"It's a test," Nhila, suggested. "It's always some sort of test when it comes to the Council."

"What type of test?" Madrin asked.

"A test of your usefulness. They want something from you. Why else would they call upon you at such a strange hour?"

"He should hope," Veran said with a hint of delight in his strained voice. "Being in the good graces of the Council is a wonderful position to find yourself in. But having them in your debt, well that's something completely different."

"Let's not get ahead of ourselves. We don't know why they've requested my presence."

"There is one thing I do know for certain," Veran said, "the Council of Seven doesn't send invitations to the Chamber for simple banter. Regardless of why they sent for you, this is a major opportunity, and opportunity is always the vehicle of power. I climbed these steps with your father when he was called before the Council for the first time. I was a bit more sprite back then, mind you, but you see what the outcome was for him."

Madrin thought about his father, the late Hayden Veleko. As the previous Pharus Ambassador to the Sukarian Council, he was universally admired by Humans and Sukarians alike, which was no small feat.

Veran continued, "He was the ultimate negotiator. Before him, I wouldn't say that Human-Sukarian relations were horrible, but there was certainly room for improvement."

Madrin leaned toward Nhila and cupped a hand over his mouth. "Here's the part where he tells us about all the miracles my father performed."

Veran stopped to rest a hand on one of his knees. Beads of perspiration were forming beneath his gray hairline, and his collared shirt was damp.

"You joke about it, but it was nothing short of miraculous," Veran said. "You see, Sukarians value decorum and levelheadedness above all, and they weren't entirely convinced that we Humans possessed those qualities. Your father convinced them. He understood how to show just enough deference to the Council, but not so much as to alarm our government. It was a masterful balancing act."

Madrin chuckled. "He neglected to teach me that little trick. My own people distrust me, and I've no idea what the Council thinks of me."

"It wasn't my intention to suggest you're lacking in any way Ambassador," Veran said sheepishly as they continued their climb.

"I know, but father's shadow is difficult to escape."

"Trying to live up to something you're not meant to be is to die a slow death," Nhila said. "You're not your father, you're Ambassador Madrin Veleko. You have your own path to forge."

Madrin looked at her with a smirk on his face. "If you keep that up, I'll have to add the titles of philosopher and motivational speaker to your already impressive list of qualities."

"And I'd have to ask for a pay increase," she said with a sly grin.

As they reached the summit of the stairs, Madrin turned to them. "So, how do I look?" he asked, tugging at his overcoat.

"Your attire is fine, but you look as if you're barely holding down your supper," Veran said.

Nhila shot Veran a stern glance prompting him to raise his hands in mock surrender.

"It's okay Nhila," Madrin said, "I keep him around precisely for his brutal honesty."

A Korchak attendant approached from the entryway. His waxen face and pale blue eyes were shrouded beneath a hooded cloth tunic, and his forearms were tucked into the sleeves of his robe.

"Welcome," he said, removing the tunic to reveal a completely bald head. He touched an index and middle finger to his forehead in the traditional Korchak greeting. "I am Dannus Prie, servant to Prefect Vicaryn Gayne. The Council of Seven is pleased by your punctuality. Please, allow me to escort you to the Great Hall."

They each returned the greeting. Madrin knew the way to the hall, but formality and ceremonial gestures were important here, so he fell in line behind Dannus, followed by Veran and Nhila.

This just may be the highlight of his day, Madrin thought as he stared at Dannus' back.

Acting in service of the gods was the pinnacle of pride for any Korchak, and the reverence they held for the Sukarians had always disturbed him. He was personally grateful for all the Sukarians had done for the Human race, but he'd lived among them his entire life, and he knew they were anything but deities.

Dannus led them down a wide marbled hallway, his long robe dragged along the floor as he walked. They stopped at a massive wooden door engraved with intricately detailed patterns.

"We have arrived," Dannus said. "Please wait here and the Council will see you in short order." He bowed slightly, then turned and vanished around the corner.

After a short wait, the thick wooden door to the Great Hall swung open slowly. Madrin walked inside, followed closely by his party. He'd been to the Chamber before, but never inside the Great Hall. He was immediately awestruck by the sheer enormity of the rotunda. The cavernous interior was adorned with Sukarian cultural, historical, and religious artifacts, but the space was so voluminous that it still felt sparse and underutilized. The high domed ceiling only served to exacerbate the effect. The carpeted aisle that bisected the room was a deep purple, bordered by an elaborate pattern of gray symbols. Rows of empty curved wooden pews lined each side of the aisle.

Three-quarters of the way down the walkway, a podium, cut from a single diamond crystal, sat atop a small platform.

Straightening his back and slightly tilting his chin upwards, Madrin separated from his entourage and approached the platform. From the podium, he looked out across the considerable distance to the area where the Council of Seven was seated.

The Council stage was the undisputed centerpiece of the monstrous hall. Like the pews, it too was wooden, and every inch was covered in ornate carvings depicting various Sukarian historical events and generally honoring the benevolent Sukarian spirit. He was once told about the devout Korchak artist who'd carved the piece, but the name escaped him now. He did remember being told the story of how the sculptor had gouged out his own eyes immediately upon completing the work to ensure it was the last thing he would gaze upon, thus searing the image in his mind for all time. He was fairly certain the tale was nothing more than Sukarian propaganda, but the more he considered the devotion of the Korchak, the less he could entirely dismiss the story's credibility.

A small amplification device sat atop the podium, and his fingers trembled slightly as he picked it up and affixed it to his collar. He silently cursed his nerves. Sukarians were exceptionally observant, and it never boded well to show weakness in their presence.

The prefects of the seven Sukarian houses sat stoically upon the stage watching his every move. The crest of each great house was etched in the stage beneath where its corresponding prefect was seated. Each of the houses represented a facet of Sukarian society, and the prefect of each house was tasked with the responsibility of overseeing its function.

He took a sip of water from a crystal glass sitting at the corner of the podium. After replacing the glass, he tugged at the hem of his overcoat. He stared at the prefect sitting at the center of the dais, his seat slightly more elevated than the others. The crest beneath his position displayed the silhouette of a Sukarian battle cruiser on a dark brown background with the word "TELK" written above the ship in black Sukarian lettering. The Prefect of House Telk was the currently appointed leader of the Council of Seven, a fact that he let no one forget.

As if on cue, Prefect Tycus Athket of House Telk spoke in a crisp voice dripping with formality. "This Council recognizes

Madrin Veleko, Ambassador for the Pharus Confederation."

Tycus was short for a Sukarian, though that meant he was still several inches taller than the average Human. He had a stern face with sagging features that made him appear even older than his three-hundred-plus years. Madrin found it disconcerting that his dull charcoal eyes never really seemed to fix on whomever he was speaking to. They appeared to pierce through to some unseen object in the distance.

He looked at each Council member in turn before returning his gaze to Tycus and uttering the obligatory greeting, "It is my great honor to appear before this esteemed High Council of the First Race. Your invitation is most welcome and humbling."

Tycus adjusted himself in his seat, appearing appeased with Madrin's salutation. "Very well then. In the interest of efficiency, I will get right to the subject at hand and tell you why you are here. As a Human emissary, we wish you to relay certain information to your people. Consider it a show of our good faith in the spirit of cooperation with your government."

"Of course, I am at your disposal," Madrin said as his curiosity piqued.

"What I'm about to tell you is not yet widely known," Tycus said.

"Then I will use the utmost discretion with its dissemination," Madrin said.

Tycus nodded his satisfaction and said, "This Council has received troubling reports of an incident in the Tyros system."

"Your Excellency," Madrin said, "if this concerns another incident between the Forrack and the Norvekians, I assure you that Pharus has had success in the past in mediating their strained relations, perhaps—"

"The situation is far beyond territorial quibbling," Prefect Vicaryn Gayne of House Elgeen, cut in. "We have lost communication with both Dullestoon station and Caristo."

"Lost communication?" Madrin asked. "Is the station experiencing mechanical issues? I understand it has been undergoing—"

"No," Vicaryn interrupted again. The issue is not mechanical. We've credible reports that an attack has been perpetrated upon the station, and that fighting continues on the planet as we speak."

Madrin's mind raced as he tried to make sense of the information. "I don't understand, why would the Norvekians suddenly escalate hostilities to such a degree? I was under the impression they were working jointly with the Forrack to refit Dullestoon and improve conditions on Caristo. The reports I've seen have been largely positive regarding their current relations."

Tycus spoke up, "Our reports provided us with the same information Ambassador, but our intelligence indicates there is a third party involved in this attack."

"What third party?"

"We received a holographic transmission from the station shortly before all communication ceased," Tycus said, motioning to his ward, Allyon Corbo.

Allyon stepped onto the stage and retrieved a holographic disk from Tycus. He took it to a nearby holographic terminal and tapped a sequence into the control panel.

As Allyon worked, Madrin noticed Vicaryn studying the ward intently. After a few moments, a holographic image materialized a few feet in front of his podium. The image resolved to show what appeared to be a scene from a ship or space station. A uniformed figure lay prone on the floor near a door. He couldn't make out the blood-soaked uniform, but he immediately noticed that the body was headless. The Forrack's head lay close by in a puddle of dark liquid. A tall soldier, with a torso clad in battle gear, stood at the door's entrance holding a short-handled weapon with a glowing blue blade at one end. A glistening, scaled, serpentine coil extended from his torso to the floor. Even though the still image only showed the soldier's back, he immediately recognized what he was seeing.

No one spoke a word for a long time before Madrin broke the silence with a shaky voice, "Could this be a deception, some sort of hoax maybe?"

Minva Olantus, of House Appox, was seated to Tycus' left. She shook her head and said, "There are survivors of the attack who conclusively confirm what you are seeing."

He looked back to the image. "But how did we not see this coming? The Cohannic have been gone for centuries. Why would they now suddenly reappear to attack a space station?"

Vicaryn leaned forward and rested his elbows on the tabletop. "The why is unimportant. What you see before you is unequivocal proof that the Cohannic have perpetrated an attack upon a sovereign race. A race that is under the protection of this Council I might add."

Tycus shot Vicaryn a sharp glance before looking back to Madrin. "Our response to this treachery will be severe, but also measured," he said. "And despite Prefect Gayne's opinion, the why is important. Before we act, we must first ascertain the motivation for this aggression."

"Motivation?" Vicaryn said incredulously. "They are Cohannic, aggression is in their nature. They require no motivation."

Tycus scowled, but before he could respond, Vicaryn added, "But if motivation is truly what you seek, then maybe the audaciousness of this attack means that the Cohannic sense weakness in this Council's leadership. Perhaps they question our continued ability to protect Vizaria."

The scowl on Tycus' face deepened and he slammed a frail hand down on the tabletop. "We have dispatched the Cohannic before, and we will do so again if it comes to that! The Forrack forces are regrouping on Caristo and preparing to retake the station. I see no need at this time to commit our full force to a situation that may prove to be nothing more than a minor incursion."

Sweat slicked Madrin's palms as he watched the prefects' argument and considered the political angles. Since House Telk commanded the Sukarian military, he knew Tycus could stall military action if he desired. But he couldn't quite shake the feeling that this threat was more substantial than Tycus was ready to believe. Hijacking a space station and attacking a planet were serious actions, especially considering the culprits.

Wringing his hands together, he glanced at Vicaryn, then back to Tycus. "What would you have me do Your Excellence?"

"Implore your government to dispatch a military contingent to convene with the Forrack forces on Caristo. Have them ascertain the true level of threat the Cohannic pose to the Tyros system. And most importantly, you must convince them to share with us any information they might obtain."

More sweat began to accumulate under Madrin's collar. "With respect, Your Excellency, my government may not agree to such a request. They might not deem it to be in their best interest to get involved in this conflict, especially if you are not willing to commit forces."

"We are not asking that Pharus get involved militarily,' Tycus said. "Situational intelligence is all that we request. Your Confederation forces at Fenghou station are nearest to Tyros and can accomplish the task much quicker than we."

He understood Tycus' reasoning but remained unconvinced that Pharus would agree to assist. "My apologies, but I must be blunt," he said. "I am not held in the highest regard within my government. I fear that President Baruke may be disinclined to do what you ask simply because I am the one asking."

Tycus tilted his head slightly. "I do not recall your father ever saying such a thing in this hall. It makes me question why you are here if a small request such as this presents so much of an obstacle."

Madrin glanced at Vicaryn, who wore an impassive expression on his face even though Tycus' comment was an obvious jab at him. It was he who'd groomed and endorsed Madrin to take up his father's post upon his death. Tycus had only reluctantly acquiesced to the appointment.

I've found a way to remind everyone I'm not my father yet again, Madrin thought as beads of sweat now formed on his temples.

He pulled a square of cloth from his breast pocket and dabbed at his forehead. "Of course, Your Excellency, my apologies. I will see it done."

"Excellent. We will await your prompt response," Tycus said sneering. "You may go."

Madrin offered a slight bow before stepping from the platform. He stumbled slightly on the final step before regaining his composure. Veran and Nhila fell in wordlessly behind him when he reached the exit.

Once they were clear of the Chamber, Veran clapped Madrin on the back. "Are you alright?"

Madrin grunted. "You were there. Surely you didn't fail to see that debacle."

Veran waved a dismissive hand. "It wasn't as bad as you think. Besides, if you can convince President Baruke to do what they're asking, all will be forgiven."

"I admire your optimism Veran, but I fear dealing with the President is going to be exponentially more difficult than what I just endured in there," he said, thrusting a thumb back toward the Chamber.

Veran studied him as they descended the stairs. "It will certainly test your political skill, but I know you're up to the task."

"It's shameful that our people treat you as an outsider simply because you were raised among the Sukarians," Nhila said bitterly. "If they were smart, they'd see it as an asset rather than a disadvantage."

Madrin grinned. "It's not my upbringing they fear Nhila, they're all simply jealous of my overwhelming charisma and striking good looks."

She rolled her eyes as they reached the bottom of the stairs. "I'm being serious," she said.

"I know," Madrin said. "But I'm not going to spend my time trying to convince my own government that I'm on their side. Besides, as long as the Council backs me, it doesn't matter what they think. Defying the Council's preferences isn't worth a fight to the President."

Nhila looked doubtful. "Maybe the news of the Cohannic returning will prompt her to agree to assist the Council without the need for much persuasion," she suggested.

"We'll find out soon enough," he said looking at them. "Get some rest; we travel to Somnus first thing in the morning."

Madrin arrived back at his quarters to find that she was already waiting for him in his room, sitting on the edge of the bed. She was always punctual for their encounters, and more importantly, she was always very discreet.

She greeted him with a wry smile as she rose from the bed. "I was beginning to think you weren't going to show."

Tanyara was almost a foot taller than him. She had a slender frame and dark gray eyes that contrasted with her slate gray skin tone. She was as beautiful as any Sukarian female he'd ever seen, including his wife.

"I'm sorry," he said. "I had an important meeting this evening."

"How did it go?"

He sighed heavily. "You don't want to know."

She moved behind him, removed his overcoat, and began to massage his shoulders. "I'm sure it was very stressful. But that's why you have me, no?"

"That's precisely why," he said, turning and pushing her up against the wall. He gently kissed her neck, while she moaned softly. He inhaled her scent as he pressed his lips to hers. She smelled of sweet carabali spice from the outer reach systems.

For the next twenty minutes, they pleasured each other until they lay spent across the large bed. Her fingers traced his navel as she rested her head in the hollow of his shoulder.

He gazed up at the ceiling, his breathing slowing. "What do they say about me?" he asked suddenly.

"How do you mean?" she asked, gazing up at him, still caressing his stomach.

"I mean, I'm sure you hear a lot of things in your line of work. What do you hear about me?"

"I hear many things about you. You're one of the most famous Humans on the planet."

Her voice was like silk, and it put him at ease. He supposed it was a common trait among all pleasure workers, but he didn't know for sure; he'd only had experience with her.

He smiled down at her. "My father was famous. I'm more infamous."

She giggled. "They do say that you aren't much like your father. But that's not a bad thing I don't think. True, your father was admired by my people, but he didn't immerse himself in our ways as you have."

"You mean the fact that I took a Sukarian wife and fathered children with her?"

"Yes, and I know that is a very taboo thing among your people, but it's not only that though. You were raised among us. You observe our traditions and adhere to our ways. My people appreciate that about you. I would say that most Sukarians view you as a friend."

"I've straddled the line between our two races for most of my life, and the only thing I've earned for my effort is the mistrust of both. What your kind see as a friend, mine perceive as nothing more than a puppet of your government."

"Well, do you feel like a puppet?" she asked.

He thought about her question. "I pretty much do what I'm told to do by those who desire power and control. So yes, I suppose I do feel like a puppet most of the time."

She raised herself onto her elbow and looked into his brown eyes. "Then do as I have done and cut your strings, Ambassador."

"How?" he asked.

"Do you know what people say about me? They say that I am a simple pleasure girl, and they're not wrong. But what they fail to understand, is that my status makes me privy to all the dark and dirty little secrets they don't want to come to the light. They tell me things they would never tell their wives, their superiors, or their friends. That makes me powerful."

His body stiffened at her words. President Baruke was already looking for any reason to remove him from his post, and here he was, readily supplying the ammunition for her to succeed. He'd always realized this, yet he persisted.

The great Hayden Veleko wouldn't have been so reckless, he thought.

She sensed his tension. "Don't worry Ambassador. I would never seek to destroy your career, not unless you forced me to. You've been nothing but kind to me. I'm just saying, those who only seek power often underestimate those they wish to control. That is where our power lies. So, what makes you powerful Ambassador?"

He didn't have an answer. But he did realize one thing in that moment. Veran was right. Opportunity was the vehicle of power, and doing the Council's bidding was a rare opportunity indeed. Now the only question was, how could he seize upon it to make him powerful?

CHAPTER FIVE
Vicaryn

Aegus: Flux Star System

Vicaryn sat stewing in silence in his solar above the Great Hall. He swirled his glass of Setgu tonic as he mentally admonished himself for sparring so openly with Tycus at the Council meeting. He prided himself on his superior self-control, and he seldom failed in that regard, but Tycus' cowardice and incompetency brought him to the very limits of his restraint. He had to remind himself that openly opposing the leader of the Council did little to advance his agenda. Brazen opposition would only invite stifling political infighting, and that would not be beneficial to his cause.

Something at the Council meeting nagged at him. He waved a slender hand over the holographic terminal and the face of Dannus Prie materialized a moment later.

"Master, how may I serve?" Dannus asked, touching his index and middle fingers to his forehead.

"What do you know of Allyon Corbo?"

Dannus appeared to search his memory. "Corbo? You speak of Master Athket's ward."

"Yes, the same."

"I know little of him. Master Athket only recently appointed him as his ward."

"Did you know him prior to his appointment?"

"Only by reputation. As I recall, he has a decorated military background. I have seen him in passing around the Chamber, but I have not had the honor of making his acquaintance."

Vicaryn sipped at his drink. "Nor have I."

"Has something troubled you, Master?"

He didn't answer the question. Instead, he asked, "Did you notice anything strange about him this day?"

"No, Master. I cannot say that I did."

He set his drink on the desk and leaned closer to Dannus' image. Lowering his voice, he said, "I want you to gather any information you can on Allyon. I want to know everything there is to know about him. Do it quickly, but be discreet."

Dannus' pale eyes widened slightly. "Yes… yes Master," he said after an uncertain pause.

"Don't worry yourself Dannus," he said. "I'm not asking you to defy your oath. You must take my word that what I'm commanding of you is in the best interest of the Sukarian race."

Dannus' countenance relaxed, and he offered a slight tilt of his head. "I exist to serve and obey."

"Tell no one else of your task, and report your findings to me expeditiously."

Vicaryn disconnected the transmission and sat back in his chair, placing his elbows on the armrests and interlacing his fingers. He pictured Allyon at the Council meeting, mentally recalling the ward's movements and mannerisms.

Those hunched shoulders, and that strange gait; something isn't right, he thought.

All Sukarian prefects had wards who were groomed to one day succeed them, it was their way. Vicaryn's ward, Jeffla Lannis, was away on an assignment. Wards were never less than impeccable in presentation. Their posture, attire, and speech would invariably be displayed perfectly in a public setting. Yet this Allyon Corbo exhibited subtle lapses that caught his attention. He couldn't yet explain what, but there was more to Allyon than the eye could perceive, and he intended to discover what it was.

CHAPTER SIX

Altar

Caristo: Tyros Star System

Altar cradled his left arm to his chest as he trudged across the sandy dunes of the Gaholie Desert. A dull ache pulsated from his shoulder to his elbow, and two of his fingers were beginning to go numb. The escape capsule was damaged during launch, resulting in a much harder landing than he'd expected. The arm wasn't broken, but he would need to tend to it soon.

A light sandstorm was sweeping in from the northeast, and he had to use his uninjured arm to shield his face. He activated his wrist communicator when he was at a safe distance from the escape capsule. He didn't want to be around if anyone came to inspect the crash site.

"Damu, can you hear me?"

He waited for a few beats, then repeated the transmission. "Damu, respond."

"Commander?" Damu's voice answered. "Sir, is that you?"

Altar exhaled a sigh of relief. "You've no idea how good it is to hear your voice. I wasn't sure if you made it off the station."

"We barely did," Damu said.

"I thought they were jamming communications," Altar said.

"They've jammed off-planet communications, but local comms seem to still be operational for now."

"Well, that's a bit of good news at least. What's your position?"

There was a momentary pause on Damu's end before he said,

"We're just south of Umraad City. It's bad sir. The entire area is crawling with Cohannic and Norvekian troops."

"How many are with you?"

"Twenty-six."

"Only twenty-six?"

"Most didn't make it off the station. The attack was highly coordinated. They simultaneously attacked the station and our main ground force in Umraad, and it appears that the Norvekians have thoroughly turned against us."

Altar felt a rush of anger at the betrayal. "Have you heard from High Command?"

"Just before off-world communications were jammed, we were informed that High Command had ordered a full retreat to Yorinar. Most of our remaining soldiers escaped from the Seppian military base before it was overrun. Those who couldn't escape fled into the desert and were slaughtered."

Altar squeezed his eyes shut, thinking about his next course of action. "Okay, the first order of business is to find a way off the planet so we can regroup with the main force on Yorinar. Can your group make it to the Hole?"

"The Hole?" Damu said apprehensively. "But sir, Fallis D'Pah will almost certainly be working with the Cohannic. He's no more trustworthy than the Norvekians."

"I'm not counting on his trustworthiness Damu. It's his greed I'm banking on. We can try to bargain with him for a way off the planet."

"What do we have that he would want?" Damu asked.

"I'll have to figure that out in route," he said. "If he's not in the mood to negotiate, there's someone else I'm hoping might be of assistance. We don't have any other options at this point; Fallis is our only play. Can you make it?"

"I think so."

"I'll meet you there. Travel fast and keep a low profile. Avoid the Cohannic soldiers at all costs, they're more likely to kill you than take you prisoner."

"We're moving out now. Good luck sir."

Altar closed the channel as he looked toward the sky. There were no ships overhead, but he knew he needed to vacate the open desert and find cover if he was to avoid an encounter. He was in no condition for a fight. He knelt and pulled a canteen and a medical kit from the pack he took from the escape pod. He downed several gulps of warm water before applying a medical compression strap to his shoulder. He glanced up at the Tyros star blazing down from above, baking the sandy landscape, and judged that he could make it to the Hole in less than two hours if he moved fast.

The damned Hole, he thought.

At first thought, it didn't seem like the optimal place to seek refuge in a situation like this. Its very name was derived from a bad omen. The tavern's full name, Myric's Hole, alluded to the fable of a disgraced warlord named Myric Dyson. As the Collikan legend went, centuries ago, Myric and his foreign hoard invaded the Collikan ancestral homeworld, Vesbon. In the face of insurmountable odds, the Collikans managed to defeat the invaders. Instead of falling honorably in battle, Myric fled to save his own life, but he was betrayed by his men and delivered into the hands of the Collikan emperor. As punishment for his cowardice in battle, he was sentenced to dig his own grave in preparation for his execution. But as he scooped dirt from the hole, it would instantly refill, not allowing Myric to complete his task. Even though it meant he would never face his execution, he ended up suffering a fate far worse, an eternity of arduous and meaningless labor. The term 'Myric's Hole' was now commonly used throughout Vizaria to refer to any laborious but pointless act.

Altar checked his energy pistol and inserted it into his holster, hoping he wouldn't have to use it on his trek. He set off at a brisk jog, thinking about his destination.

No matter how ill-fitting the name, Myric's Hole is our best chance to get off this planet.

Altar arrived at Myric's Hole just as Tyros was slipping below the northern horizon. His arm throbbed and his eyes burned. He'd drank the last of his water a half-hour ago, and his mouth was as dry as the warm desert air. Catching his breath, he crouched behind a dilapidated outhouse and studied the shabby building in the distance. The discolored exterior clay walls were crisscrossed with hairline cracks that spread over the surface like varicose veins. Wispy tendrils of smoke rose from vents on the roof and mingled with the swirling dust.

Four armored hover tanks were parked in the sandlot on the side of the building, and several mercenary types milled about the grounds. he was relieved to see no Cohannic soldiers slithering about.

He activated his communicator. "Damu, do you copy me?" he whispered.

The voice that answered him was not Damu's. "Rest assured, he can hear you, Commander. He's just not in a position to respond at the moment."

The voice sounded gruff and scratchy, like rubbing coarse sand across a smooth stone. He immediately recognized the speaker as the tavern's proprietor, Fallis D'Pah.

"Listen Fallis—" he began to say before his words were cut short.

"No, I think you should be the one listening right now," Fallis said smugly.

There was a brief pause, followed by a commotion and the sound of a muffled scream. Altar tensed at the noise but remained silent.

Fallis' voice returned to the channel. "Ah, it seems I have your full attention now, good. I'm curious Commander, what unholy desperation brings someone like you to my fine establishment?"

Altar gritted his teeth. "I'm sure you're well aware of the situation."

"Quite so, quite so, but the question remains, why come here?"

"I came because I have a proposition for you," he said.

Fallis made a sound like he was sucking his teeth. "Propositions offered from the shadows are so… disingenuous. Wouldn't you agree? I'm the type who likes to look a person in the eyes when I'm being propositioned."

He slowly stepped from behind the outhouse. He raised his right arm in the air and kept his left arm pressed to his chest.

"Here I am," he said.

He saw movement through the thin layer of gray soot coating the back windows. Two spotlights swiveled in his direction, dousing him in an intense white light. He moved his hand in front of his face to shield his eyes from the harsh glare.

"There he is, in the flesh," Fallis said. "Your weapon, toss it over."

"He reached down cautiously and pulled the pistol from its holster. He tossed it toward the back door of the building before raising his hand back into the air."

"Thank you. Now come a little closer," Fallis instructed.

As Altar warily stepped toward the back door, three mercenaries appeared at the left corner of the building, their energy rifles trained on him.

The back door creaked open and Fallis stood in the entrance. He was a wiry Ragominnian dressed in a black, heavily pocketed, military jumpsuit. His thin green dreadlocks cascaded around his shoulders, and his harsh yellow eyes almost glowed within the shadow of the doorway. He held twin energy pistols, one aimed at Altar, the other at the head of a Forrack soldier with the name 'ASSILEM' embroidered on his uniform.

Fallis stepped from the doorway to within arm's length of Altar. "This is much better, right?" he said.

Altar raised his hand a bit higher into the air. "The weapons are unnecessary. We've not come here as adversaries, we're simply seeking assistance."

"In my experience, assistance is typically rendered by friends," Fallis said. Then he took an exaggerated look around. "Do you see any friends here Commander? It looks to me like you've traveled all this way just to die."

"Come now, Fallis. You claim to be a businessman, don't you? Assistance is a commodity like anything else. It can be bought and sold. I'm looking to buy."

A flicker of interest flashed in Fallis' eyes. Though he moonlighted as a tavern owner, he was still a mercenary through and through. He'd sold his services to so many different sides of so many different conflicts, that Altar seriously doubted if he even bothered to consider right and wrong anymore. He understood that for people like Fallis, the equation was simple. If compensation was involved, it was always right.

Fallis looked around with a smile. "Why not? Let us hear what the good Commander has to offer. I'm in the mood for a bit of entertainment."

Altar stole a glance at the female Sukarian standing just behind Fallis. Her name was Vascha Norn, and his next words would be indirectly aimed at her. She'd always struck him as a maternal-type figure to Fallis, maybe an advisor of some sort. He didn't fully understand the dynamics of their relationship, but he suspected she curbed some of Fallis' more sadistic tendencies. He'd appealed to her sensibilities in the past when dealing with the Dark Hand, and he believed her to be a reasonable and reliable resource. He was silently hoping his assessment of her would prove true.

He looked Fallis in the eyes and said, "Here's where we stand Fallis. We've lost Caristo. Anyone with eyes can see that. I know you and your Dark Hand will play some role in the Cohannics' future plans, but ask yourself, what happens when they're defeated? You know as well as I that they've tried this before, and it ended with them paying a steep price. Everyone else who sided with them paid a price too. It's taken them over two and a half centuries to crawl off that sweltering rock they call a homeworld."

Fallis licked his lips but said nothing.

Altar continued, "All I'm asking is that you provide us safe passage from Caristo. The Cohannic don't need to know you allowed us to leave. In return, I give you my word that the Forrack government will take no action against the Dark Hand when this is all over. You can keep your operation, as well as your life."

The strike came so fast that Altar didn't have time to react. He gasped as Fallis struck him in his injured shoulder with the butt of the energy pistol, causing him to drop to one knee and sending a torrent of pain shooting from his shoulder to the tips of his fingers.

Fallis glared down at him over the end of his gun. "You presume to offer me my life when it's clearly yours that hangs in the balance. Okay then, here's my official response to your offer."

He discharged his energy pistol into Assilem's temple. Half of the soldier's head disappeared in a spray of crimson and gray as his lifeless body crumpled to his knees and fell onto his side.

Altar sprang to his feet, but the Dark Hand mercenary behind him kicked his legs from beneath him, sending him sprawling onto the ground.

Fallis leveled both his pistols at Altar's head and moved his fingers to the trigger. "Your proposal is rejected," he said.

"Wait!" Vascha's voice called from behind Fallis.

She stepped beside him, keeping her eyes on Altar. She leaned in and whispered something into his ear that Altar couldn't hear. After she finished, Fallis looked at her questioningly and she nodded slightly.

Keeping the pistols aimed at Altar, he asked, "Do you value the safety of your soldiers, Commander?"

Altar grimaced as he nodded. "They have families. And as I said, this planet is lost to us; there's no need for further bloodshed here."

"Would you die for them?" Fallis asked.

He struggled back onto his knees. "Without hesitation," he said.

Fallis holstered his energy pistols. "There's a small transport vessel at my hangar just east of here. It'll comfortably accommodate you and fifteen of your soldiers. Take it and leave this planet. If your people survive this fight, I expect you to hold to your word and fully pardon me and my organization for any actions we pursue during your fight with the snakes."

"Fifteen?" Altar asked. "But there are twenty-seven..." Altar stopped himself, glancing at Assilem's body, his legs still twitching. "Twenty-six of us."

"The others will remain here with me," Fallis said. "They won't be harmed as long as you keep your word. But if I suspect that you have plans to break your promise, it will be them who pay the price. And trust me, Commander, it will be an awfully slow and painful price. You say they have families, well then I urge you to remember that."

"I'll stay as one of the ten then," Altar said.

Without a word, Fallis drew and pointed one of his pistols at the nearest Forrack soldier and fired. She let out a stunned groan as she clutched the singed hole in her stomach. She glanced at Altar with fear and despair in her eyes before collapsing onto the ground, her dark blood soaking into the sand.

Vascha flinched and Altar shouted a stream of obscenities at Fallis.

Fallis aimed at another of the Forrack soldiers. "You still seem to believe you are in a negotiation Commander. You are not. I'm calling the shots and I've told you what to do. Now, unless you want me to press this trigger again, I suggest you get moving… now. You'll be traveling with one less, so you'll have more legroom."

He holstered his pistol and twirled an index finger in the air. A group of mercenaries shoved fifteen of the Forrack soldiers out the door toward Altar, while another group held the ten hostages at gunpoint.

As the door closed, Altar took one more look at Vascha. Her onyx eyes conveyed a helpless apology and he could only hope she would look after his troops.

With rage in his eyes, Damu reached down and helped Altar to his feet as he growled, "I'm going to kill that bastard."

"No. You aren't," Altar said. "I struck a bargain and I intend to honor it."

"You can't be serious sir. He killed Assilem and Eener like they were nothing. He'll kill the others too."

"I understand your frustration Damu, I do, but we were all condemned to death when High Command left us behind. We have a second chance now, a ticket off this planet. A ticket that Assilem, Eener, and all the others paid for with their blood. Fallis is a problem for another day. I need you with me on this."

He extended his good arm. Damu chewed the inside of his cheek as he eyed the outstretched arm, then he grasped Altar's forearm and said, "Of course I'm with you. Always will be. C'mon, I know where the hangar is, follow me."

Altar didn't budge. Instead, he looked at the soldiers assembled around him. "Today was brutal," he said. "It was a stark reminder that we live in a cruel and unforgiving universe. It was a reminder that came at the expense of our fallen comrades. But I swear to you, when the time comes, and we defeat the Cohannic, we'll show this universe that we learned our lesson well. We'll have our vengeance." He stared at the Myric's Hole tavern. "I intend to start here."

He turned and started walking east, his soldiers followed.

CHAPTER SEVEN
Tolbin

Janus: Pharus Star System

Tolbin Mako hated this city. Upsonna was nice enough, as sprawling metropolises went, but it wasn't the aesthetics that unnerved him, it was that damned dome. A shiver traveled up his spine as he walked down the dark alleyway.

The only thing preventing me from being crushed by trillions of gallons of seawater is an energy barrier the width of my thumb.

He cringed at the thought as he glanced up nervously at the shimmering domed barrier. The view of the blue-green blanket of water was interposed by skytower summits and transport tubing. He could almost hear the rushing water above the bustle of the city, but it was likely just his imagination playing tricks on him.

He spotted the meeting place up ahead on the right, and as he approached the sturdy iron door, he noted that it looked out of place among the other shabby wooden doors lining the alleyway. He expected nothing less from the Admiral. She preferred to meet in person for his mission briefings, and never in the same location more than once.

I hope this is the last meeting in an underwater city, he thought as he banged his fist on the thick door.

A computerized voice spoke from the intercom. "Authorization code?"

Tolbin placed his eye close to the retinal scanner as he spoke. "Alpha, eight, twenty-eight, seven, five."

"Authorization code acknowledged; welcome Agent Mako."

The door slid open vertically and Tolbin stepped into the sparsely furnished room. The cold air caused goosebumps to rise on his forearms. The walls of the room were padded from floor to ceiling with signal-disruption mesh designed to prevent surveillance and communications interception. A holographic communicator sat on a metal desk that was pushed up against the left wall, and a small couch was positioned against the right wall near an accent table.

Sado Felix rose from the couch and walked toward him sporting a forced smile. "Good to see you again Agent Mako."

He was thin with a tanned complexion, and his clean-shaven face and keen blue eyes made him look younger than his actual age. He was smartly dressed in business attire, as usual, and not a strand of the blond hair on his head was out of place.

Tolbin didn't bother returning the smile. "Sado, it's been a long time, though not quite as long as I would have liked unfortunately."

Sado clasped his hands in front of him. "Trust me, the feeling is mutual."

"Where's the Admiral?" he asked, looking over Sado's shoulder toward the hall leading to the rear of the residence.

"Regretfully, she had other pressing matters to attend to, so she sent me to conduct this meeting."

"What matters?"

"She didn't say, and I didn't ask. You know how Phalanx business goes."

Tolbin sauntered over to the couch and plopped down, placing his feet on the accent table. "So, what are my orders then?"

Sado touched his wrist communicator and a holographic image of Caristo materialized above the metal table. "Deep cover assignment on Caristo."

He rolled his green eyes. "What the hell have the Forrack and Norvekians gotten up to now?"

Sado chuckled. "Do you really think we'd send an asset to Caristo over a petty dispute?"

"Who's we exactly?" Tolbin asked with a raised eyebrow. "The Admiral does all the sending. You're just the glorified errand boy for the Phalanx."

Sado visibly stifled a retort before regaining his composure.

"We'll have to agree to disagree on that point. You're being sent to infiltrate the Dark Hand."

Tolbin rubbed at the course stubble of his beard. "The Dark Hand is old news. We know all about them. Why do I need to join up?"

Sado touched his communicator again, and the image of Caristo was replaced by an image of a Cohannic soldier standing over a decapitated body.

"You probably weren't aware, since the errand boy hasn't informed you yet, but the Cohannic are back. They've taken the planet with the help of the Norvekians, and there's little doubt that the Dark Hand will be working with them in some capacity."

Tolbin removed his feet from the table and leaned forward with his elbows on his knees. "Bullshit," he said. "There hasn't been a Cohannic sighting in nearly two hundred years."

"More like two hundred and seventy years," Sado corrected. "Either way, we'll need to reset the clock, because they're most definitely back, and the Dark Hand is exactly the type of organization they'd utilize to advance their agenda."

"And what agenda is that?" Tolbin asked.

"We don't know yet. The Admiral believes it's in our interest to have someone on the inside so we can find out."

He studied the holographic image, intrigued. "What are the mission parameters?"

"Strictly non-lethal observation and reporting. We just need to know what they're planning next. Are they content with Dullestoon station and Caristo, or are they set on galactic domination again?"

"You do realize that Fallis D'Pah isn't among the most trusting despots," Tolbin said. "Infiltrating his organization will take time."

"Don't worry about that. We suspect they'll be recruiting heavily to stay in the Cohannics' good graces, and they don't exactly discriminate."

Tolbin grunted. "The hell they don't. They'd never accept a Forrack."

Sado handed him a datapad. "Good thing you're not a Forrack then. They'll take members of any other race as long as they're disreputable enough. You should fit right in," Sado said clapping him on the shoulder.

He looked down at his shoulder, then back at Sado. "Please don't touch me."

Sado cleared his throat. "We've already prepped your cover. You'll find everything you need on that pad. You'll be using the Dergon Santon identity."

Tolbin grinned with delight. "That one's my favorite. The disgruntled Pharus military defector turned independent smuggler and mercenary."

"The mercenary part does come quite naturally to you," Sado said.

Tolbin ignored the slight. "What's the mission duration?"

"You'll remain there as long as the Admiral needs you to be there. We need a lot more intel before we can decide on the appropriate action to take."

"When do I leave?"

"Two days, so get comfortable. You'll be departing Janus with a small survey team leaving from Griner Military Base. They'll take the Unity portal to Ilmad station for a refitting operation. At Ilmad, you'll detach from the survey team and board a small freighter that'll be waiting for you. It'll be loaded up with a small cache of military-grade weapons, and two cases each of fintra and diamond crystals."

Tolbin whistled. "That's a lot of riches, even for a smuggler. But why fintra crystals? What would the Dark Hand need with cloaking technology?"

"We don't know yet, but our best guess is that they plan to sell them on the black market as funding for their operation. We'd be ever so grateful if you'd use only what's necessary to accomplish the mission."

Tolbin winked. "Don't worry Sado, I'm a thrifty type of fella."

Sado looked unconvinced, but he continued, "You're to only use secure quantum communication channels, and then only if absolutely necessary. From Ilmad, you'll take the relay to Caristo and make contact with the Dark Hand. Your cover will be in place well before you arrive in the Tyros system. The rest is up to you."

"No sweat," Tolbin said, memorizing the information and simultaneously dreading spending two more days in the underwater city.

"I hope so," Sado said. "This is a top-priority black operation. And do try to remember the non-lethal bit, will you? We only need information. It wouldn't do for you to blow your cover trying to live up to the myth of your legendary badass status."

"That myth is what helps me survive out there," he said.

"Just try not to die on this one," Sado said. "Not that I'd lose a wink of sleep. I just don't want us having to explain what we were doing to the President."

"Don't fret Sado, I won't disappoint the Admiral. And I sure as hell won't be giving you the satisfaction of dancing on my grave."

Sado smirked. "I'd gladly take dance lessons for the occasion."

He glanced again at the back hallway, then he turned and walked from the residence. He could almost feel the hole Sado's stare was boring into the back of his head.

After Tolbin was gone, Phalana Maldon stepped from the darkened hallway at the back of the residence. She was tall with a lithe figure and a smooth olive complexion. Her slightly graying, cornrowed hair was gathered into a long braid that hung to the middle of her back.

Sado turned to her. "Well, what do you think?"

"I think it went well," she said. "I know you don't care much for him, but he's perfect for a mission of this type. The Phalanx needs him."

"Then why did you avoid meeting with him?" Sado asked.

"Detachment. Tolbin is as cold and callous as they come, but he harbors a soft spot for me because of what I did for him. It makes him weak sometimes. I need him at the very top of his game for this."

"Do you not think it's wise to at least send a secondary asset, just in case?" he asked.

"No. He needs to feel completely alone, without friends and without backup, because that's exactly what he'll be. Once he gets to Caristo, it's out of our hands. We'll have to rely on him to get the intelligence we need and relay it to us whenever he can."

Sado shook his head slowly. "I think you put too much faith in him."

"Perhaps, but the Forrack won't be able to stop the Cohannic by themselves. When they inevitably fail, we'll need every advantage we can get to contain the threat."

"How much of what we learn from this operation do you plan on sharing with the President?"

"We'll share what we must, but no more. President Baruke has her own agenda. The Confederation will seek to avoid this war if possible, but they lack the foresight to see that it's inevitable. While they bicker amongst themselves, the Phalanx will continue to do the heavy lifting behind the scenes to stave off disaster."

"If she ever discovered what we're really doing, that will be the true disaster."

Phalana fixed her dark brown eyes on him. "Make no mistake Sado, the Confederation knows what we're doing, they just don't know *how* we do it. Truth be told, they don't want to. Baruke and the Assembly get to keep their hands clean and their consciences clear. Meanwhile, we'll do what needs to be done. Frankly, I prefer it that way."

Sado nodded and started for the door. "I'll work on getting everything ready for the mission."

"Sado," Phalana called out to him, "make sure he gets whatever he needs; expenses be damned. But keep a close eye on him."

CHAPTER EIGHT
Madrin

<u>**Somnus: Pharus Star System**</u>

"Ambassador Veleko, what an honor," Surman Aletto said with the practiced smile of a politician.

"Senator," Madrin said, shaking Surman's outstretched hand.

Surman was the longest-tenured senator in the Pharus Assembly, and his wrinkled hands and weather-beaten face bore witness to that fact. Despite his age, he was a spry man with energetic blue eyes, and he was widely expected to be President Baruke's successor.

"How was your trip?" Surman asked.

"Uneventful," Madrin said.

"Incredible, isn't it?" Surman asked, his steely blue eyes twinkling.

Madrin twisted his face in confusion. "Excuse me."

"From one star system to another in less than a day, what would we do without the wonders of Sukarian ingenuity?" Surman said, still smiling.

"Oh, yeah, the portals are something else," Madrin said.

He wondered if Surman was simply making small talk, or if he was trying to gauge his level of infatuation with the Sukarians.

Every interaction is a test here, he thought.

"Has the President arrived yet?" he asked.

The Senator's smile widened. "Always so quick to get down to business. Never one for chit chat."

"My apologies. I suppose I'm just a bit uneasy considering the circumstances."

"Ah, yes. This business in the Tyros system has us all a little on edge. What's your assessment of the situation?" Surman asked.

"It seems pretty serious to me," Madrin said.

Surman pursed his lips, exponentially increasing the wrinkles around his mouth. "What are the Sukarians going to do about it?"

"That's what I'm here to discuss with the President. Has she arrived yet?" he asked again.

Surman glanced around the waiting area and said, "I was told she would be with us shortly. Until then, let's catch up. How are your wife and children?"

"They're well."

"I do hope I'll get to meet them someday. I've heard nothing but wonderful things."

"I look forward to giving them a tour of the planet someday soon," Madrin lied.

He could hardly think of anything he wanted less than to parade his Sukarian wife and half-Sukarian children around as a spectacle for gawking onlookers. Laudrin had only accompanied him to the Pharus system once, to see the Palacia Gardens, before the children were born. The curious glances and judgmental stares were enough to ruin the entire trip. She vowed never to return, and he hadn't pressured her to do so.

The President's holographic secretary materialized near a smoked glass door on the opposite side of the room. "President Baruke will see you now," it said in a pleasant voice.

Surman gestured toward the door. "After you Ambassador."

The presidential conference room was a simple affair. A few portraits of past presidents decorated the walls, alongside the framed facsimiles of several important historical documents. A large wooden desk sat near the room's only window. The floors were dark hardwood partially covered by a circular rug upon which the President's desk sat. A high-backed leather chair was positioned behind the desk, and two smaller leather chairs, separated by an accent table, sat facing it.

President Jastine Baruke rose from her seat and approached the men as they entered. Her shoulder-length auburn hair swayed with her long strides, and her hazel eyes conveyed power and competence. Her manufactured smile was of the same sort Surman had greeted him with, and he began to wonder if he too subconsciously employed the insincere politicians' smile in his greetings.

"Ambassador Veleko, Senator Aletto," she said shaking their hands in turn, "I apologize for the wait. I had to tend to an important matter."

"Understandable," Surman said taking his seat. "Thank you for taking the time."

"Yes, thank you," Madrin echoed, unconvinced. He was all too familiar with the power play of making attendees wait past time for a meeting. He'd employed the tactic once or twice himself.

Jastine took a seat at her desk as Madrin settled into his chair. "So, Ambassador, I understand that you've come at the behest of the Sukarian Council."

He cleared his throat before saying, "Yes ma'am. I'm sure you're well aware of the situation in the Tyros system. It has introduced a substantial amount of chaos throughout the spiral arm."

"Indeed it has," she said.

He continued, "As you're also well aware, the Council of Seven doesn't do well with chaos. As such, they're requesting an intelligence-sharing arrangement with us in order to better assess the situation."

She glanced at Surman, then looked back to Madrin. "We always share information with the Council, why should this situation be different? We all have a common interest in resolving this matter promptly."

"That's just it," Madrin said, "we don't know exactly what the matter is, do we?"

She put two fingers to her chin. "Well, we know that an aggressive race has engaged in an unprovoked hostile action against a sovereign system."

"We also know that the Norvekians helped to facilitate said hostile actions," Surman added.

"But I'm certain the Sukarians know all this too, and possibly more," Jastine said. "So exactly what intelligence does the Council wish us to share?"

"They're looking for more specific information. Things like targets, troop numbers, objectives, and actionable intelligence. They would like the Confederation to take steps to gather it."

She sat back in her chair. "I see. The Council would like us to go to the Tyros system, knock on the Dullestoon station hull, and ask the Cohannic to please tell us what they're up to. Then, after they explain their master plan, they would like us to report back to them. Is that the gist of it?"

He said nothing in response to the sarcasm.

She fixed him with a bemused stare. "And what was their response when you politely explained to them that the Confederation isn't a Sukarian subject to be ordered around?"

"It wasn't an order Madame President. It was more of a request in the spirit of galactic cooperation."

"I wonder," she said, narrowing her eyes, "if the roles were reversed, would the Sukarians be so helpful to us? They seem to always be on the demanding end of these so-called requests in the spirit of galactic cooperation."

He shrugged his shoulders. "They did provide us with unrestricted access to the data logs they received from Dullestoon. That's not information they had to share with us. I take that as evidence of their good faith."

"Good faith would have been contacting me directly with the information, but instead they sent you to deliver both the logs and their request."

Madrin tilted his head. "Is that not the role of an ambassador?"

"Quite so," she said, "but I often find myself wondering just whose ambassador you are. One would think you'd be lobbying the Council on behalf of the Human race, but here you are doing the opposite."

He shook his head. "My allegiances are clear. Everything I do is for the benefit of the Human race."

"I beg to differ," she said. "For instance, what concessions did you negotiate on behalf of the Confederation in response to the Council's request?"

He adjusted himself in his chair, keenly aware of Surman's eyes locked on him in anticipation of an answer. "As I said Madame

President, it was a simple enough request. I didn't believe myself to be at a bargaining table."

Surman broke into a condescending chuckle. "When dealing with the Sukarians, you're always at a bargaining table," he said.

Jastine abruptly rose from her seat and said, "Well then, if it's only a request, kindly inform the Council that we respectfully decline to operate as their scouting party."

Madrin felt a nagging pressure at his temples as he felt his goal of securing the Confederation's cooperation slipping away. He understood the President's sentiments well enough, and he shared her frustrations. The Council of Seven could be extremely aloof at times, almost certainly a byproduct of their exalted status and self-aggrandizement. But that's why he viewed his position as so important. He was supposed to be the filter that rendered the Council's haughty disposition more palatable to the Human government.

It's hard to be a filter when all they see is a Sukarian trapped in a Human body when they look at me.

"If I may," he said, raising his hands in a conciliatory gesture. "Please."

She reluctantly sat back down.

"I know you don't think much of me," Madrin said. "But regardless of your opinion of me, I only have Pharus' best interest at heart. I know the Council can be difficult at times, but I honestly believe that working with them on this is best for everyone involved, including us. This threat is too serious to allow political bickering to hamper our efforts. Besides, even if you decide to go it alone, the next logical step would be to gather intelligence anyway, would it not?

"That's a reasonable assumption," she conceded.

He continued, "Then what's the harm in proceeding to do what you would naturally do anyway? That will allow you time to both gauge the true extent of this threat, as well as to ascertain the Council's level of commitment to cooperation."

"You believe they will continue to act in good faith if we give them what they want?" Surman asked.

Madrin nodded. "I do. Let's not forget, they've faced down the Cohannic before and won. Practically alone, I might add. Pharus should be a part of the victory this time."

Jastine drummed her fingers on the desk as she stared at him. "I knew your father, you know. More by reputation than by personal experience, mind you, but I did cross paths with him a few times. He was as great a diplomat as he's given credit for. I do see some of him in you Ambassador, but the one thing you would be wise to remember about Hayden Veleko is that he never forgot who he was. He was a Human. You may technically be a Pharus ambassador, but you clearly serve at the leisure of the Council of Seven, not mine. So, you can report back to your handlers that we'll take steps to ascertain the severity of this Cohannic threat, but we'll do it on our own time, and of our own volition. Unlike you, I am not a puppet of the Council of Seven. So, until Pharus is treated as a partner, and as an equal, We'll determine what intelligence we choose to share, and with whom we choose to share it."

With that, she and Surman rose from their seats, indicating that the meeting was over.

Madrin stood up slowly and straightened his jacket. He nodded curtly at them both. "I will ensure the Council receives your official response to their request. Thank you for your time."

He exited the Presidential Headquarters building and was joined by Nhila and Veran. The look of anticipation on their faces was palpable.

"Well? How did it go?" Veran finally asked, falling in beside him.

"Better than expected," he said.

A broad smile spread across Veran's face as the tension drained away. "Excellent! So, what's the President's action plan?"

"To go it alone."

Veran's smile faded in an instant. "I thought you said it went well."

"I said it went better than expected. Meaning that at least they didn't hurl me from the top floor window."

"This is disappointing news. The Council won't be pleased, not one bit." Veran said.

Madrin ran a sweaty palm over his short black hair. "The Council doesn't necessarily need to know the details."

Veran stopped in his tracks. His face went pale, and his mouth hung open. "Ambassador, I strongly recommend against attempting to deceive the Council in any way. The consequences would be dire."

"It's not deception. The Confederation will do precisely what the Council wishes. They'll simply be doing it of their own accord."

"And what happens when the Council calls on Pharus to deliver the intelligence they've gathered?" Veran asked, the color not yet back in his cheeks.

"When that time comes, our government will cooperate with the Council as they always have. I'm certain of it. Right now, I see no need to alarm the Council with technicalities."

Veran resumed walking, but his posture didn't portray confidence in Madrin's reasoning. "You're playing a risky game. For all our sakes, I hope you win."

"I always win," Madrin said with a wink.

Veran placed a hand on his shoulder. "Now that we have that bit of business behind us, your mother awaits you on Arcus."

Madrin turned to Nhila and asked, "Is the transport ready?"

"Ready and waiting," she responded. "Shall we leave now?"

He glanced back at the Presidential Headquarters building. "Yes. Now is very good," he said.

Arcus: Pharus Star System

"Prepare for atmospheric entry," the pilot said over the transport's intercom system.

"Finally," Veran grunted as he activated his shoulder harness.

Nhila engaged her own harness. "Oh stuff it Veran, it wasn't that bad."

"Wasn't that bad! The pilot went out of his way to hit every distortion pocket in the relay. I'm surprised we made it in one piece."

"And how many ships have you piloted in your life?" she asked sarcastically.

"You should be asking the pilot that question," he shot back.

She rolled her eyes. "You're insufferable."

"No, he's just an old man," Madrin said yawning and rubbing

his eyes. "Space travel can be tough on the elderly."

"You just wait until you get a few more years on your ledger, then we'll see who's laughing then," Veran said.

The transport ship shuddered slightly as it dove through the atmosphere of Arcus. Madrin peered out the window at the landscape passing by below. Dense forests gave way to flat plains dotted with lakes and ponds. Then came the industrial zones, pockmarked with massive processing plants and hulking manufacturing hubs. He silently marveled at the efficiency of it all. How all of the smaller moving parts worked together to keep the entire planet humming along. He correlated this with his existence as a mere cog in the vast political machine.

Those at the controls of the machine wield the real power, he thought.

The first skytowers moved into his field of vision as the transport approached the outskirts of the city. Though not quite as tall as those on Aegus, the towering buildings made for an impressive sight as ships of varying sizes weaved above and around their summits. They fell in line behind a large refuse-disposal vessel bearing the corporate logo of the Jennash Corporation.

"Approaching the Thoman City landing field," the pilot said over the intercom system.

Veran tapped Madrin's arm. "How does it feel to be home?" he asked, pointing out the window.

"Good, but it doesn't feel quite like home anymore."

Veran glanced out of the window. "I know what you mean. Things have changed a lot. The skytowers keep getting taller, and the traffic lanes keep getting slower."

"It's not just about how much things have changed over the years, it's also the fact that I don't get back here often enough," Madrin said.

Veran chuckled. "That's the cost of being a big shot ambassador."

The pilot's voice returned. "Touchdown in five. Four. Three. Two. One."

There was a slight thump as the metal landing struts contacted the landing pad and the docking clamps locked the ship into place.

"Vessel secure," the pilot announced. "It was a pleasure to provide for your travel needs. Have a wonderful visit to Thoman

City."

Nhila kneeled next to Madrin's seat. "Sir. Please remain here while my team secures the route to the hospital."

He nodded, then pulled out his datapad to search the hub. "Let's see what's going on around Vizaria," he said scanning the feed.

He tapped on a feed labeled 'Breaking News' and his face gradually soured as he read the article.

"What is it?" Veran asked.

"The Forrack have lost Caristo."

Disbelief shrouded Veran's features. "The entire planet?"

"It appears so," Madrin said as he continued reading. "The Norvekians have allied with the Cohannic, and it says here that the Forrack forces have withdrawn to Yorinar."

"This is getting more serious by the day," Veran said.

"More serious by the minute is more accurate," Madrin corrected. He glanced up to see Veran grinning. "I don't like that look. What sinister thoughts are you having?"

Veran clasped his hands together and pressed them to his lips. "Hear me out," he said. "This problem has escalated well beyond what the Forrack can handle alone. There needs to be a galactic response. Now imagine you," he pointed a finger at Madrin, "the esteemed Ambassador Madrin Veleko, spearheading the effort to coordinate a united galactic response to quash this threat. That sort of publicity would be all but guarantee you a senatorial seat in the Pharus Assembly."

Madrin sat back in his seat and rubbed a finger back and forth across his eyebrow. "I'm not sure if you noticed Veran, but I couldn't even convince our own government to cooperate with the Sukarians. How do you expect me to bring the entire galactic community together for a common cause?"

"I have confidence in you my boy. I know what you're capable of, even if you don't."

Madrin's communicator chimed, and Nhila's voice said, "Sir, the route has been vetted. We can leave whenever you're ready."

He stared at Veran. "You're right. This is a serious situation that requires a very serious response. When we get back to Aegus, I'll try to convince the Council to act with or without our government's intelligence. If the Sukarians make a move, everyone else will follow."

Veran grinned. "That's the spirit. But remember, it's all about perception. You'll have to make sure you get the credit for any coalition that's formed."

Madrin stood and clapped Veran on the shoulder as he started toward the transport exit. "That, my friend, is what I pay you for."

The hospital was only a short distance north of the landing field, but Madrin was grateful for the reprieve. He felt like he'd been running a non-stop marathon, and it was starting to take a toll on his mind and body.

I wish I could see Tanyara, he thought longingly.

He surreptitiously watched Nhila as she sat across from him. She sat motionless, staring out the window of the hover car. Her jaw was slightly clinched, and her light eyes shifted constantly, scanning the terrain. He could almost feel the tension radiating from her. She looked like she was ready to uncoil and spring into action at a moment's notice.

"Do you ever miss it?" he asked.

"Sir?" she said, pulling her attention from the window.

"Your time at Sagis… and the stuff before. I'm sure it was all a bit more exciting than chaperoning a mid-level politician around."

She smiled. "I can't argue that point. But if you're asking if I ever long to go back into that life, my answer is an emphatic no."

"Why not?"

She sighed softly. "The life of a mercenary is treacherous; I'll never go back to that. I did a lot of things back then that I'm not proud of now. I justified it all by constantly telling myself that I only did what I had to do to survive. But to be honest, I actually enjoyed a lot of it, and that's what scared me the most. I was young and impulsive, and I got a rush from all the excitement, but for all of my adventuring, I didn't end up with a lot to show from that time in my life."

Madrin nodded his understanding. "That's what led you to Sagis?"

She nodded her head. "At first I thought Sagis saved me from that world. Being a security specialist for a major corporation had its perks, and it paid well of course. But then the scandal happened, and it made me realize that I'd never really escaped my demons, I'd only changed their scenery."

He could see the pain behind her eyes, and he regretted broaching the subject. Her prior involvement in the slave trade would forever be a stain on her reputation, but he didn't believe it should define who she was for the rest of her life.

He leaned forward and rested his forearms on his knees. "You made a terrible mistake, but you also corrected it. You're the one who exposed Sagis' actions and put a stop to what they were doing. That counts for something."

She chuckled bitterly. "It certainly hurt me a lot more than it hurt them," she said.

Madrin remembered when news of the salacious incident broke. He monitored the hub closely as each new development surfaced. Though he wouldn't admit it to Nhila, he secretly marveled at the way Sagis navigated its way through the fallout. After sacrificing a few low-level executives to take the blame, they then embarked on a whirlwind public relations campaign and doled out some modest fines. The whole sordid affair faded into obscurity within a few short weeks.

Politics at its finest, he thought.

He reached out and placed a hand on Nhila's knee. "My father used to say that the only cure for shame was redemption. Regardless of what you did in your past, it was you who singlehandedly ended the largest slave-trading operation in recent memory. If that's not redemption, then I don't know what is."

"I appreciate you saying that, and I'll be forever grateful for the opportunity you gave me when no one else wanted anything to do with me. I know it cost you a lot, politically I mean."

He waved a dismissive hand in her direction. "I'd pay the price a thousand times over. If you haven't realized it yet, my political image has never enjoyed very favorable reviews."

She chuckled again and the bitterness had evaporated. "Even so, I still believe that you'll be president one day, and when you do, it'll continue to be my honor to protect your ass," she said with a smile.

The Karmend Medical Facility was the largest hospital on Arcus. It sported twin skytowers seventy-four stories tall that were comprised almost entirely of opaque glass. Karmend was renowned for its exceptional diagnosis and treatment of a wide variety of trauma and diseases. It was here, nearly three years ago, that Madrin's father was unsuccessfully treated for Nalick's disease, a rare central nervous disorder that was almost always fatal.

As the private car hovered into the parking station of the facility's south wing, an automated voice greeted them. "Welcome to the Hayden Veleko Disease and Infection Treatment Ward. Your assigned space is located on level one, lot eleven dash two. Have a pleasant visit."

Carrine Veleko beamed as Madrin stepped stiffly from the car. She moved in and hugged him tightly, then stepped back and assessed him.

"Let me look at you," she said.

He raised his hands out to his sides and spun in a circle. "Do I pass inspection mother?" he asked smiling.

She turned to Nhila and asked, "Has he been getting enough rest? He looks exhausted."

"He never rests ma'am," Nhila said looking at him.

Carrine pursed her lips. "Just as I suspected."

"How are you mother?" he asked.

"Oh, you know, one day at a time and all that."

"It's good to see you. You look well," he said.

"It's good to see you too." She pointed an accusatory finger at him. "You must visit more often."

His brown cheeks blushed purple. "I know, and I will."

She looked at him doubtfully. "Well then," she said, "come up to my office. We have much to discuss."

She shot a final glance at Nhila before interlacing her arm with his and guiding him toward the elevator as Nhila issued directives to her three-man security team.

They entered the elevator, and when the doors slid closed, Carrine turned to him and said, "I'm delighted to see Nhila hasn't yet slit your throat from ear to ear."

"Don't start mother," he groaned.

"I'm just saying, you can't always trust those ex-mercenary types."

"You sound like Veran when I first brought her on," he said.

"Veran is wise. There's a reason your father trusted his counsel. You should think about that."

"She's been with me for over a year now mother. You'd think if she was going to rob me blind or murder me, she'd have done it by now. She's not in that life anymore."

Carrine shrugged but said nothing further.

They exited on the forty-sixth floor and walked the short distance down the hallway to Carrine's office. The suite was well-appointed, and a large digital portrait of Hayden Veleko hung on the far wall above the desk. The broad smile and intense brown eyes were exactly as Madrin remembered.

The man even exudes charm through a picture, he thought.

The panoramic window to the right offered a spectacular view of downtown Thoman City. The platinum dome of the provincial capitol building gleamed brightly as it reflected the afternoon light from Pharus. He could even make out the curved roof of the impressive Cultural History Museum, which purported to preserve the remembered history of the Human ancestral star system.

That is until we managed to find a way to destroy it.

Carrine ushered him toward a sitting area with two plush chairs and a semi-circular table holding a water carafe and two drinking glasses. They each took a seat.

"So, tell me," she began with a twinkle in her eyes, "how is that family of yours that I hardly ever get to see?"

"Laudrin and the kids are doing fine. I promise I'll bring them to see you soon."

She seemed satisfied with his response as she picked up a glass of water and sat back in her chair. "Well, get on with it then. I know you didn't travel all the way from Aegus just to visit your dear old mother. How bad is it?"

"How bad is what?" he asked, bringing his glass to his lips.

"The situation in the Tyros system of course. What else? It's all the talking heads on the hub have been blathering about lately."

"It's probably much worse than what they're reporting. It's

almost like no one wants to accept that this invasion is happening."

"Is that why you met with the President, to make her accept it?"

"Sort of. The Sukarians aren't sold on the magnitude of the problem yet. They want the Confederation to do some digging."

"And what do you think?"

"I don't think we have the luxury of sitting on our hands. We should be acting right now. All of us."

"What did she say when you explained the urgency of the situation?"

"Let's just say she wasn't in the mood to hear Sukarian words coming from my Human mouth. She essentially reminded me that I'm not father and sent me on my way."

"And you accepted that?" she asked.

"What could I do but accept it? I can't very well force the President to act on behalf of the Sukarian Council just because I think it's the prudent thing to do."

Carrine held an index finger in the air. "Correction, you *can* force the President's hand, you just can't do it from your current position as ambassador. You need more leverage. You need a senate seat."

"The Assembly is out of the question for me. You know that. I'd never win in an election, not in a thousand years. You'd stand a better chance than I would."

"So, that's it then? You're just going to accept that the ambassadorship is as high as you go, and wallow in obscurity while the galaxy burns?"

"Did you ask my father that question?" Madrin snapped, then immediately regretted it. "I'm sorry mother. I shouldn't have said—"

"No, no, don't apologize. It's a fair question, one that deserves a response."

She rose from her seat and walked over to the portrait of Hayden. She stared at it for a long while. Without turning, she asked, "What did you think of your father?"

"He was a superb ambassador," he answered.

She shook her head, still looking at the picture. "No, not as a political figure, as a man, as your father."

He thought about the question, then said, "I practically worshiped the ground he walked on; you know that. I always thought I'd be lucky to become just half the man he was."

She continued staring at Hayden's visage. "All of that sounds good, but it only reflects the narrative Hayden carefully weaved for himself. It's a narrative that the public, and you, spout until this very day. The truth is, Hayden was an abysmal ambassador."

"What do you mean?" asked Madrin.

"I mean the job of an ambassador is to act as an envoy between governments. An ambassador is simply a mouthpiece for governments that can't seem to speak directly to one another. That wasn't what your father was."

"What was he then?" he asked.

"Your father was a liar, a cheater, and a thief. He did any and everything to get results, including deceiving our own government at times."

"Are you saying he was a traitor?" Madrin said rising from his chair and barely containing the anger in his voice.

Carrine turned and stared at him. "Heaven's no son. I never knew a greater patriot than your father. What I'm saying is that Vizaria wasn't set up for anyone but the Sukarians to truly thrive. Your father understood that, and he used it to his advantage. The reason that you and everyone else still hold him in such high regard to this day is because he got the job done, even with the odds stacked against him. You, on the other hand, insist on playing by the very rules created to hold you back."

"Veran counsels me to play by the rules, and you just said he is wise. So which is it? Am I to be the callous politician who gets results, or am I to follow Veran's wise, but cautious advice?"

She walked over to him and placed her hands on his shoulders. "Veran's instincts are good when it comes to character. That's why I continue to urge you to be wary of that bodyguard of yours. As for politics, he doesn't have the stomach for it. He's wise, but you must be wiser, as your father was. He followed Veran's advice when it was prudent and ignored it when he thought it best to do so."

"Why did father never aspire to more than just the ambassadorship?" he asked.

She sighed and retook her seat. "Hayden understood where he could do the most amount of good and where he had the most influence. His role was to keep us in the good graces of the Council because that was what was best for us at that time. Now, this invasion has changed the landscape, and remaining in the Council's good graces is no longer what's most important. Critical decisions, that will affect the Human race for generations, will soon need to be made, and they'll be made in the Assembly. You need to find a way to be in the room when they happen."

He glanced at his father's portrait and muttered, "By any means necessary."

She lifted her glass. "How do you plan on getting into that room?" she asked before taking a sip of water.

"Veran believes that if I can spearhead an effort to form a galactic coalition, I could set myself up for a senate seat in the Assembly."

She shrugged. "That could work, but it would take time, and that's the one thing we don't have."

He nodded slowly, thinking. "Urgency is key," he said.

She smiled knowingly. "Tell me, what do you know of the Cohannic?" she asked.

"They're ruthless," he answered.

"Yes, but that's a bit of an understatement. They are savage beasts unlike any other race in Vizaria. They know only conquest; they have a blood lust for it. They summarily execute most of the prisoners they take, including women and children. The ones they leave alive are sold into a life of slavery. They don't look at the order and harmony of Vizaria and marvel; they look at it with disgust and revulsion. They yearn to watch everything we hold dear burn to ash, and they clamor at the opportunity to provide the flame."

"You think that's why they've returned? To destroy what we've built?" he asked.

"I don't claim to know," she said. "But what I do know is that they won't stop until they're thoroughly defeated, or until they win. Where are their forces now?"

"At last report, they'd taken Caristo with the help of the Norvekians. They're on the planet right now."

She raised her thin black eyebrows. "They won't stay there. When they leave, where do you suspect they'll go next?"

He allowed his imagination to take over his thoughts. He pictured a fleet of Cohannic ships writhing in flames as they lifted away from the surface of Caristo, lighting the sky on fire.

Where would they go next?

He lifted his head, his eyes meeting his mother's. "Yorinar," he said.

She nodded her agreement. "A fire tends to leap from branch to branch as it spreads. The snakes live on Fulmaren, and now they've taken Caristo. Yorinar is the last habitable planet in the system, the last branch. Not to mention, that's also where the Forrack will be making their last stand to keep control of the system. It's only logical that's where their next attack will be focused."

"If Yorinar falls, the Cohannic will have complete control of the Fire portal and the entire spiral arm would be vulnerable," he said.

"Indeed," she said. "The enemy is not only at the gate, they're about to breach it. Now tell me, my son, will you hide behind rules and procedures while the likes of the Council of Seven and President Baruke use you in their incessant squabbling?"

He gazed at the portrait of his father. "No, I won't. But if I'm to get anything done, I'll have to get creative with my approach."

She leaned back and folded her arms across her chest. "Do whatever you must, but do it quickly."

CHAPTER NINE
Zanna

Regalus: Chalpin Star System

The girl's violet eyes fluttered open. At least, she thought they were her eyes. She wasn't certain. She felt disconnected from her body, and her mind didn't feel completely under her control. She had a sensation of floating, but at the same time, she sensed she was confined to a specific point in space and time. The fingers of her right hand twitched uncontrollably, but when she looked down to inspect them, there was nothing there but a purple void stretching into infinity. She frantically looked around, but the void was all there was. She raised her nonexistent hands in an attempt to feel her face, but there was nothing there.

A sense of dread blossomed inside of her. "What is this?"

She thought she said the words out loud. She could hear them, but it was as if they came from somewhere else, somewhere outside herself.

The feeling of dread was quickly joined by terror and confusion as she struggled to comprehend what was happening. It was disconcerting not to know who you were, where you were, or if you even existed.

The sound of a light breeze swept through her consciousness. It brought with it a soothing voice that said, "Calm yourself, child."

The voice was that of a male, and it sounded both very distant and very near. It resounded from everywhere and nowhere all at once. She didn't think it was a voice she'd ever heard before, but she couldn't remember anything from before now.

Her voice trembled as she spoke. "Who's there?"

"There?" the voice replied in a quizzical tone. "Words like there and here, above and below, now and then, hold no true meaning here. You no longer inhabit an existence that has use for such terms."

"Why can't I remember anything?"

"There is nothing of consequence to remember. All you need to know will be revealed."

"Does all this mean I'm dead then?"

"Death is merely a meaningless construct. If you choose to be dead, then that is your reality. If you choose not to be dead, then that will be your truth."

The girl struggled to clear her mind. Something was prying at the edge of her thoughts. A revelation perhaps. No sooner than she felt it, it was gone, replaced by the dense fog of uncertainty.

"I don't belong here," she said.

A long pause ensued before the voice responded, "You don't even understand where *here* is, so how can know that you don't belong?"

She was stumped. "Who am I? What's happening to me?"

"You are no one, and you are everyone."

"That doesn't make sense."

"Little here will make sense until you have undergone the change."

"Change? What change?" she asked.

"You must ascend to a higher plane of consciousness. It is there that you will ultimately decide what you will become."

She tried to still her mind. She focused on remembering who she was and how she arrived here, wherever here was. She considered the tangible clues.

My voice is female and feeble, like a child's. And he did call me child, hadn't he?

"I'm a female child," she said, less confidently than she'd intended.

"If that is your desire," the voice responded.

"And what should I call you?" she asked.

There was a pause. "You may call us Zurin."

"Is that your name, or your race?"

"Both and neither."

Frustration began to swell inside her. "Must you insist on speaking in riddles?"

"Riddles are naught but a lack of comprehension. The information is always there. You simply cannot yet access it. Your mind is trapped child. You cling desperately to a reality to which you may never return. You must let go."

"How can I do that?"

Another long pause ensued. "That is for you to decide."

"Will you help me then?"

"We will guide you along the way, but this is a journey you must take alone."

A journey? That sounds familiar somehow, she thought.

Another nagging sense of revelation taunted her. But, again, it proved elusive.

"What must I do to undergo this change you speak of?"

"You are not yet ready. You may never be. You are but the latest in a long line seeking to travel this path. But first, there are hard decisions you must make, and harder truths you must accept before you will be ready. There is much we have to show you. "

The girl looked around at the endless purple void and asked, "What do you have to show me?"

"All," the voice said. "Now, shall we begin?"

CHAPTER TEN
Cassyn

Janus: Pharus Star System

"Ensign Spreen?"

Cassyn started and looked up from her datapad, almost choking on her wafer crisp. She cleared her throat and said, "Yes, sir. I'm Cassyn Spreen."

"I didn't mean to startle you," the uniformed soldier said extending a hand toward her. "I'm Yuen Bo. Commander of the Vengeance."

He was tall and slender with close-cropped, midnight black hair that looked even blacker against his smooth tanned skin. His hairless face featured a wide nose that contrasted with his thin lips, but most of her attention was drawn to his eyes. One was black, the other hazel.

Handsome, she thought as she grasped his hand.

"Pleasure to meet you, sir."

"Ready to see your new home away from home?" he asked.

"Absolutely."

He turned toward the concourse. "Well then, walk with me."

She eyed him as they walked. "So, do you always provide a personal escort for new crew members?"

Yuen smiled, displaying a set of straight white teeth. "As a matter of fact, I do. One thing you'll quickly notice around here is that we do things a bit differently than you may be used to. We're Confederation soldiers working for Sagis, but we operate more like their security personnel than typical soldiers. It's a bit less formal, and it'll take some getting used to, I know it did for me. For starters, you can dispense with the titles. Just call me Yuen."

"Yuen. Noted," she said

She took in her surroundings as they continued through the concourse. Natural light from Pharus filtered through the partial glass ceiling and bathed everything in a stark, reddish-yellow hue. The sprawling concourse floor buzzed with activity. A group of young soldiers moved hurriedly past them, and crowds of weary passengers congregated around common areas throughout the area. Automated material retrievers zipped around the floor ferrying equipment and tools to various locations.

A news anchor appeared on one of the public holographic feeds. She spoke in a monotone and appeared bored as she reported the latest information about the terrorist attack on Dullestoon station and Caristo in the Tyros system.

Cassyn tapped Yuen on the arm and pointed at the feed. "What do you make of that?"

He studied the feed. "I think the term 'terrorist attack' is inaccurate. Terrorists usually make demands. Or they at least have a political or religious agenda. From what I've heard of the Cohannic, they don't negotiate. Their only agenda is conquest."

A sense of foreboding swelled inside her as she stared at the anchor. Her concentration was broken by a familiar voice coming from her right.

"Cassy? Is that you?"

She and Yuen stopped and turned. Tolbin Mako approached, repositioning a large rucksack from one shoulder to the other.

Her heart tightened in her chest. "Tolbin. Wow, what a surprise."

"Yeah. For the both of us," he said glancing at Yuen.

She looked at Yuen. "Um, sir… I mean, Yuen. This is Tolbin, Tolbin Mako. We attended Halvert together."

Yuen raised his eyebrows. "Halvert Academy huh? Which graduating class?"

Tolbin closed one eye and looked to the ceiling as if he was thinking. "Let's see. That would have been the year nine ninety-never. I wasn't exactly what you would call Confederation soldier material." He gestured toward Cassyn. "This one here though, she's as good as they come."

She shifted from one foot to the other, tugging at her right earlobe. "So, uh, what brings you to Griner?" she asked.

"Oh, I'm just passing through," Tolbin said. "I've linked up with an engineering firm and we're headed to do some retrofitting work on Ilmad."

"Engineering? I didn't know you fell into that line of work," she said.

Tolbin stared at her. "Well, you know, when everyone you love abandons you, you sorta have to adapt and learn new tricks as they say." He turned to Yuen. "You know what I mean Yon?"

"It's Yuen. And no, I can't say I do."

"Well, that's fantastic Yon. It really is. Consider yourself lucky. A bit of friendly advice though, watch the company you keep, and you might never have to find out."

Tolbin shot Cassyn a wink before turning and walking back in the direction from which he came.

Her right eye twitched as she watched him stride across the concourse. She hadn't seen him in over three years, and she hadn't spoken to him for almost as long. Yet, this brief interaction stirred up emotions she forgot she held for him, with hate being the predominant one at the moment.

"What was that all about?" Yuen asked.

She resumed walking. "It's nothing."

"It's none of my business, but you two seem to have a history."

"You're right," she said, "it's not your business."

"Say no more," he said raising his hands in surrender.

She shook her head. "I'm sorry. There's just a lot to unpack there."

He smirked knowingly. "I get it. Affairs of the heart and all that."

Her tension melted away under Yuen's disarming smile. "So, how long have you been stationed on the Vengeance?" she asked.

"Nearly two years now. I've served under Brasif the entire time."

"How is he, as a captain I mean?"

"Most would probably say he's an acquired taste."

She chuckled. "Most Cortarans are."

"True," he conceded, "but Brasif is, let's just say, especially peculiar."

"Is that why he's here instead of with the Cortaran fleet?"

"We're here, so I suppose the same question could be asked of us."

"It could," she said, "but I'm sure you've read my dossier. You know my story."

"I only know what the file says, but I'd rather let people show me who they are, rather than rely on a file. Some come here as a steppingstone to something greater, and some come for their careers to die. I'm sure you'll show me why you're here in due time."

They rounded a curved corridor that terminated at a large metal door inscribed with the words 'HANGAR #3, SAGIS INCORPORATED'.

Yuen approached the control panel to the left of the door and entered a code. As the hangar door slowly began to rise, he turned to her and said, "Welcome to the Vengeance."

Cassyn marveled at the sight of the ship. The Vengeance had a sleek profile with contoured edges, and its hull was a brilliant display of chrome plating that reflected the bright lights of the hangar. Maintenance crews swarmed around the vessel checking and rechecking pre-launch safety protocols as their reflections danced across the ship's mirror-like surface. She savored the astringent and faintly sweet aroma of the ethnelene fuel hanging in the air. She inhaled slowly and deeply as an intense longing for aggie gripped her.

"Magnificent isn't she," Yuen said as they walked toward the ship.

"I'll say," she said. She reached up and brushed her fingertips along the underside of the hull as she moved toward the forward section of the ship. "This is a Cortaran ship."

"Yes, it's a modified Pegasus class frigate," he said.

"Modified? How so?"

"Well, for starters, there's no cloaking technology. Also, the dimension drive has been removed. The Cortarans aren't very charitable with their technology."

She cringed as she thought about the dimension drives Sagis Incorporated had developed. She remembered her father once explaining how the drives gave Cortaran ships the capability of traveling almost as quickly as using a portal. Like other Cortaran technological advances, the dimension drive had unnerved many within the galactic community.

"What about weapons capabilities?" she asked, still studying the ship's hull.

"She has a standard complement of photon and disruptor missiles. There're a couple of focused energy beam turrets. Oh, and there's an electromagnetic pulse cannon. Our weapons specialist, Fosh, is as good as they come. We can handle ourselves in a fight."

"Have you had to do much fighting?"

"Nothing major. Most raiders and pirates have been deterred by the presence of military vessels guarding the convoys, rather than just the Sagis security ships."

She felt a wave of relief, then instantly felt guilty for it. Her father never had ships like the Vengeance to protect him during his time with Sagis.

If he had, he might still be alive, she thought.

"You ready to see the inside?" Yuen asked.

"Sure."

She stole a glance at him as they walked to the opposite side of the ship. He had a wonderful physique, and she liked the way he carried himself. She enjoyed his easy-going manner and his wry smile.

He's certainly not a typical military officer, she thought.

They approached the port side of the Vengeance and stepped onto the anti-gravitational lift, which elevated them to the access door. She followed him through the personnel hatch and onto the landing deck.

She was struck by the dramatic change in temperature as compared to that of the hangar. "Why is it so cold?" she asked, rubbing her forearms.

Yuen chuckled. "I almost forgot. You're not accustomed to serving on a multiracial vessel. Sagis may be a Cortaran company, but it employs a wide variety of races. Take the Vengeance for example. She has a crew of eighty-nine. In addition to the Cortarans, that number also includes Humans, Dumians, Ragominnians, and Gorgans. There's even a Venganese on board if you can believe it. So, in true Cortaran fashion, the common areas are set to the precise median preferred temperature of each race."

She rubbed her hands together. "I thought I'd escaped the cold when I left Ardhamn."

"Sorry to disappoint," he said.

He led Cassyn into a lift and pressed the panel for the bridge. He turned to her and smirked. "Time for you to meet Brasif."

The bridge was smaller than she expected, and the matte gray walls absorbed much of the bright lighting. It was as cold as the landing deck was, and the air held a faint chemical odor. The navigators' station, which was comprised of two pilot chairs, navigation controls, and a panoramic view screen, was situated at the front of the ship. The weapons station was to her left, and the engineering and communications stations were across from it on the opposite wall. The command station sat in the middle of the bridge, and it included chairs for the captain and the commander.

The high-backed chrome captain's chair swiveled in her direction and a Cortaran rose from the seat and approached. He was slender and he moved with an almost imperceptible limp to his gait. His two-lobed cranium was pockmarked with dull-green freckles, and his bright eyes shone a light gray. She took notice of his missing left arm, but she didn't allow her eyes to linger.

He stopped in front of her. "I'm Brasif Mantalor," he said without extending his hand. "You are Cassyn Spreen I presume."

"Yes, Captain."

He stared at her for so long, that she began to wonder if he'd lapsed into a seizure of some sort.

"Please, Cassyn, repeat to me the name by which I just introduced myself," he finally said.

"Pardon me, sir."

"My name, repeat it to me please."

"Brasif Mantalor," she said uncertainly even though she knew she'd given the correct response.

"Exactly, very good, very good indeed. You see, my parents did not name me Captain, and they did not name me sir. They named me Brasif... B-R-A-S-I-F," he said, spelling out the name slowly.

"Understood sir, I mean... uh, Brasif."

"Thank you kindly," he said, pivoting on his heel and returning to his chair.

She looked at Yuen who had a bemused smirk on his face. "I warned you," he mouthed.

She leaned in close to him and asked, "What happened to his arm?"

"I've never asked, but rumor has it that he was once a member of the Regalus Guard. I heard he lost it during the Krion Order terrorist attack on Seven Spires in eighty-six."

She chuckled, then realized he wasn't laughing. "You're serious? A Cortaran in the Regalus Guard? Highly doubtful."

"Hey, I'm just telling you the story as it was told to me. Come, let me introduce you to the rest of the rabble."

She followed him to the weapons station where a gangly Ragominnian was fiddling with a device that she didn't recognize. He looked up from his tinkering as they approached.

He brushed a long thin dreadlock from his face. "Dis her? Da new one?" he asked in a thick accent.

Yuen extended a hand in his direction. "Cassyn, meet Lieutenant Commander Fosh Credeel, our weapons specialist."

"Pleasure da meet ya," Fosh said inclining his head in greeting.

"Likewise."

"Fosh here is one of the best weapons specialists in Vizaria," Yuen said.

"Now, now Yuen. Flattery won't get ya outta da eighty credits ya still owe me." He looked at Cassyn with a wide grin. "He's right tho. You fly me close enough to a target and I'll remove it from existence."

"I'll keep that in mind," she said. "What's that you're working on?" she asked, indicating the device in his hand.

"Dis, dear Cassyn," he said holding the spherical device at eye level, "is a low yield personal explosive device."

She studied it closely. "A grenade? It doesn't look like one."

"It don't look like one ya ever seen because it's my own special design."

"What's so special about it?"

He looked around the bridge as if to ensure no one was listening. Then he whispered, "Magnets."

"Magnets?" she repeated.

"I call it da mag grenade," he said brushing another errant dreadlock from his forehead. "Ya see dese?" he asked, holding the grenade closer to her and pointing to it.

She examined the small flat disks covering its surface. "What are those?"

"Very powerful seeker magnets. Dey activate after ya throw dem and dey stick to any nearby metal surface. After a three-second delay, dey go boom. Very nasty business."

"I'll have to take your word for it," she said.

"Let's leave Fosh to play with his toys," Yuen said guiding Cassyn across the bridge to the engineering station.

They stopped behind a large Gorgan who had his back turned to them. His thick, unkempt fur was matted in spots and thinning in others. She was unsure what to make of this since Gorgans generally took great pride in the condition of their fur.

Yuen tapped him on the shoulder and the Gorgan turned and flashed a welcoming smile, notwithstanding the sharp, yellow-tinged incisors.

Yuen gestured toward Cassyn. "Soldaan, allow me to introduce you to our new pilot Cassyn Spreen."

"So, you're the one everyone's been raving about," Soldaan said.

"I suppose," she replied.

"I, for one, am glad you're here. Dajin hasn't had a proper pilot for weeks and I'm not sure how much more the ship can take. We could use someone who knows how to properly navigate the relays."

"That's why I'm here," she said. "Don't worry, I'll get us to where we need to go in one piece."

Soldaan exhaled a deep breath. "Thank the Helia. Every time Dajin hits one of the space-time tunnel walls, it causes circuit overloads in some of the systems. I wasn't sure how many more access conduits I could crawl through before I completely lost my fur. Have you ever seen a hairless Gorgan?"

She chuckled even though she wasn't entirely sure he was joking. Still, the mental image was amusing all the same.

"I can't say that I have," she said.

He shook his massive head. "Trust me. It's not a pretty sight."

A voice sounded from behind Cassyn and Yuen. "What nonsense is he filling your heads up with over there?"

Cassyn turned to see a squat Dumian standing with her hands on her hips. "Hello. You must be the navigator," she said.

"Hello yourself. And yes, I am. The name's Dajin."

"I'm Cass—"

"I know who you are," Dajin said, cutting her off. "Seems like all anyone can talk about is the new Human pilot who's come to help me fly the ship."

Dajin spread her thick arms out to her sides and looked dramatically around the bridge. "Here she is everyone. Now, can we all get back to work? We have things to do." She turned and stalked back to her station at the front of the ship.

Cassyn turned to Yuen. "I don't think she's impressed by me."

"I'd say she was especially courteous by Dumian standards," he said.

"Dajin is quite right," Brasif spoke up from his chair. "We do have things to do. We've just been cleared for departure. So, if we're quite finished with the pleasantries, everyone take your stations so we can get underway."

Cassyn crossed the bridge and sat in the pilot's chair. Though she could pilot a wide variety of vessels, including most Cortaran ships, she appreciated that the navigation panel was configured to Pharus Confederation standards. She closed her eyes and slowly exhaled. She felt like she was on the cusp of embarking on a new chapter of her life. Excitement and fear wrestled for control of her emotions, and she found herself yearning for the mental escape that only aggie could bring.

Brasif's voice pulled her from her thoughts. "The convoy is prepared for departure. Set relay coordinates for Fenghou interstellar space station."

Dajin entered a series of formulas into her navigation terminal. "Relay coordinates entered and synchronized with the convoy," she said.

"Coordinates received," Cassyn reported.

"Let's go then," Brasif said.

Cassyn took the controls and piloted the ship from the hangar and toward the blinking relay beacon off the ship's starboard bow. The four transport ships in the convoy entered the relay and vanished and she piloted the Vengeance in after them.

She knew the trip wouldn't take long. In the matter of a few hours, she would guide them through the relay past Arcus. Then they would pass beyond the gas giants Fortuna and Nemesis to the outer reaches of Pharus Confederation space where they would use the Unity portal to travel to the Fenghou interstellar space station. The Vengeance would patrol the area while the transports loaded supplies. Afterward, the convoy would use the relay network to travel back to the Unity portal and proceed to the Carmo system, the place where Devlin Spreen drew his final breath. She felt the moisture pooling at the corner of her eyes, but she quickly wiped it away before any tears could fall.

A new chapter indeed, she thought.

Sphercal: Carmo Star System

The Vengeance emerged from the relay behind the convoy, and the small fleet settled into a low orbit above Sphercal. From this distance, the large quarries and excavation sites were visible between the gaps in the thick layer of cloud cover. The red giant star, Carmo, blazed in the distance, its light glinting off the space station orbiting the planet.

Cassyn checked her navigation terminal and verified the convoy's flight path to the Sagis facility in the southern hemisphere. The building's official designation was Refinery A8-2, but most simply referred to it as the Carmo facility since it was Sagis' only installation in the system. As the Vengeance dove through the thick atmosphere, Cassyn took manual control. She deftly maneuvered the ship past the convoy vessels toward the continent in the southernmost ocean. As the ship drew nearer to the landmass, she spotted the Carmo facility in a clearing encircled by a dense concentration of towering burboran trees.

The site was more akin to a compound. Dozens of interconnected buildings were joined together by covered walkways, footbridges, and access tubes. Workers, machinery, and vehicles were in constant motion throughout the complex. The sprawling compound was massive, easily occupying several hundred thousand square meters of land area.

"Set us down there Cassyn," Brasif said pointing.

She saw the landing area he was motioning to and banked the ship to the right. Moments later the Vengeance settled down with a muted thump near a building labeled 'Metallurgical Research & Processing'. The cargo ships passed overhead, heading to their designated landing points throughout the complex. Security drones began scanning the ship as Dajin powered down the engines.

"Our welcoming committee has arrived," Yuen said rising from his chair.

She looked out the window and saw several automated material retrievers emerging from the building, heading to unload the newly arrived cargo ships. Exiting the building behind the retrievers were Yero and a female Cortaran dressed in research garb.

"Cassy!" Yero said, grasping her by the shoulders as soon as she stepped from the anti-gravitational lift. "It's wonderful to see you."

"You as well," she said.

He nodded his head at Yuen. "She's everything I said she would be, isn't she?"

Yuen appraised her with a sly grin. "She got us here in one piece. I think we'll hold on to her for now."

Cassyn reddened at being the focus of attention.

"Cassy, allow me to introduce you to Doctor Mirren Chastoma," Yero said, placing his hand on his companion's shoulder. "She is the head of our metallurgical research and processing operation here on Sphercal."

"Very nice to meet you," Mirren said with a slight nod. "Yero has told me a lot about you. Would you like a tour of my department?"

"I'd love that," Cassyn said looking around.

Mirren eyed Yuen. "You too Commander. I don't believe you've seen our latest project."

Yuen inclined his head. "I'd be delighted," he said.

"Excellent," Yero said, "I'll go speak with Brasif while Mirren gives you two the grand tour." He leaned close to Cassyn and whispered, "Come and find me when you're finished. There's much I wish to discuss with you."

Cassyn and Yuen followed Mirren into the building. They ascended a narrow ramp to the second story and walked to a control room at the end of a brightly lit hallway. Mirren placed her three fingers and thumb onto an access panel and the door slid open.

"What do you know of mentarium Ensign Spreen?" Mirren asked as they walked into the large room.

Cassyn looked at Yuen and smiled. "Please, just call me Cassyn," she said.

Yuen returned the smile with a knowing grin of his own.

"Mentarium is the strongest known metal in the spiral arm," Cassyn said surveying the room. "Many races use it for armored hull plating on their warships."

"Quite correct," Mirren said as she walked over to an interior wall that rose several stories high. "Mentar is a naturally-occurring metal that can be found throughout Vizaria. It is quite durable, but extremely fickle when mixing with other metal compounds. Chromium is the only known element that will bond with mentar without drastically compromising its strength and durability. The atomic bond of the mentar and chromium is the strongest we've been able to create."

"Is this the new project your team has been working on, making a metal stronger than mentarium?" Yuen asked.

"We've done better than that," Mirren said with a sparkle in her teal eyes.

She pressed a panel and the towering gray wall transformed into a clear pane of glass. Yuen let out a low whistle, and Cassyn craned her neck to take in the view. Behind the glass was a circular walkway surrounding the rim of an enormous vat. Dozens of scientists, dressed in full hazardous-materials suits, moved about on the platform tending to various terminals and machinery. A long cylinder protruded from the vat and extended high into the air to where two machines were affixed to the chamber's ceiling, pumping molten liquid into the slowly rotating cylinder.

"What is it?" Cassyn asked, her mouth hanging open.

"You know of artros, correct?"

"Yes. A rare, heat-resistant metal," Cassyn answered.

"Exceedingly rare," Mirren corrected. "It's only found on Fulmaren and a small percentage of the meteoroids in Vizaria, which are thought to be from fragments of Fulmaren's crust that were dislodged via celestial impacts."

"So, what's it got to do with this?" Yuen asked, motioning to the apparatus.

"What you're witnessing is the first successful attempt at combining the mentarium alloy with artros. My team and I have developed an alloying technique that allows for the successful bonding of the two metals. We call the resulting compound artarium. It retains the yield and impact strength of mentarium and the extremely high thermal resistance of artros."

"So, it's basically a metal that's hard to break and hard to melt," Cassyn summarized.

Mirren's giggle sounded almost child-like. "That's an oversimplification, but yes. If I had to put it simply, I'd call it a nearly indestructible compound."

Cassyn and Yuen shared a look. "Can it be used as hull plating for a ship?" he asked.

Mirren smiled. "Now you're beginning to understand the implications."

She walked over to a workbench and picked up a rectangular piece of dull-gray metal and handed it to him. He examined it and passed it to Cassyn. She ran her hand over the smooth surface; it was cold to the touch.

"You're holding one of the first pieces of artarium ever produced," Mirren said. "The compound is lightweight enough to be used on warships. The problem is that we have access to precious little artros, not nearly enough to mass-produce the artarium on a scale to outfit an entire fleet."

"Why is it so cold?" Cassyn asked.

"It's a result of the tightly bonded atoms. There is almost no movement at the atomic level, thus minimal thermal energy is generated. That's also the reason it can tolerate extreme temperatures."

"Can it withstand the heat around the Cohannic homeworld?" Cassyn asked, handing the metal back to Mirren.

Mirren looked at Yuen and Cassyn in turn. "It can withstand the heat of Fulmaren, and then some."

A half-hour later, Cassyn knocked gently on the doorway of Yero's office. He looked up from a holographic pad he was studying at his desk and waved her in with a smile. She sat in the chair opposite the desk.

He rose and circled the desk, taking a seat on the corner. "Did you enjoy your time with Mirren?"

"It was enlightening, to say the least."

He chuckled. "I know, I know. The wonders of metal processing can be dull at times, but I assure you that the work Mirren and her team are doing is cutting edge. It will be an absolute game changer, especially given the current state of affairs in the Tyros system."

His deep purple eyes twinkled as they caught the light. She was amused by the giddiness in his voice. Nothing seemed to get a rise out of a Cortaran quite like a new and intriguing scientific breakthrough.

"I just fly ships Yero," she said. "I'm afraid that most of the things you guys do here are beyond me. But I'll take your word for it."

"How's your mother?" Yero asked, changing the subject.

"She's well. We haven't spoken much lately. But she was pleased to hear I took this assignment. I guess she thinks I'll be safer here than on a military vessel. Plus, you're here to keep an eye on me."

He crossed his legs. "Family affairs can be troublesome. Especially when your Human emotions are involved."

She supposed he was right. She couldn't deny she wore her emotions on her sleeve, and she always appreciated Yero's directness. It reminded her of her father. He'd inherited that same directness during his years working among the Cortarans.

She looked around the office. "I thought it would be more

difficult."

"How do you mean?"

"Coming here, to Sphercal, to this facility," she said, waving her hand in the air. "He died here. I guess I just thought that everything here would remind me of him. But when I look around, I don't see a trace of him anywhere. It's like he was never here, and I think that's even worse."

"I assure you that Devlin's spirit permeates this entire place, all the more now that you're here. He touched many lives here, and he'll always be remembered."

"Thank you, Yero. That's reassuring."

"So, what do you think of your new assignment?" he asked, clasping his hands together.

"It's, um, different. They're an interesting crew."

He pointed at her. "You mean *you* are an interesting crew. You're a part of the team now Cassy."

She smiled. "I suppose I am. At any rate, it beats the hell out of my icebox prison on Ardhamn. I want to thank you again, Yero, for everything. I know it couldn't have been easy to pull the strings you must've had to pull to get me here."

"Say no more," he said with a slight nod of his bulbous head. "It was the very least I could do for the daughter of old friends. Besides, it's going to be nice having you around more often. How are you faring with Brasif?"

She exhaled audibly and widened her eyes in mock exasperation. "I can honestly say that I've never met a Cortaran quite like him. He exhibits the cold rationality I'd expect from your race, but his penchant for sarcasm is limitless."

"If he's heaping it on, that can only mean that he likes you," Yero said.

"What's the story about his missing arm?" she asked. "He could be easily fitted with a biomechanical prosthetic."

"He's never spoken to me on the matter."

"Which one," she asked, "how he lost it, or why he chooses not to replace it?"

"Neither," Yero admitted. "However, I did hear a rumor that he contracted a rather aggressive case of tranculispa, a nasty flesh-eating bacteria. I heard that the limb was removed to prevent it from spreading to other parts of his body."

"Are all of your security fleet captains so mysterious?" she asked with a smirk.

"I don't know about mysterious. But I can assure you that there are none like Brasif. Despite his odd personality, he's as good as they come. That brings me to why I wanted to speak to you. I've briefed him on your next escort run, which incidentally won't be for two more weeks."

Her eyes lit up. "So, we'll have an extended stay on Sphercal?"

"You will indeed. And that will allow us time to catch up properly."

"I look forward to it," she said.

He raised an index finger in the air. "But I wanted to tell you personally that the next assignment will take the Vengeance into the Sifton system."

"Sifton," she said surprised. "Isn't the fighting still ongoing there?"

"The situation between the Intergalactic Coalition and the natives is complex. The conflict has cooled down in the past few weeks. Enough so that we've been able to broker a deal to secure an important shipment that's been stranded on the Patrinah station."

Her eyes widened in disbelief. "Are you telling me that a cease-fire was called just so Sagis could go in to pick up a shipment?"

He stood and walked back around the desk. "It's not quite as simple as that, but yes, a deal was struck, and we've been assured safe passage in two weeks to retrieve our property. Nevertheless, the prospects for danger are always present there, so I wanted to tell you myself."

"I appreciate that," she said. "We'll get the job done."

"I've no doubt."

"What type of shipment could be so important as to risk going into an active conflict zone?" she asked.

"An extremely valuable one. But I won't bore you with the technical details. You should rest and enjoy your downtime for these next two weeks. You've earned it."

She left Yero's office feeling more rejuvenated than she had for a long time. She had a new mission, and a new, albeit strange,

family. Things were headed in the right direction.
New beginnings, she thought with a smile.

CHAPTER ELEVEN
Altar

Yorinar: Tyros Star System

"Come home now Altar. This has gotten serious. And look at you, you're hurt," Alara said with fear evident on her holographic face.

Altar rubbed the dressing on his shoulder. "Alara, listen to me. I'm fine."

"You're not fine! There's dried blood all over you."

"It's not my blood my love."

"Is that supposed to make me feel better? A war is starting and you're right in the middle of it."

"It's not a war. It's more like a terrorist attack. The situation will be under control soon, I promise."

She looked unconvinced. "Where are you now?" she asked.

"A transport ship."

"Going where?"

He diverted his eyes for a moment and then cleared his throat. "We're headed to Yorinar to join the main fleet there."

"Yorinar, are you insane! There're already reports of fighting around Telsia and Averan-Ginest. You barely escaped Dullestoon, then you almost got caught on Caristo, and now you're heading right back into danger."

"That's the job Alara. The fighting around Yorinar is precisely why I must go there. Don't you understand? If Yorinar falls to the Cohannic, they'll have complete access to the Fire portal. The portals are linked to every system in Vizaria, they could strike anywhere."

"You said yourself that you have less than thirty fighters. What possible difference would your presence make? You have a family to think about. For the love you say you have for us, please come home now."

His chest tightened under the pressure of the unspoken ultimatum. A potent mixture of fear and frustration welled up inside him. He understood her concern, but it was an impossible choice.

Why can't she accept that this is the life I chose? he thought.

He looked through the small window into the transport's cabin where his troops sat. Some were talking to each other while others were getting some much-needed rest. All were dedicated to the mission. He could see the resolve on their faces and the determination in their eyes. They had oaths to uphold and friends to avenge. Most of them had families too, and they were depending on him to help protect them. They were all in.

How can she expect me to abandon them at a time like this? he thought. *The Cohannic struck a devastating blow against us, and now we must strike back. Hard.*

He regarded Alara's shimmering image and said, "I can't come home, not yet. Going to Yorinar is how I protect you and Halmon. We're going to end this. I swear it to you."

She looked as if he'd punched through her stomach and ripped her hearts out. "I see," she said momentarily casting her eyes away from him. "Well, I pray for your safe return, whenever that may be."

She severed the connection.

He stared out the transport window and sighed, silently questioning if it was all worth it. They'd just been violently expelled from a planet his race took from the Norvekians generations ago. Now, here he was, hurtling through space to fight for another planet the Forrack were not native to. He wasn't the type to engage in political discourse, but it sure felt like imperialism to him.

Exactly what we purport to be fighting against now, he thought, not allowing the irony to escape him.

Altar was speaking with Supreme Commander Gailius Rhandu through the holographic terminal when he heard a soft knock at the cabin door. Damu was looking through the window, and Altar waved him in.

"What is your current position?" Gailius was asking.

"We'll be entering Telsia orbit in approximately twenty minutes," he said.

"Good," Gailius said with palpable relief.

"What's the current tactical situation, sir?" Altar asked.

"The damned snakes hit us hard. What's left of our main battle fleet is engaged with the enemy near the moon as we speak. Our fleet and the moon's surface defenses are holding up for now. Orrick Klemo is leading the fight personally. He arrived while you were making your way off of Caristo."

"What about the station?" Damu asked.

"We were in contact with the station's chief, Halen Gunt, just before their communications ceased. He reported that Averan-Ginest was able to avoid the same fate that Dullestoon suffered. He said they stopped the Norvekians from taking the station from the inside, but now they're struggling to hold off the waves of Norvekian fighters coming up from the planet. He's requesting immediate assistance."

"So, Yorinar is lost?" Altar asked.

"Yeah," Gailius said somberly. "The Norvekians have captured most of our ground assets, and Cohannic forces are attacking the population centers. It's a total nightmare. We were caught completely off guard."

"How could this happen?" Damu asked.

Gailius' jaw tensed before he spoke. "The Norvekians opened the door and let the snakes in. Seems they've been planning this for some time too. Their leadership has pledged themselves to the Cohannic, and they've declared open war on us. We sent saboteurs to neutralize Yorinar's planetary defensive capabilities so at least those can't be used against us. The moon and the station are all that's left. If they fall into enemy hands, the entire system is lost."

"We'll be arriving in a transport ship. We'll need a military vessel so we can join the fight," Altar said.

"It's already arranged," Gailius said tapping at a console outside of Altar's field of view. "The Traegar is standing by for your arrival. You'll assume command of the battle group from Benart Dresco. The station is the priority; I need you to join in its defense. I'll remain aboard the Holstrek and coordinate our resources. Once the station is secured, we can use it to retake Yorinar and get its planetary defenses back up. From there, we'll crush the Cohannic fleet between our forces at Telsia, the station, and Yorinar's planetary defenses."

"Sir," Altar said, "with all due respect, we could use the Holstrek in the fight. It's the largest ship and most well-equipped vessel in the fleet. This battle is much too important for it to remain on the sideline; we should hit them with everything we've got."

Gailius shook his head. "Negative. If things go wrong here, we'll need the Holstrek back in the Bartos system."

Altar's eyes grew wide as icy claws gripped his chest. "What do you mean by that?"

"Look at the battlespace Commander," Gailius said. "This Cohannic-Norvekian alliance is much stronger than we anticipated. They're not going to stop here. Why would they? Orrick Klemo is hell-bent on galactic conquest, just like the snakes before him. That means their forces will need to be sustained with fuel, medical supplies, crystals, forward bases, and most of all, food. Bartos is the hub of agriculture in this sector. If they take the Tyros system, Bartos is the logical place they'd go to convalesce before continuing their assault."

The realization crashed down onto Altar all at once. Of course Gailius was right; Bartos was the closest system to Tyros with the resources the Cohannic would need to carry on their campaign.

Why didn't I see this? he chastised himself.

He looked at Gailius with urgency swirling in his eyes. "This is it, sir, our last chance. If we lose this engagement, we don't have a hope of stopping the Cohannic in the Bartos system. We need the Holstrek in this fight."

"No," Gailius said bluntly. "I've issued my orders and I expect you to carry them out. I'll be in touch."

The holographic transmission ended abruptly and Altar slammed a hand down on the desk, sending searing pain through his injured shoulder. "Cowards! High Command is too busy planning their escape instead of bringing our full force to bear."

"We're nearing the relay exit," Damu said. "What's the plan?"

Altar looked past him through the cabin window. His soldiers were ready for this fight, and so was he. He stood and attached his energy rifle to the magnetic holster on his back.

"We make damned sure this is as far as the snakes get."

Altar and Damu strode onto the bridge of the Traegar as Benart Dresco stood by a command station issuing orders to undock from the transport ship.

Benart turned and offered a crisp salute, raising his right hand to his eyes, palm out toward Altar. "Welcome aboard the Traegar sir. The ship is yours."

Altar returned the salute. "Thank you Benart. It's good to see you again. This is my communications officer Damu Bordrigun," he said gesturing to Damu.

Benart nodded to Damu. "Nice to meet you. Please, take the communications station."

Altar had known Benart since their years serving together on a patrol vessel in the Bartos system before Altar was assigned to Dullestoon station. He was several years younger than Altar, but he came from a long lineage of career soldiers, and Altar found him to be an exceptional officer.

"What's the condition of the ship?" Altar asked, scanning the bridge.

"Excellent," Benart replied. "We've only engaged in minor skirmishes near Telsia, mostly against Norvekian ships that strayed too far away from their attack groups. Supreme Commander Rhandu has been holding our battle group in reserve awaiting your arrival."

"Brief me on the current situation," Altar said.

"Juppar," Benart called out, motioning for a youthful-looking officer to join them at the command station. "This is Tactical Officer Frin Juppar," Benart said as Frin saluted. "Show the Commander our current tactical situation."

Frin tapped a sequence into the command station and a three-dimensional holographic feed of the battlespace appeared above the table.

"We're here," Frin said, pointing to the holographic depiction of the Traegar. It was situated at the head of a four-ship formation orbiting the moon. Then he indicated an area on the opposite side of the moon and said, "Here is where our main force is engaged with the Cohannic fleet."

Dozens of ships swarmed around each other emitting green beams of light and green, blue, and yellow projectiles. Two ships, larger than the rest, held a stationary orbit at the fringes of the raging battle. They were launching oblong projectiles toward Telsia's surface.

"Is one of those Klemo's ship?" Altar asked pointing at the two large vessels.

"From the communications we've intercepted, we believe he's aboard that one, the Fire Star," Frin said, indicating one of the battlecruisers.

"They're bombarding the surface of the moon," Benart said, pointing to Telsia. "They appear to be targeting military installations and lunar defenses. Surface shields are heavily damaged but holding for now."

Altar searched the feed and located Averan-Ginest station orbiting Yorinar. A hoard of fighter ships buzzed around the station, firing from all directions. The station intermittently returned fire, occasionally hitting and disabling one of the attacking ships.

He studied the unfolding scene. *The station has much more firepower than that. Why are they holding back?* he wondered.

"Commander Unis, Supreme Commander Rhandu is hailing us," Damu reported.

"Put him through."

The tactical holographic battle space was partially replaced by a holographic image of Gailius' head and upper torso. "What's the delay Commander? You should already be en route to the station."

"Something feels wrong," Altar said. "Averan-Ginest is formidable. They should be making quick work of the Norvekian fighters, but they're barely doing any damage."

Gailius stroked his short beard. "Maybe they've sustained

damage to their weapons systems. Or maybe Chief Gunt is conserving his more devastating munitions for the larger threat. It's only a matter of time until the Cohannic fleet turns its sights on the station," Gailius reasoned.

"Perhaps," Altar said, not entirely absolved from his misgivings, but also without a better explanation.

"The best way to find out what's going on at the station is for you to get over there quickly. I'll coordinate the battle above the moon."

The feed disconnected and Altar walked over to the navigation station.

"Helmsman, make for Averan-Ginest, top approach."

The pilot punched in the coordinates. "Course laid."

"Proceed."

Altar turned to Damu as he moved back to the command station. "Relay orders for the Monmoth to follow us. Instruct the rest of the battle group to approach the station from beneath."

"Aye sir," Damu said.

The Traegar, flanked by the Monmoth, arrived above the station in a matter of minutes. The remainder of the battle group approached the lower section of the station moments later. Altar stared at the viewscreen and assessed the damage to the station's hull as the Traegar passed over.

"Three fighters on our port side," Frin called out.

"I have missile lock on the lead ship," the weapons specialist reported.

Altar's eyes lingered on the station.

Something's not right, he thought.

"Sir?" Benart called out, rousing Altar from his thoughts.

Altar tore his eyes from the screen and said, "Fire the missiles."

He turned to the command station and watched the Traegar's missiles as they impacted one of the enemy ships just above the engine. There was a momentary green flash as the shield absorbed much of the damage, but a streak of blue ionized ethnelene trailing from the engine evidenced the damage the missiles had caused.

The weapons specialist pumped a fist in the air. "Direct hit to their main engine."

"The other two fighters are veering away," Frin said.

Altar continued studying the holographic battlespace. "Hold current course. Let them go." He turned to Benart. "Does this feel a little too easy to you?"

Benart shrugged. "Norvekian ships aren't that intimidating in small numbers; they do their real damage when they swarm."

Altar sucked his teeth as he thought. "They have a steady stream of fighters coming from the surface, yet there's barely a scratch on the station. You would think they would have inflicted more damage with those numbers."

"They did disable the station's communications, maybe there's more damage than it appears," Benart offered.

Altar turned to Damu. "Put me in contact with the Oracle."

Following a short pause, the holographic image of the Oracle's captain replaced a portion of the tactical feed.

"Commander?" the Captain said.

"Captain Orrum. What's your situation?"

"We have things well in hand. We've already disabled two of the Norvekian ships attempting to attack the underside of the station."

"What's your visual damage assessment of the underside of the station?" Altar asked.

He could see Orrum scanning something outside of his field of view.

"There seems to be minimal hull damage," Orrum said.

Altar looked to Frin. "Give me a report on the enemy's movement."

Frin rotated the tactical feed to view different angles of the battlespace. "The Cohannic fleet is still engaged with our main fleet above the moon. Hmm, that's strange," Frin said, crinkling his forehead. "The Norvekian ships are moving away from the station now, and there don't appear to be any more fighters launching from the planet."

"Are they retreating?" Orrum asked.

"Commander, major power surge emitting from the station!" the weapons specialist shouted.

Altar spun toward the view screen in time to see dozens of points of light blinking on across Averan-Ginest's hull. It was as if an angry swarm of glowing chellock flies suddenly awakened to attack.

"Thank goodness," Orrum said. "The station has regained—"

Orrum's holographic image suddenly dissipated and the floor shuddered beneath Altar's feet as a deafening roar enveloped the bridge.

"What the hell is happening?" Benart shouted over the noise.

"We've lost contact with the Oracle," Damu said.

The pilot locked eyes with Altar. Fear and confusion were written all over his ashen face as he spoke the words, "Averan-Ginest is firing on us."

"It's a trap," Altar said, shouldering Frin aside and studying the holographic battlespace.

The Oracle had taken a direct hit to its bridge and was attempting evasive maneuvers as it took several more volleys of fire from the station. The two ships flanking either side of the Oracle were also taking fire as they returned fire with minimal effectiveness.

The Traegar shuddered violently again and Benart frantically studied a holographic rendering of the ship's exterior. "We're sustaining damage to our thrusters and secondary engine, but hull integrity is holding for now."

"Move us away from the station and toward our main fleet," Altar ordered the helmsman.

"We have incoming!" the weapons specialist shouted.

Altar turned back to the battlespace map and his mouth went completely dry at the sight. The Fire Star was heading straight for their position with most of the Cohannic fleet in tow.

"Get me Supreme Commander Rhandu," he said to Damu without looking away from the feed.

Within moments, Gailius' image materialized. The Supreme Commander appeared too calm considering the sudden development in the trajectory of the battle.

"Sir," Altar said, "the Cohannic had the station all along. We're in dire need of assistance."

Gailius didn't blink. "Negative Commander. I'm pulling our forces from the moon. This battle is lost. We must turn to our contingency plan now."

"The battle is not lost!" Altar shouted, slamming his fist down on the command station console causing Gailius' image to momentarily distort. "The Cohannic fleet will be on us in minutes. We don't stand a chance unless the Holstrek and its escort ships join the fight. We can turn the tide right now."

"I'm sorry Commander Unis," Gailius said somberly, "I'm ordering our remaining ships to retreat to the portal. We have to rally to Bartos. The complete loss of the Tyros system will certainly rouse the rest of the galactic community into action, it has to. This is how we save our people."

A surge of dread filled Altar's stomachs as the realization dawned on him.

We were never meant to succeed here today. Our defeat was the plan all along.

He tasted the acrid bile in the back of his throat as his head began to spin. "This was your backup plan, wasn't it? Sacrifice us to save yourselves."

"I understand your frustration Commander, so I'll pretend you never said that. We've made tactical and strategic choices to ensure our success, and I need—"

Altar disconnected the feed and turned to Benart. "Status report."

There was a distant look in Benart's eyes. Altar gazed around and saw similar looks in the eyes of the entire bridge crew. They looked utterly defeated after witnessing his exchange with Gailius.

He touched the panel for ship-wide communication and said, "This is Commander Unis speaking. We are currently under attack by hostile forces that have taken Yorinar and commandeered Averan-Ginest station. Our remaining forces are in full retreat and, in a matter of moments, the Cohannic fleet will be within attack range. Our battle group is taking heavy damage, and High Command has deserted us. We're on our own."

As if to underscore his last words, a powerful explosion rocked the bridge, causing the crew to grab hold of something to maintain their balance.

Altar steadied himself and continued, "Despite the grim circumstances, failure is not an option for us. If we lose this fight, we lose everything. The enemy will turn its attention to the Bartos system. Our homes, our families, and our very existence are at stake. Anyone who doesn't think that's worth staying alive for, put an energy pistol to your head right now and press the trigger." He paused for a beat, then said, "Since I didn't hear any shots, I'll assume you're all still with me. Now, let's give them everything we've got."

All at once, the entire bridge crew broke from their stunned immobilization and began frenetically interacting with their respective stations.

Frin manipulated the battlespace feed. "Sir the Fire Star is thirty seconds out of firing range. The Oracle is disabled and still taking heavy fire. The Monmoth, Paladin, and Yuerma are taking evasive action and returning fire on the station."

"What's the position of our main fleet?" Altar asked.

Frin rotated the feed again. "They're nearly at the relay; should we follow?"

Altar shook his head vigorously. "Running is not an option. We have to stop them here."

Benart looked at Altar. "If we can't run, and we can't win, what do we do?"

Altar contemplated the question, then an idea formed in his mind. "Helmsman, move us right above the station. Get as close as you can. Land us on top of the damned thing if you want."

The pilot tapped at the controls. "Yes sir."

Altar walked to Damu's station. "Instruct the Monmoth to follow our lead and tell the Paladin and Yuerma to get as close to the underside of the station as they can get."

"Aye sir," Damu said.

Benart's confused frown melted away as he began to understand Altar's plan. "Great thinking sir. Hopefully, this will negate the station's firepower."

"Our proximity to the station should interfere with their targeting sensors," Altar said.

"The Fire Star is in range," the weapons specialist reported.

Altar pointed at Damu. "Tell the battle group to target the Fire Star's main engine."

Lasers and photon missiles from each ship in the battle group shot out toward the Fire Star. It banked to its port side, narrowly avoiding three photon missiles. However, two particle beams strafed the shield just above its main engine.

"Minor damage to the Fire Star," the weapons specialist said.

Frin was rotating and scanning the battle map at a frenzied pace. "Twelve more Cohannic vessels entering range."

"It seems to be working sir," Benart said, barely containing his excitement. "The station is unable to effectively target us at this close range, and the Cohannic ships are reluctant to fire on us while we're this close to the station."

"This is only a temporary solution," said Altar. "I need options."

Damu spoke up and said, "The only way we can win this engagement is to regain the station. And the only way to do that is to dock with it and send in a boarding party."

"But we've no idea how many enemy soldiers are aboard the station," Frin objected.

Altar shook his head. "We wouldn't be able to dock under heavy fire, and even if we could, we don't have the manpower to take the station anyway."

"If we can't take the station, our only other option is to destroy their fleet," Benart said.

"Without the station, we don't have enough firepower to destroy their entire fleet," Frin said.

A brilliant light flashed in the battlespace map above the command station, interrupting the impromptu brainstorming session.

The weapons specialist turned in his chair. "The Oracle has been destroyed."

A thought suddenly leaped into Altar's mind and he was shocked by how quickly he embraced it. "We don't need to take the station to use it as a weapon."

"What do you mean?" Frin asked.

He pushed past Frin and zoomed in on the holographic view of Averan-Ginest. "The enemy ships will need to come into close proximity to the station to accurately target us. What if we were to move each of our ships to critical areas of the station, say engineering, the armory, and fuel storage? A simultaneous detonation of ships this size near those areas should cause the whole station to explode. Most, if not all, of the nearby enemy ships would be destroyed, or at least damaged beyond repair."

Frin's jaw dropped open as he looked around at everyone. "What you're suggesting is suicide. Surely there must be another way."

He looked Frin in the eyes. "You're the tactical officer. Look at the battlespace and tell me a scenario where we make it out of this alive."

Benart nodded his head in agreement. "The Commander is right, we're out of options. This is the only way to end this."

"Wait," Frin said. "Let's take a moment to think rationally about this. This isn't even their fleet. They still have troops and ships at Caristo."

"Merely a reserve force," said Altar. "This is their main fleet, and Orrick Klemo is leading it himself. If we can destroy the bulk of his forces, and eliminate him in the process, this nightmare is over right here, right now."

Frin motioned to the view screen. "And what about them? There're over two hundred thousand civilians on Averan-Ginest station."

"The Cohannic don't take hostages," Damu said. "Most of those people are either already dead or being massacred as we speak. The ones that aren't killed will be sold on the intergalactic slave market, and that's a fate worse than death."

Frin looked at Benart as if silently pleading for him to object, but Benart only nodded his head slowly in agreement.

Frin sighed heavily. "If this is our only choice, then we have to do it right because we'll only get one shot at this."

He started rotating the image of the station, tapping on various parts of the outer hull. "The main engineering section is here," he said, pointing to an area near the bottom of the station. He tapped another area nearby. "Fuel storage is here." Then he tapped two other areas near the station's midsection. "Munitions storage is here and here. One ship detonation midway between them should take out both locations."

"That's three ships then," Benart said. "What about us; what's our target?"

Altar pointed at the Fire Star. "Klemo. He can't be allowed to survive. Our job will be to make certain the Fire Star is destroyed in the blast."

Benart straightened and looked at Damu. "Relay Commander Unis' orders to the battle group. Tell them to get into position but hold until the command for detonation is given."

An impact rocked the bridge and the lights flickered momentarily.

"They're moving in closer and narrowing their fire spread," the weapons specialist reported.

"Shield strength is at fifty-three percent and hull plating is seventeen percent degraded," Frin said. "The other ships aren't faring much better."

Altar continued watching the approaching enemy ships on the viewscreen. "They won't destroy our ships this close to the station. They only want to disable us so they can safely move within towing beam range."

Frin looked away from the ship's status screen. "Whatever we're going to do, we need to do it fast then."

"The Monmoth and Yuerma are in position sir," Damu reported. "The Paladin is still en route, but she's taking heavy fire."

"Tell them to stay their courses," Altar said, studying the battlespace and the Paladin's painfully slow progression toward the red indicator marking the station's fuel storage section.

"We need to detonate all of the target areas, or we can't be certain the explosions will have the desired effect," Frin warned.

Altar exhaled a slow measured breath. The seconds seemed like years, and thoughts of Alara and Halmon flooded his mind.

Alara will hate me for not returning to her as I promised, but she will forgive me. As Halmon grows up, he'll eventually understand why I had to fulfill my duty, and he'll come to know that all I did was for him, his mother, and the Forrack race.

He walked toward the front of the bridge. "Helmsman, set an intercept vector for the Fire Star. Fire at will when we get in range, then lure it back toward the station. Damu, relay orders for the battle group to overload their drive crystals when the Fire Star gets close enough to the station."

The Traegar accelerated from the station and immediately began taking fire. The ship was jostled by the impacts from photon missiles and focused energy beams.

"We're drawing their fire sir," Frin reported. "Shield strength is at thirty-seven percent and hull plating is twenty-eight percent degraded."

The weapons specialist swiped two fingers across the holographic interface and tapped a blinking red panel and said, "Firing on the Fire Star."

Two disruptor missiles hit just to the starboard side of the Fire Star's bridge resulting in a shimmering effect as the polarized hull plating was momentarily weakened. An instant after the impacts, the arc of an energy beam sliced across the same area. The beam left a dark scorch line on the ship's hull.

"The Fire Star is coming about and targeting us," Frin said.

Altar wobbled slightly as the Traegar was hit by another series of enemy projectiles. "Get us back to the station now," he ordered.

Frin held tight to the command station table for balance. Shields at sixteen percent. Hull plate degradation is at forty-one percent. Critical systems are starting to take damage."

"Commander," Damu called out, "the Paladin is in position."

Benart turned to Altar. "Ten seconds until the Fire Star is within the projected blast radius."

A wave of grief flowed through Altar as he watched Averan-Ginest station loom larger and larger on the viewscreen. He silently mourned for the tens of thousands of innocent lives on the station, lives that were about to be exterminated in the blink of an eye. He mourned for the families of the brave soldiers who were forfeiting their own lives to save countless more. He didn't mourn for himself, however. Some part of him always knew his life would end in service of the Forrack race. He was honored that his sacrifice would mean his family, and his people, would live on. With no regrets, he closed his eyes and awaited his fate.

"Sir!" Damu shouted.

Before Damu could continue, there was a sudden shift in the Traegar's trajectory. Altar stumbled sideways into a wall, sending a sharp pain through his injured shoulder. He struggled to keep his footing as he held on to a nearby chair.

"Inertial inhibitors are failing," Frin shouted before being flung away from the tactical station.

Altar clung to the chair as he watched bodies being tossed all around the bridge. He turned his head and glimpsed the view screen. Alternating views of Averan-Ginest station, enemy vessels, and open space filled the screen.

The ship is spinning, he thought, frantically searching for an explanation.

He felt lightheaded and realized he was on the verge of losing consciousness.

No explosion, he thought groggily. *The Cohannic fleet hasn't been destroyed.*

Panic surged through him as he fought the overwhelming urge to close his eyes. But as sleep inevitably took him, he stole one last look at the viewscreen. Before his eyes closed, he saw a purple void stretching into infinity.

CHAPTER TWELVE
Zanna

<u>Regalus: Chalpin Star System</u>

Fragments of images raced through the girl's mind immediately after she willed the ship to be moved from harm's way. There was a frightened young woman bound in restraints, a well-dressed, one-legged man with a disfigured face, and a crumbling mountain.

She didn't recognize the faces she saw, but she felt like she knew them, or had known them in another life perhaps. She couldn't determine if the images were memories, or simply the manufactured thoughts of a deep slumber.

"Why the Forrack Commander?" Zurin asked, breaking her concentration.

She thought about it and said, "I don't know. I just have a sense he will yet be needed."

"You could have done nothing, but you chose to intervene."

"He would have died if I hadn't."

"How could you know that? You removed him from his peril, so his possible fate remains unknown."

"I... just... knew," she said.

Zurin persisted. "Did you see it in a vision?"

"I didn't see anything. It was just a feeling."

"Wisdom and foretelling are powerful gifts," Zurin said. "But the compulsion to act upon those gifts can be dangerous."

"Are you saying that I should have left him to his fate?"

"We are suggesting that you may be his fate, and that should never be the case. You must resist the desire to interfere simply because you possess the ability to do so, even if it is contrary to your feelings."

She felt like she'd just failed an important test. "I don't know why I saved that soldier. I only know that my instincts guided me. It's like I'm assembling a puzzle without seeing the image."

"You are limited to the pieces you have before you, but the possibilities of your creation are infinite. That is the danger of which we speak. You risk assembling a picture that was never meant to exist, an abomination of fate and destiny."

She absorbed the words. "You show me much, but you divulge no context to what I see. Perhaps I could get a better sense of the full picture if I knew who I was, or at least where I am."

"Tell us, child, why do you cling to the notion of material existence? Have you not seen the wonders of the Garmantua nebula? Then, in the next instant, were you not in the underwater Ormunii lairs on Phomia?"

"Yes," she answered.

"And on our travels, did you require the use of a spacesuit or underwater breathing apparatus?"

"No," she admitted.

"Did you not, with a mere thought, move an entire spacecraft from one planetary system to another?"

"I only desired that the ship be moved. It was through your power that it was done."

"Are you certain?" Zurin challenged.

She had no answer to the query. More questions flooded her mind. She felt as though her thoughts might overwhelm her, but she decided not to tell Zurin about the images she'd seen.

Instead, she asked, "So, are you saying I can control things with my thoughts?"

"We are saying that your preconceived concepts of time, space, reality, and possibilities should now be thoroughly shattered. The physical realm is but a speck in the grand collection of all things. There is much more for you to see. But you must first free yourself of these material notions. You must release your mind from its prison if you wish to experience true freedom."

"The miraculous change you keep talking about," she said in a voice dripping with sarcasm.

"It is no miracle, it simply is."

"Did you undergo the change?"

"Yes. Long ago."

"So now your purpose is to help others do the same?"

"In a sense, yes."

"So, if you have a purpose, then I must have one as well. I saved that Forrack soldier for a reason, though I may not know what it is yet."

"You are not wrong," Zurin said. "But you cannot possibly comprehend such a purpose in your current state. The answers you seek exist outside of space and time. True reality is devoid of good or evil; there is only harmony and chaos."

"You keep speaking of this change that I must undergo. Is it absolutely necessary? Can I not regain my memories, my sense of self, and realize my purpose as well?"

"Impossible," Zurin said. "Your primitive mind would collapse."

"How do you know?"

"Because we have seen it happen time and time again."

"So, I need only renounce the physical realm in order to undergo the change?"

"It is just that simple."

"And what if I refuse?"

Her question was met by an unnerving silence. She sensed that she may have overstepped her station, or committed an offense against Zurin. Just as she was about to offer an apology, Zurin's voice returned.

"We have conferred, and we accept your offer."

"Offer? What offer?" she asked confused.

"None of the others who came before you have maintained such a connection to the physical realm as you have. You are different. We believe you may be the one we have been seeking."

"Wait, what offer?" she repeated. "I've made no offers."

"But you will, we have seen it," Zurin said.

"So, what, my future self made you an offer?"

"It was more of an ultimatum."

Before she could protest or ask any other questions, a brilliant purple light obscured her vision, and a jolt of pain shot up her spine to the base of her neck. She instinctively raised her left hand to shield her eyes from the piercing light.

My hand!

She squinted against the light and studied the dark shadows that were her hands. She flexed the three fingers and thumb in awe, as if she were discovering them for the first time. As her vision adjusted, a humanoid form with a featureless face and long slender limbs resolved before her.

The light dimmed as the form drew closer, speaking in a calm voice. "You would not agree to undergo the change unless we restored you to your primitive self. Perhaps experiencing your physical existence in its entirety will assist you in releasing it for good. We have restored your physical form to its original specifications, though we fear you will not survive the change in this body. We relent only because we believe you may be the one we have been seeking."

She looked down at her stomach, her legs, and her feet. She gently caressed her arms, then her cheeks. She no longer felt confined to a specific point in space and time, now she felt confined within a physical body. She opened her mouth and drew in… nothing, yet she was breathing just fine. There was no wind on her skin, no ambient sounds in the distance, and no scent registering in her nostrils.

Disappointment replaced her elation. "You've restored my body, but I'm still in this place, and still without memories of who I am."

"Restoring your body was simple. Restoring your mind will take a toll on you. Should you emerge from the restoration process with your senses intact, your mortal form must then endure the change. You will not be able to return to the physical realm until the process is complete."

"How long will—,"

Zurin reached out and touched her forehead before she could finish her question. The edges of her vision flooded with blackness, and the strength in her newly formed legs faltered. She collapsed into the infinite purple void as a tidal wave of memories rushed into her mind. She saw her mother's smiling eyes, her father's stoic face, and her brother's mischievous grin. She saw her fellow Potentials walking the halls of the Academy, and Bolvaanar's stout form standing watch over them. She glimpsed her reflection in a mirror and the sight brought a smile to her lips. She remembered.

My name was Zanna Yuturi.

CHAPTER THIRTEEN
Vicaryn

Aegus: Flux Star System

Vicaryn stared at the informant's holographic image for a long time. "Are you certain?" he asked.

"Yes, he told me himself," the informant said.

Vicaryn drummed his fingers on the desktop as he contemplated how to use the information. "If he so openly speaks of misleading the Council in your presence, then there is no doubt you enjoy his full confidence."

"I have his complete trust, I'm sure of it."

"Good," Vicaryn said.

The informant wrung his hands together nervously. "What shall I do next?"

"Nothing. Let him come before the Council and spread his misinformation. It's better that he suspects nothing."

The informant bowed his head slightly in acquiescence. Then he glanced to the left and right as if he wanted to make certain no one was in earshot of his next words.

"And our agreement remains intact?" he asked.

"Most certainly," responded Vicaryn. "You've exhibited your loyalty to this Council, and to me personally, on many occasions. It's past time that you reaped your reward. You'll be his replacement after he is disposed of. Your long years counseling his father, and now him, make you a natural selection for the post. No one would question it. Veran Gauld, Pharus Ambassador to the

Sukarian Council. It sounds fitting, wouldn't you agree?"

"Certainly, Your Excellency. You honor me."

"Then the matter is settled. Make haste back to Aegus, there's much for us to discuss."

A wide grin spread across Veran's face as the transmission ended.

Vicaryn leaned back in his chair and looked up at Dannus who was standing at the corner of the desk. "I'll soon have another task for you. But first, tell me everything again, from the beginning."

Dannus slid his forearms into the sleeves of his robe. "I surreptitiously accessed the file on Corbo using the backchannel you provided. I was able to decrypt the redacted information and found that Allyon Corbo is in fact of House Telk. On further investigation, I discovered that he previously held the rank of Olgran within a Sukarian special forces unit. By all accounts, he served admirably as the unit commander of a mixed Korchak-Saunta force during the skirmishes with the Velderians in the Golmir Cluster."

Vicaryn stroked his long chin as he processed the information. "He must've been a very impressive soldier indeed to have been entrusted with command over Sauntas. Continue."

"During an engagement with Velderian ground forces on Engata Prime, Corbo and his entire unit disappeared. A total of ninety-three soldiers, all presumed killed. Three weeks later, Corbo arrived in a stolen Velderian fighter at one of our checkpoints near Regus II. In his after-action debriefing, he claimed his entire unit was ambushed and he alone escaped the carnage. He claimed to have evaded the enemy until he found a way to escape the system."

"I assume he was thoroughly screened when he arrived," Vicaryn said.

"He was, and no signs of Velderian DNA were detected. Though he was cleared, he never returned to combat service. Instead, he was awarded a Valorous Conduct gem and elevated to the rank of First Tridor. According to what I could find, he has served in an administrative capacity within House Telk since that time."

Vicaryn steepled his fingers beneath his chin. "No doubt Tycus was enthralled by Corbo's impressive service record. Enough so that he raised him up to serve as his ward."

"It would appear so," Dannus agreed. "May I be so bold as to inquire about your suspicions Master?"

Vicaryn placed his elbows on the desk, his coal-black eyes darting rapidly from side to side as he considered everything Dannus had relayed. "I have a theory Dannus, and I will share it with you. But first, were you able to procure the sample?"

Dannus stood and fished a small cylindrical vial from his tunic. He handed it to Vicaryn and took a seat. "I collected it from a utensil that Corbo used in the dining hall just this morning."

Vicaryn studied the vial for a moment, then he pressed a hidden panel on the wall behind him which opened a recessed compartment. He lifted an onyx cube from the compartment and pushed the panel back into the wall. He gently placed the cube onto the desk and tapped a sequence of symbols inscribed on one side. The top of the cube opened, revealing a small circular port into which he carefully inserted the cylinder. He pressed one of the symbols to close the top.

A computerized voice emitted from the onyx cube, "Genetic profile detected, analyzing data."

Vicaryn gazed at the box as if in a trance. Though he was only playing a hunch, deep down, he already knew what the next words from the cube would be. He sat in awe of the sheer eloquence and audacity of the scheme. The patience it took to devise and execute such a plan was beyond admirable. The Velderians were, without doubt, the most frightening race he'd ever encountered, but they were also the one he respected above all others. He often wondered why his ancestors chose to settle such a cunning and uniquely talented race within Vizaria.

Perhaps they were unaware of the Velderians' shapeshifting abilities, or maybe they naively believed the Velderians wouldn't use their skills for treachery.

Either way, they were here now, and Vicaryn waited with barely contained patience for confirmation of his suspicion.

A low chime sounded from the box and the computerized voice said, "Data analyzed. The presence of Velderian genetic material is confirmed."

Dannus sprung from his chair, his pale blue eyes wide with

alarm. "Velderian treachery! Master, I will take a contingent from the Krion Order and purge this spy immediately."

"You will do no such thing," Vicaryn said, still staring at the box. "Retake your seat."

Dannus unsteadily lowered himself back into his chair. "But the scan confirms that Corbo is a Velderian mimic Master. How is this possible?"

"They've obviously found a way to evade the scanners," Vicaryn surmised.

Dannus shook his head in disbelief and said, "If that's true, that would mean they've had this capability for several months at least. We need to immediately obtain genetic samples from all Council members and their staffs."

Vicaryn shook his head. "Not yet. We have the precious element of surprise, which we can use to our advantage."

"But Master, we have a Velderian mimic in our midst. The entire Council is in danger."

"There is no danger Dannus," Vicaryn said calmly. "The mimic has been among us for a few months now. Had its orders been to assassinate, it would have already struck. Besides, they would have surely sent Cressix had they wished to assassinate a member of the Council."

"Then what do you believe to be its purpose?" Dannus asked.

Vicaryn licked his thin lips. "This one has been sent to gather information about us, and it has presented me with a most exceptional opportunity."

"You would feed the mimic false information to report back to its handlers?" Dannus asked.

Vicaryn snapped his head up and stared directly into Dannus' eyes, coal-black meeting pale-blue. "No, my servant. The mimic cannot be allowed to step foot off of Aegus." He gently rested a hand on the onyx cube. "I have a more creative plan in mind. Listen carefully, this is what I need you to do…"

CHAPTER FOURTEEN
Tolbin

<u>Caristo: Tyros Star System</u>

Tolbin stepped from the freighter and his nostrils were immediately assaulted by the dry, acrid desert air of Caristo. He adjusted the FEB rifle strap across his chest and pulled his dark shirt down over the small energy pistol tucked into his trousers at the small of his back. He carried a rucksack in his right hand, the words 'You Touch, You Die' were prominently displayed on either side. He offered a broad smile as he approached the three Dark Hand mercenaries standing outside of Myric's Hole tavern.

"Not another step," the mercenary on the right growled.

He was a short, but powerfully built, Ragominnian with close-set beady eyes and a heavily scarred face. Unlike most Ragominnians, he had no dreadlocks, instead, matted green tufts of hair covered his large head.

He motioned to the other two sentries. One was a young Ragominnian with her dreadlocked hair twisted into a single braid that hung over her shoulder. The other was a much older Rematon who appeared as if his mercenary days should have been long behind him.

They approached, and the female gestured for him to raise his arms out to his sides. He complied and the Rematon produced a hand-held scanning device and methodically walked around him waving the scanner over his body as he went. Tolbin couldn't tell if his slow pace was due to his thoroughness, or if it was simply as fast as the elderly mercenary could move.

"I'm definitely armed," Tolbin said. "Heavily."

Scarface sucked his teeth. "Ya weapons don't cause us no concern Human. They more than welcome here."

"He's clear," the old mercenary said.

"Stay wit his ship 'til we get back," Scarface said to the old mercenary as he turned.

The female placed her hand on Tolbin's shoulder and shoved him roughly toward the tavern door.

Tolbin stopped and looked at her over his shoulder. "Push me again, and I'll be wearing that hand on a necklace by sundown," he said.

She looked at Scarface.

Scarface stared at Tolbin, then jerked his thumb in the direction of the open door. "Inside," he demanded.

Tolbin crossed the threshold into the tavern and immediately noticed the oppressive heat. Unlike the desert heat outside, the air in the tavern was thick and humid. It carried a musty scent that reminded him of an old, dank attic. As he was guided through the dining hall toward a back hallway, he took mental notes of his surroundings.

To his left, in the back corner of the room, there was a semi-circular bar with nine patrons sitting and standing nearby. The patrons appeared to be exactly what he'd expect to see in a place like this. They were an eclectic mixture of ex-mercenary types, wannabe toughs, and drunkards who looked to be on borrowed time.

The Sukarian bartender, however, was an odd sight. She was well past her youthful years, which wasn't saying a lot of a race whose average life expectancy was measured in centuries. Still, Sukarians were a notoriously haughty race. They were rarely found frequenting establishments such as Myric's Hole, let alone being employed by them. He made a mental note to learn more about her.

Scarface stopped at a large, nondescript wooden door at the end of the hallway. He turned to the female and said, "Wait here."

She nodded curtly as he slid the door open and ushered Tolbin through.

The room was larger than he would have expected of a back-room office. Two couches were pushed up against the wall to his left. A row of holographic transmitters lined the ceiling above an absurdly large desk sitting near the middle of the room. The holographic feeds were broadcasting real-time footage of various areas in and around the building. He caught a glimpse of the Sukarian bartender on one of the feeds, and his freighter, with the old mercenary standing nearby, was displayed on another.

There was an elevator door located on the wall beyond the desk. It led to the second story of the room. The second floor was framed on three sides by a glass banister, which allowed viewing access down to the first floor. To the right of the elevator door was a panel-controlled door that presumably led to another room.

The door slid open and Fallis entered the room, his dual energy pistols strapped to his thighs. His stringy dreadlocks waved slightly with the motion of his stride. Though he was within his own confines, his shifty yellow eyes constantly scanned the room as he walked. It was as if he was expecting threats from any direction at any moment.

The life of a mercenary, Tolbin thought. *He's not even comfortable in his own home.*

As Fallis approached, movement at the door caught Tolbin's attention. Despite being a seasoned operative who'd seen his fair share of strange things, he struggled to maintain his composure at the sight. A Cohannic soldier slithered through the door and a cold chill traveled down his spine.

He'd grown up hearing the bedtime stories about the monstrous Cohannic and how they would bite off the heads of misbehaved children and suck their insides out. Preadolescent Tolbin never believed the ridiculous tales. His great-grandfather claimed to had seen a Cohannic in the flesh, but Tolbin hadn't believed that either since the Cohannic had been driven back to their homeworld long before his great grandfather was ever born.

Still, the sensational descriptions of the Cohannic utterly failed to capture the true awe that this real-life specimen inspired. The soldier was a full two feet taller than Tolbin. He wore a yellow and brown tactical vest that was covered with blinking amber lights. His head, which seemed disproportionately small compared to his body, was covered by a visored helmet that obscured his facial features. His arms were bare from the shoulder to the forearm, and the dark green and black scales covering his body glistened as they caught the light. His forearms and hands were fitted with dull-gray metallic gauntlets, which also had blinking lights.

A utility belt around the soldier's midsection held various devices and tools Tolbin didn't recognize. He did, however, take notice of the short-handled energy blade hanging from the belt behind the soldier. Instead of legs, the Cohannic's lower half was comprised of a single mass, which was also covered in the glossy scales. The tail curved to the floor and moved in a rhythmic motion, propelling the soldier toward him.

The soldier slid to within a few feet of Tolbin and drew up to his full height as he looked over to Fallis. "Is he the one?"

"So he claims," Fallis said.

Tolbin tore his eyes away from the Cohannic soldier and looked at Fallis. "What do you mean, so he claims?" he said mocking Fallis' voice. "Of course I'm the one."

He turned back to the Cohannic soldier and tossed the rucksack at his tail. "Dergon Santon, at your service."

The soldier looked past him to Scarface. "Were his biometrics thoroughly scanned?"

"Yes, everything checked out."

"Leave us," the soldier said to Scarface.

Scarface offered a slight bow, then turned on his heel and exited the room.

Tolbin looked at Fallis curiously. "My biometrics? Ah, you wanted to make sure I wasn't a Velderian spy. I get it and I take no offense. I hope you're satisfied that I am who I claim to be because that would've been awkward."

The soldier removed his helmet and said, "I'm called Ongbo Dutt."

Tolbin shuddered internally at the sight of Ongbo's scaly face. His serpentine eyes blinked slowly, and his glistening forked tongue slid in and out of his lipless mouth. Tolbin was disappointed that the soldier wasn't Orrick Klemo himself. He might have shot him in the head right then and there if he were.

Instead, he said, "Good to meet you."

Fallis stooped, grabbed the rucksack, and hefted it onto a nearby table. He let out a low whistle as he reached into the bag and pulled out a gray and white FEB rifle.

As he manipulated various components of the weapon, he looked over his shoulder at Ongbo. "It's military grade, the good stuff."

Tolbin smirked. "There's a lot more on my ship."

Ongbo look over at the table where Fallis was now inspecting an energy pistol. "How did you come by these weapons?" he asked.

Tolbin leaned in closer to Ongbo and lowered his voice. "I could tell you, but then I'd have to kill… him," he said pointing a finger at Fallis.

Ongbo slowly turned his gaze back in that direction.

"So, we have a comedian?" Fallis said, aiming the energy pistol at Tolbin.

"Just joking," Tolbin said, raising his hands and chuckling. He looked back and forth between Fallis and Ongbo who were still awaiting an answer. "Truth is, it wasn't difficult. Tyros is crawling with two-bit smugglers. I simply find out which ones aren't the real deal, then I expertly relieve them of their ill-gotten gains." He pointed to the holographic feed showing his ship. "I got that particular freighter from a small band of Ertani pirates who were more than happy to give me what I wanted if I would only spare their lives. I kindly informed them that I already had what I wanted, and now you can find five headless Ertani floating in space somewhere between here and Jaft if you're so inclined to search."

"If you're supposed to be such a big deal, then why have I never heard of you?" Fallis asked, still pointing the energy pistol at him.

"Well," he said, "for one, I generally steer clear of your particular organization, for obvious reasons. And two, if you had heard of me, that would mean I wasn't particularly good at what I do, now wouldn't it?" He carefully lowered his hands. "Now. If you'd be so kind as to point that thing away from me, I would appreciate it."

Reluctantly, Fallis replaced the pistol in the rucksack.

"Thank you," Tolbin said. "Now, back to business. As I was saying, that freighter out there is full of the same high-quality weapons as are in that bag. Take them as a token of goodwill. Just know that I can get more. I also have a substantial amount of these."

He reached into a pocket concealed under a flap on his trousers and retrieved a small container. He slid the top open, revealing a small tray of sparkling gems.

Fallis walked from the table and inspected the tray. He removed one of the deep violet-colored crystals and held it up to the light. It was vibrant with a smooth texture.

"Fintra," he said to no one in particular.

He replaced the crystal and picked up another. This one was jagged, with clean, sharp edges. It was as clear as glass.

"Diamond," he said, this time looking at Ongbo.

"Correct, and correct," Tolbin said. "Unlike the weapons, no one was harmed in my acquisition of these lovelies. I merely bartered for them."

"Bartered with whom?" Ongbo asked.

"That's more of a complicated question than you realize, but it does bring me to why I'm here. You're going to need weapons and other supplies for this little venture of yours." He looked at Fallis. "No offense, but you're sort of a... um local gang, shall we say." He looked back to Ongbo. "I have a relationship with both the unsavory," he jerked a thumb toward Fallis, "and the more reputable elements of Vizaria. That's what you're missing, and that's what the Dark Hand can't give you."

"So, what exactly are you proposing?" Ongbo asked.

"I'm proposing that I work with the Dark Hand to procure more weapons. You keep some for your... crusade, and I'll sell some to those in need, say the Intergalactic Coalition, or maybe one of the mercenary groups. With credits in hand, I can get more of those sparkly crystals from the Ormunii."

"So, you're claiming to have a direct trade relationship with the Ormunii?" Fallis asked skeptically as he placed the diamond back in the tray.

Tolbin shrugged. "Who else do you know to possess large stashes of fintra crystals?"

"Just because you have them, doesn't mean you got them from the Ormunii," Fallis said.

"Fair point," Tolbin conceded. "But if I were to introduce you to my Ormunii contact, that might alleviate your doubts."

Ongbo's forked tongue flicked out and back into his mouth. "This is a meeting you can arrange?" he asked.

"I can," Tolbin said confidently. "The Ormunii are notoriously neutral in matters of galactic affairs, so they're not averse to doing business with my type. There is one caveat though."

"That is?" Fallis asked impatiently.

"The time and place of the rendezvous will be completely up to her," he said. "That's non-negotiable."

"Set it up," Ongbo said.

He tucked the tray of diamonds back into his pocket and said, "Consider it done. I'll be in touch."

As he turned to leave, A vice grip clutched his left shoulder. The pain was sharp, but his instincts didn't register the grab as an attack. He looked down at his shoulder and saw Ongbo's gauntleted claw. He turned back to face him.

Ongbo's slick tongue flicked from his mouth. "In addition to the weapons, we'll also take the crystals as a, how did you put it?

"A token of goodwill," Fallis offered with a smirk.

He sensed the menace in Ongbo's voice and that cold chill returned. He removed the case from his pocket and slipped it into Ongbo's open claw.

Ongbo kept his grip on his shoulder and leaned down to his ear. "If I find out you're not who you claim to be, I'll personally remove your head and disembowel you."

He locked eyes with Ongbo and suddenly the ridiculous stories from his childhood no longer seemed so far-fetched.

He cleared his throat and said, "I have a feeling this is the start of a very lucrative business relationship."

CHAPTER FIFTEEN
Cassyn

<u>Sphercal: Carmo Star System</u>

Cassyn stared up at the ceiling as her thoughts raced.

This was a mistake. Oh, who am I kidding? I've been making the same 'mistake' for the past three weeks now.

She looked over at Yuen's sleeping form and the yearning returned. He lay on his back with the sheet draped across his waist, one bare leg exposed. She didn't feel guilty for how they'd been carrying on. After all, neither she nor Yuen was in committed relationships. And though he was her superior, her time on the Vengeance had numbed her to such formalities.

He had been right when he warned her that things would be much different working for Sagis, but she never expected this. Or did she? She was attracted to him from the moment she met him, but she'd never intended to end up in his bed. For his part, he didn't seem at all awkward about their relationship.

Damn. Have I gone and gotten myself into an actual relationship? she wondered.

She rose from the bed and slipped on her blouse and pants.

"You're leaving me again?" Yuen said, rousing from his sleep.

She smiled. "And you're pretending to be asleep again."

"Admittedly, it's very difficult to get any sleep when I'm near someone so beautiful," he said with a wink.

"Nice try, but I have to go. I'm on shift in thirty."

"I'm not a quitter you know; I'll get you to stay with me one of these nights," he said.

She crossed to his side of the bed and sat on the edge. "What are we doing?" she asked.

He reached out and softly caressed her arm. "We were doing some very naughty things. Shall I recount the highlights?"

"I'm serious," she said. "Where is all this going? We don't really talk about it, it just… is."

He sat up on one elbow and adopted a more serious demeanor. "Where would you like it to go?"

"I'm not sure exactly, but I don't think our little secret is much of a secret anymore. We've been sloppy."

"You assume that I care about the crew knowing about us."

"Don't you?" she asked.

He sat up and propped his back against the headboard. "I like you Cassyn, like really, really like you. I'd love nothing more than for our… thing, to be something real. But I sense you're holding back, and I get it. You're concerned about our ranks and how it all may look to the others. I don't want to rush you." He reached out and took her hand in his. "But I don't want to lose you either. So, just know that I'm ready whenever you are, not a moment sooner, not a moment later." He planted a soft kiss on her hand.

She leaned in and gently kissed his lips. "Thank you, that means a lot to me."

She stood and finished getting dressed, and as she reached to press the button to leave, she turned back to him and said, "I'll see you on the bridge later."

He flashed his signature smile. "It's a date."

Back in her quarters, Cassyn buried her head in her pillow as the effects of the aggie worked its magic on her. She hadn't lied about having to be on shift, but she needed this. The pressure was beginning to get to her. Yuen was right. She was concerned about how a potential relationship with him would appear to everyone else. Informal as things on the Vengeance were, he was still her superior, and there would be constant whispers about their relationship.

Yero gave me this opportunity as a fresh start, as a way to get myself back on the right track, and here I am finding a way to ruin things like I always do.

As she felt her body slowly levitating, she thought about her feelings for Yuen. He was everything she'd ever wanted in a mate. He was kind, attentive, and emotionally available, all the things Tolbin hadn't been. Perhaps most important, he was honest, which was something she'd not completely been with him.

How would he feel knowing he was gallivanting around with an insecure drug addict with mommy and dead daddy issues? she wondered.

She thought she knew the answer, but she always thought she knew the answers to everything, and she'd proved herself wrong time and time again.

Her mind splintered into a million pieces whenever she tried to process her complex emotional thoughts, and the aggie always brought the shards back together again. The euphoria stretched its tentacles and touched every part of her body as she wallowed in its embrace. She rolled onto her back and craned her neck to look at the small plant conservatory she'd brought with her from Ardhamn. She felt a pang of guilt for not tending to the plants as much as she once had. Spending time with Yuen necessitated cutting back on her hobby.

She wasn't sure why she activated the call feature on her wristband. Perhaps it was because the plant habitat reminded her of home, or maybe it was the effects of the aggie, or just plain loneliness.

"Call mother," she said.

Pharie was stifling a yawn as she answered the call. "Cassyn? It's the dead of night here. Is everything okay?"

She paused for a long time before speaking. "Everything's fine Mom. Just a bit homesick I guess."

"Homesick? Honey, you hated Ardhamn."

"Not Ardhamn Mom, home, Mintellis."

"Oh, I see," Pharie said.

There was a low mumble in the background. She presumed it was Tamon asking who was calling at such an obscene hour. Her blood heated up as she imagined that impostor lying in the spot where her father used to lie.

She took a calming breath. "I'm sorry, I don't know why I called."

"No, no, don't apologize. I'm happy to hear from you, Cass. Really, I am."

Cassyn sighed heavily as her head swirled and she fought against a bout of uncontrollable giggles. "I might be falling for someone," she blurted out.

"Oh?" Pharie responded in a prodding tone.

"He's very sweet, and he treats me well. Nanna used to say that's all you needed from someone to be happy."

"Nanna said a lot of things, sweetie. Sometimes she was right, sometimes she wasn't."

"But you and Dad were happy once, weren't you?"

There was a long pause before Pharie asked, "Where are you going with all of this Cass? Are you sure you're okay?"

Cassyn ignored the question. "It's just… you always wanted me to follow in your footsteps and go to Belcanor Academy and become an educator or a researcher. You wanted me to find a nice young man and settle down, get married, and have kids, just like you did. But the more you wanted those things for me, the more you pushed for them, the harder I fought against them. Dad never pushed, he just wanted me to be happy, but I couldn't even do that because I was too busy trying to make sure I was the opposite of what you wanted me to be."

"It's true that I wanted a different life for you," Pharie said. "But is that so terrible? After your father died, I couldn't bear the thought of losing you too. I just wanted you to be safe. And I did want you to be happy, but you chose to run off and join the military where you almost let Tolbin ruin your life. You've made your choices Cass, and now you're living the exact opposite life I wanted for you. You won. The life I'd envisioned for you is never going to happen. But I don't know if the path you've chosen is conducive for a future with whoever this… someone is."

"So, there it is," Cassyn said. "The truth. The inevitable fact that I can't have anything good in my life because I didn't do it your way."

"Oh Cass, that's not it. The truth is, you can't have what you want because you don't even know what that is yet. You're lost in a fantasy, and you're constantly clinging to things that aren't real. As long as you stay trapped like that, anything you touch will only fall apart. You must see that."

The words slashed Cassyn to her core and she disconnected the transmission without another word. The warm, soothing sensation she'd been feeling devolved into an icy cold numbness. Tears cascaded from her eyes, and she buried her face into her pillow screaming as loud as she could, for as long as she could. Breathless and lightheaded, she rolled onto her back and closed her eyes.

She's right about me, she fretted.

That thought is what she feared the most. Tolbin hadn't almost ruined her life, it was the other way around. To this point, her life had been a sad series of bad choices. Her career was made up of nothing but constant clashes with her superiors, which only landed her on a frigid outpost planet with no path toward advancement.

Maybe I don't know what I want. Maybe I am destined to live out my days in loneliness and obscurity. Or maybe my mother doesn't know what the hell she's talking about.

Being with Yuen felt right to her. It felt... different. For the first time in her life, she'd stumbled upon something she both wanted *and* needed, and she deserved it.

Cassyn's head swirled, and her stomach lurched as she checked her wristband.

"Shit!"

She sprang from her bed, threw on her uniform, and grabbed her things. She ignored the annoyed looks as she sprinted down the hallway to the lift.

"Nice of you to join us," Brasif said as she scurried onto the bridge.

She hurried to her seat. "I'm sorry Cap..., I mean Brasif. I overslept. It won't happen again."

She was slowly becoming acclimated to the ways of the Vengeance, but calling her superiors by their first names was taking some time to get accustomed to.

Brasif didn't bother to look in her direction as he spoke. "That's what you said the last time, and the time before that."

She knew enough not to respond.

He continued, "In your absence, our next assignment was

expedited. We're going to be retrieving a shipment from Patrinah Station and transporting it to Fenghou Station. It's quite a distance and I'd like to get underway immediately, that is, if your schedule permits."

"We're transporting the shipment ourselves, not escorting a convoy?" she asked.

"I'm told that it's a fairly small shipment and there is no need for a full convoy."

"Why are we leaving three days earlier than planned?" she asked.

He turned in his chair and looked at her. Speaking in a calm, instructive tone, he said, "We transport and escort shipments; we don't set the schedules. Now if you don't mind, may we go now?"

She bit the inside of her cheek and took a moment before she replied, "Ready."

"Excellent. The relay coordinates have been set, now please get us to Patrinah."

"Course confirmed," she said before guiding the Vengeance into the swirling space-time tunnel of the relay.

As the ship crossed the threshold, a wave of nausea hit her. Her stomach lurched and her throat tightened. The shimmering tunnel walls seemed to close in around her, causing her heartbeat to quicken.

"Correct your trajectory," Brasif said.

Her head thundered over the muted whirr of the engines. She closed her eyes tightly, then opened them again, but she found no respite. Her skin felt clammy as beads of sweat formed at her temples and her fingertips and toes started to tingle.

"Course correction, now Cassyn!" Brasif barked.

She was vaguely aware of commotion all around her. She heard Brasif shouting something through the haze, but she couldn't make out the words. She felt as if she'd suddenly been submerged in a warm pool of murky water. Her vision narrowed and her thoughts slowed. She turned her head and the effort was far more taxing than it should have been. Dajin has arisen from her chair and was headed straight at her with facial features contorted by fear and panic.

What's happening to me? she wondered.

The impact of Dajin's large shoulder sent her crashing to the floor, but she felt no pain. She looked on as Dajin frantically interacted with the holographic controls, her hands moving over the panels with urgency.

Why is everyone going crazy? What's wrong?

Strong hands gripped her under her armpits and lifted her bodily to her feet.

"Get her off my bridge," Brasif demanded with rage in his eyes.

Her legs dragged uselessly along the floor as Soldaan hauled her toward the lift. His breath was hot on her ear and his coarse fur scratched against her neck.

"Hey! Put me down," she said, struggling weakly in his arms until her strength faded and she went limp.

The next thing Cassyn saw was Yuen's mismatched eyes staring down at her with concern. Her head was pounding, and she squinted against the bright lights. She realized she wasn't in her bed.

"Where am I?"

"Medical ward," he said. "You gave us quite a scare."

Fragments of memory flashed in her head as she struggled to raise herself from the bed. "Oh no, the relay tunnel."

He placed a hand on her shoulder and gently pushed her back down onto the bed. "It's handled. Everything's okay."

"Was anyone hurt?" she asked.

"Everyone's okay."

Tears pooled in the corners of her bloodshot eyes. "What have I done?"

He sighed. "Well, I know that's probably a rhetorical question, but it deserves an answer. The condensed version is that you got high out of your mind. Then you proceeded to almost maneuver the Vengeance into the wall of a relay tunnel, which, of course, would have obliterated us all. You also left Soldaan with a few scrapes and scratches, but I think he'll live." He squinted one eye and looked toward the ceiling as if trying to recall something. "Yeah, I think that pretty much sums it up."

She groaned and let her head fall back onto the pillow. "I've just thrown away my entire career, haven't I?"

"You've certainly not done yourself any favors," he responded. "How long have you been on aggie?"

Her cheeks flushed at the question. She'd always considered her drug use to be her dark little secret and a deep source of shame. It was an ever-present reminder of her inability to control her more self-destructive impulses. For her, it symbolized and legitimized all the negative perceptions she already felt people held toward her.

Despite her shame, she forced herself to look at him as she spoke. "I started shortly after my father's death. I guess it started as a coping mechanism, but I've obviously failed to cope adequately."

He just nodded and listened in silence.

"You must hate me now," she said.

"Why would I hate you?" he asked.

"Keeping something like this from you must feel like a betrayal. I know it would feel that way to me."

He nodded slightly and said, "I'll admit that it's a lot to take in. I wish you'd have let me know so I could have helped before it got to this. But none of this changes the way I feel about you. I love you Cassyn."

Studying his eyes, she could practically feel the sincerity radiating from him. She was at a loss. She'd never felt for anyone the way she felt about him in that moment. If her stomach wasn't performing acrobatics, and her head wasn't spinning, she'd grab hold of him and kiss him. Instead, she just stared quietly at him as the tears flowed down the sides of her face and dropped onto her neck.

"I love you too," she said. "So, what happens next?"

He shifted in his chair. "Brasif was less than happy, but I was able to talk him out of jettisoning you from the airlock. And thanks to Yero, he agreed to allow you to remain aboard the Vengeance until Pharus military command decides what to do with you."

She looked around the medical bay as if she'd just remembered something. "Where are we going?"

"Yero talked Brasif into continuing on our way to Patrinah, despite the incident."

Her shoulders slumped. "I can only imagine how disappointed Yero is in me."

He smiled that wry smile she loved so much. "There's no doubt you let a lot of people down, but redemption is in your future Cassyn Spreen, I know it. I'll be here for you every step of the way. Now, get some rest, we'll talk again when we get to the station."

He kissed her forehead before leaving the room. She lay there for a long time enduring waves of emotions ranging from disappointment to hope. She was awestruck by how quickly she went from feeling certain of her future to having no idea what was would happen to her. She was fairly certain her piloting days were over, and she hadn't entirely ruled out expulsion from the military altogether.

She dreaded the next conversation with her mother almost as much as she dreaded the next one with Yero. But if Devlin Spreen had taught her nothing, it was to attack adversity head-on.

Come what may, I won't let this be the thing that breaks me.

She rolled onto her side planning to sleep the rest of the way to the Sifton system, and as she lay there, the absurd desire for aggie taunted her.

CHAPTER SIXTEEN
Vicaryn

Aegus: Flux Star System

Vicaryn sat listlessly as the verbal barrage between Siverion Muld and Pentanus Derva ensued.

"You would alienate our entire race just to satiate your god complex?" Pentanus was saying.

"It's hardly a complex if it's factual," Siverion shot back.

Pentanus looked around the Council table and said, "We are not gods Siverion."

Siverion pointed a crooked finger toward one of the far walls. "Tell that to the Korchak, or the Quaduni, or the dozen other races that would consider what you just said to be blasphemous."

"They are not the only ones who matter. Holding ourselves up as deities would undermine every advantage we enjoy as the First Race. It's lunacy. How do you think the Humans or the Dolbans would react to such a declaration? Not to mention the inevitable religious war it would spark with the Cortarans."

"They are all unworthy and ungrateful," Siverion said smugly. "They wouldn't even be in Vizaria had we not saved them from certain extinction, yet they pretend to be on equal footing with us. The worst part of it all is that we allow it. So, I suppose you are correct Pentanus; we aren't gods. Gods would never tolerate the things we have come to accept."

"Ungrateful as they may be, we still enjoy high status among almost all the races of Vizaria, even those who choose not to deify us. We should be satisfied with that."

Siverion harrumphed loudly as he looked at Pentanus. "Listen to yourself. Do you think we should be satisfied with the modicum of respect they show us? We built the relay network. We brought them here. We should be demanding tribute and servitude from these inferior races; that's what we should be doing."

Pentanus rested his elbows on the table and leaned in Siverion's direction. "Here are the facts," he said, ticking them off on his fingers as he went. "The Cortarans have eclipsed us in technological advances; the Humans remain free-spirited and independent as ever, and would never acquiesce to such subjugation; the Dolban population outnumbers ours four to one; the Ghansans possess one of the best and most well-equipped militaries in Vizaria; the Velderians continue to be an ever-present threat to galactic stability; and, in case you've forgotten, the Cohannic are making a play for galactic domination as we speak. So, tell me Siverion, when are you going to snap your godly fingers and make these realities disappear?"

Pentanus has the right of it, Vicaryn thought. *Declaring ourselves gods would be our undoing. Siverion, and those who think like him, are fools.*

"Enough of this," Tycus said, leaning forward to rest his elbows on the bench. "While I do enjoy a lively debate, we have more pressing matters to discuss. I've been informed that Ambassador Veleko has arrived. I expect him to confirm that the Humans have agreed to assess the extent of this invasion and share any resulting intelligence with us."

Vicaryn raised his eyebrows. "Are you certain that will be his report?" he asked.

"Can you imagine any other?" Tycus shot back.

"I can imagine a great many things. I'm simply wondering what this Council is prepared to do should the Ambassador's report returns... unfavorable."

Tycus stared at him for a long moment, and he could tell the Council leader was assessing him, trying to figure out the angle he was playing at. For his part, Vicaryn's face gave nothing away. Outwardly, he was simply curious about a potential backup plan should things not proceed in the Council's favor.

Tycus maintained his stare and responded, "Should that

happen, I'll personally talk some sense into President Baruke."

Vicaryn offered a small nod knowing that every prefect gathered around the dais recognized the response as simple bluster. There had only ever been one prefect who'd personally spoken to a non-Sukarian government leader, and he was promptly removed from the Council for his effort.

Tycus would never risk such a thing, he thought.

"Very well," he said to Tycus. "If the Humans have agreed to do our bidding, what will the next step be?"

Val Jurga of House Holm spoke up. "Why do we need the Ambassador to tell us what we already know? The Forrack have fled the Tyros system. The Fire Portal is fully under Cohannic control now. They could show up anywhere in Vizaria, even here. How can there be any response other than war?"

Siverion waved a dismissive hand in the air. "Tyros means nothing. The entire system is nothing but vagrants and criminals. We allowed the Forrack to govern there, and look what's happened. I say good riddance. Let the whole system rip itself apart."

Pentanus looked at Siverion. "So, you're content doing nothing while the Cohannic possess a portal?"

Siverion did not hesitate in his response. "Yes. The First Portal is well defended. The snakes wouldn't dare strike at Flux. It would be their undoing."

Pentanus raised his voice. "And what of the dozens of other systems that have no hope of fending them off?"

Siverion kept his tone even. "The ones who have shown us the proper respect have nothing to fear. The others… well, they might want to reconsider their allegiances."

Pentanus shook his head in pity. "And by allegiances, I take it you mean the gods they serve."

"Take it however you please," Siverion said.

Val looked around at the other Prefects. "Surely we cannot be considering allowing the snakes to retain the territory they've taken. Especially when it gives them access to a portal."

"Why not?" asked Minva Olantus of House Appox. "Prefect Muld is quite correct when he says we have never shown an interest in the Tyros system before. We only went there in the past to quell the Cohannic's first attempt at taking the system, then we handed everything over to the Forrack and left. We've not meddled in their affairs since, so why should we do so now? Who knows, maybe the Cohannic will impose order there on a scale that the Forrack couldn't."

"The words *Cohannic* and *order* do not belong in the same sentence," Val said. "The snakes know only war and savagery. Once they're finished with the Tyros system, they will surely move on to another."

Jamun Enchavi of House Enchavi spoke for the first time. "What of the costs? he asked. "We speak of war as if there is no price. In addition to expending our soldiers, we stand to bankrupt ourselves and deplete our resources by entering this conflict. We're already heavily burdened by our proxy war with the Velderians."

"While I appreciate your penchant for counting credits Prefect Enchavi," Pentanus said, "finances mean very little when a Cohannic claw is gripping your throat."

Jamun chuckled softly. "That sounds like fearmongering to me. The Cohannic didn't even get past Caristo the last time they attacked, let alone make it out of the system," Jamun said.

"Yes, but last time they were not allowed to pillage unchecked," Pentanus pointed out. "Now, they have the entire system under their control and they have the Norvekians as allies. There are even credible reports that the Dark Hand is in league with the snakes. It would be folly to measure this current situation by our last success."

"We simply do not have enough information to formulate an effective response at this time," Tycus said. "The intelligence from the Humans will shed more light on the situation."

There it is. His cowardice surfaces, Vicaryn thought.

Remembering his last confrontation with Tycus, he decided to take a more measured approach in this debate. He needed to voice his support for joining the war, but not too much as to sway Tycus from his erroneous course.

He placed his palms flat on the table. "Prefect Jurga is right," he said. "The Cohannic are expansionists by nature. They pose a threat that I do not believe we can leave unchecked."

Tycus glowered as if he was about to offer a retort, but Vicaryn continued before he had the chance.

"However, I also agree with Prefect Athket that we cannot yet fully ascertain the enemy's true motives in this current conflict. It might well be that they are satisfied with their conquest of the Tyros system. They may view it as their empire, and perhaps their campaign will come to an end there. Without more intelligence, which Prefect Athket believes to be forthcoming, we should not make any hasty decisions."

He almost dry heaved at the distaste the words left in his mouth. He knew there was no chance the Cohannic would halt their advance at Yorinar, but he needed to reinforce Tycus' flawed logic to better lay his trap. From his peripheral vision, he saw Tycus eying him suspiciously.

His guard is up, good. Let him remain focused on me.

Val and Pentanus glared at Vicaryn but held their tongues.

Minva straightened in her chair and lightly tapped her palms on the table. "I, for one, am satisfied with the consensus. Shall we bring in the Ambassador?"

Tycus reached out and placed his hand over a glowing green orb. Moments later, the clone of Allyon Corbo entered the Council chamber and approached the dais.

Vicaryn studied the mimic keenly as it traversed the long aisle. He admired the grace with which it moved. The attention to detail was truly impressive.

Only a tiny fraction of the Velderian population possessed the gift of mimicry, but the carnage that a mere handful of skilled mimics could inflict was catastrophic. Still, he looked on in wonderment. It was the first time he'd ever knowingly observed a mimic in action. It both amazed and frightened him. He wondered what fate the real Allyon Corbo had met. He supposed that any being whose identity was claimed by a Velderian mimic would have surely been permanently disposed of. He'd considered taking the mimic alive, but that wouldn't comport with the design of his plan, and to his knowledge, no mimic had ever been captured.

It's a shame. I would relish the opportunity to interrogate one of them.

Tycus whispered something in the mimic's ear and it exited the Great Hall, returning several minutes later followed by Ambassador Madrin Veleko. Just as the last time, the Ambassador's two companions took seats at the back of the room near the entrance door. Madrin approached the podium and waited to be addressed.

Tycus issued the standard greeting. "This Council recognizes Madrin Veleko, Ambassador for the Pharus Confederation."

Madrin ran a palm over his hair and said, "It is my honor, once again, to appear before this esteemed High Council.

Tycus offered a slight tilt of his head. "When last you were before this Council, we tasked you with convincing your government to assist us in assessing the Cohannic threat. What news do you have for us?"

Vicaryn noted a slight hesitation in Madrin's voice before he answered, "The news is favorable. The Pharus Confederation has accepted your request to further investigate the enemy's intent. Military and diplomatic attaches will be dispatched to coordinate with the Forrack government."

Tycus shot a triumphant glance in Vicaryn's direction. "And what of the information-sharing agreement? May we expect full and detailed reports on your government's findings?"

Madrin nodded. "The Pharus Confederation will share any intelligence gathered with this Council."

Vicaryn delighted in Madrin's boldness. It was a serious offense to knowingly speak untruths to the Council, and he knew Madrin understood the graveness of such an act. The last offender to commit the crime was still wasting away in Deljadun Prison.

The Ambassador is playing a perilous game, and he didn't flinch. It's good to see that he learned some of the lessons I taught him, though it's a shame he's misplaced his trust.

He looked in Veran's direction and saw the man staring back at him.

Now that the Ambassador has perjured himself before the Council, he looks to me to strike the death blow.

He'd always secretly despised Veran, but he also held a grudging admiration for his ambition. The way he aided in legitimizing Hayden Veleko on the galactic stage was nothing short of masterful. He helped the elder Veleko ascend to heights that no Human had ever achieved in Sukarian-Human relations. He'd taken a background role with Hayden, but it seemed he was unwilling to do the same with his son.

Tycus began to rise from his seat. "This Council is pleased with your report, and we look forward to the first intelligence briefing."

Madrin cleared his throat. "If I may?"

Tycus paused, then hesitantly retook his seat. "You have more to say?"

"A small request," Madrin said.

Tycus glanced uneasily toward Vicaryn, then back to Madrin. "You may proceed."

Vicaryn could tell that Tycus assumed the next words from Madrin's lips would be of his design, but it was a misplaced assumption. Vicaryn was just as eager as the other Prefects to hear what the Ambassador was going to say.

"Even in the absence of detailed intelligence reports, it's become clear that the situation in the Tyros system is grave," Madrin began. "The Forrack have been expelled, and now nothing stands between the Cohannic-Norvekian alliance and the rest of Vizaria. This situation will be exponentially more difficult to handle if the Cohannic are allowed to spread outside the Tyros system."

"This Council has urgent matters to discuss," Siverion interrupted. "What are you asking of this Council?"

"A military alliance," Madrin said.

There was a low murmur around the Council dais and Vicaryn suppressed the urge to smile.

He's even bolder than I thought.

Tycus motioned for silence. "Your request is premature, is it not? The reason we sent you to confer with your government was precisely so that we could ascertain if war was even necessary. We still don't have that answer."

"That is true, Your Excellence, but at that time the Cohannic had only taken a space station. Now, they control an entire star system, including a portal. I believe the calculus has changed dramatically."

Pentanus leaned forward to speak. "Is this an official request from Pharus?"

Madrin hesitated. Though he'd already lied to the Council about Pharus' willingness to share intelligence, Vicaryn knew he would understand that lying about an official request for a military alliance would be going too far.

"No," he admitted. "This is a request of my own volition in light of the imminent threat we all face."

"What makes you think we need Pharus to defeat the Cohannic and the Norvekians?" Minva asked.

Madrin bowed his head slightly. "I meant no offense Prefect Olantus. Of course the Sukarian military is more than capable of dealing with this threat alone, but I wasn't suggesting an alliance solely with Pharus. This menace threatens all of Vizaria; therefore, I propose a galactic alliance."

Minva scoffed. "And who would lead such an alliance, the Humans?"

Madrin shook his head. "You are the First Race. You led the fight against the Cohannic and drove them back to Fulmaren generations ago. You could do the same again, this time at the head of a much larger coalition."

"It isn't an unreasonable request," Val said.

"I agree," Pentanus added.

Siverion abruptly stood from his seat. "This is outrageous! Are we now going to let the Humans dictate when and how we declare war?"

"Siverion is right," Jamun said. "We're not here to consider alliances."

Vicaryn remained impassive as the scene unfolded before him. He'd not anticipated Madrin's proposal, but it all made sense now. The Ambassador wanted to orchestrate an alliance to gain notoriety, which he could then use as political capital to advance his career. He wondered if Veran knew of this scheme.

Of course he knew. He was probably the one to concoct it.

He looked again in Veran's direction to see him staring back, silently pleading for him to expose Madrin's deceit and end this spectacle. Vicaryn wasn't so inclined.

Tycus raised both arms in a call for order in the Chamber. "Retake your seat Prefect Siverion."

Siverion complied, but he never took his eyes off of Madrin.

Tycus addressed Madrin and said, "While this Council does appreciate your view of the current state of affairs, we've already discussed the matter at length. It is doubtful the Cohannic will leave the Tyros system, but if they should, we will deal with them expeditiously. Your request for an alliance will not be considered at this time." He narrowed his dark eyes. "I do wonder how your government will receive the news of what you've attempted to do here today, but that is a matter to be resolved between them and you. This Council expects full intelligence briefings from the Pharus Confederation per their agreement. You may go."

All of the Prefects stood in unison, signaling an end to the conference. Vicaryn could see the defeat written on Madrin's face as he looked at him for a last-second reprieve. He offered no such hope. He watched Madrin's shoulders slump slightly as he turned and stepped from the podium. Veran glanced back at him once more before following Madrin from the Great Hall.

Don't fret Ambassador, I'll soon be ridding you of at least one of your problems, he thought.

CHAPTER SEVENTEEN
Madrin

<u>Aegus: Flux Star System</u>

Madrin descended the steps two at a time as Nhila and Veran struggled to keep pace.

"Sir, please slow down," Nhila pleaded.

"Yes, for heaven's sake," Veran said panting heavily.

Madrin paused at the landing and rested a hand on a nearby wall. Sweat drenched his collar, but it was more from the ordeal he'd just endured rather than physical exertion. He clenched his eyes tight and let out a guttural scream as he struck the wall twice with his fist. Pain erupted in his knuckles and traveled up his forearm to his shoulder.

"I'm finished," he said. "I risked everything in there, and I lost."

Veran caught up to him and placed a reassuring hand on his back. He took a moment to catch his breath. "You took a risk, and it didn't pay off, but all is not lost. We just have to find a way to spin this."

"Spin!" he screamed, looking at Veran in disbelief. "There is no spinning this Veran. I lied to the Council, and it won't be long until they discover it. The only chance I had was convincing them to take the fight to the Cohannic, and I failed. The President will relieve me, and who knows what the Council will do. It's over."

He leaned against the wall and slid down into a sitting position as he clutched his bloody hand to his chest.

Nhila looked back up the stairway to make sure no one was watching him in this vulnerable state. "What do we do now?" she asked.

He looked up at her with sorrow-filled eyes. "There is no *we* anymore Nhila. There's a major storm coming my way, and I don't want you or Veran around me when it hits."

Her face hardened. "Bullshit. We're not abandoning you at a time like this."

Before there could be any more discussion, footsteps echoed from around the corner, farther up the stairway. Someone was approaching. Nhila stooped and helped Madrin to his feet as Veran brushed dirt and debris from his clothes. Dannus Prie turned the corner and seemed slightly startled by the trio's presence before quickly regaining his composure. He eyed Madrin and stole a glance at his bloody hand.

"Greetings, Ambassador," he said, "my Master would like to speak with you." He looked at Nhila and Veran in turn and added, "Privately."

"Not a chance, I'm coming too," Nhila said.

Madrin straightened his jacket. "It's okay Nhila, I'll be fine. You and Veran wait for me at the transport."

"But sir—" Nhila began to protest.

Madrin held up his uninjured hand. "I'll be fine." He looked at Dannus and said, "Lead the way."

Vicaryn exited the elevator and walked swiftly down the corridor. He'd set Dannus to his task, and now his timing needed to be precise. He rounded a corner and spotted Tycus several feet ahead, the Allyon Corbo clone close by his side.

He called down the hall, "Prefect Athket, a moment of your time."

Tycus turned with a look of annoyance. "What is it?"

He approached the pair, looking the mimic in its eyes.

Marvelous. Truly marvelous, he thought.

He tilted his head apologetically. "Excuse the intrusion. Ward Corbo, a pleasure. I would like a private word with the Prefect if you would be so kind as to excuse us."

The mimic looked to Tycus for approval. Tycus gave a curt nod and the mimic turned to leave.

Vicaryn held up a slender finger in its direction. "Oh, I almost forgot, the Ambassador requested your presence at his transport, something regarding a message from Pharus."

The mimic again looked to Tycus, who waved his hand dismissively. "Go, see what he wants."

"May we?" Vicaryn asked, gesturing to a small conference room off the main hallway.

Tycus stepped into the room and turned toward Vicaryn. "What's the meaning of this?"

Vicaryn touched a panel and the door slid down. He walked to the far side of the room and stared out a large window facing the south courtyard. Tall, spindly skytowers simultaneously reached for the clouded heavens and stretched into the distant horizon. The transport sat near the center of the courtyard, appearing as a speck from this height.

He continued staring out the window as he spoke, "I understand your reluctance to get involved in this conflict with the Cohannic, but the situation has become dire. Things have progressed more quickly than we could have imagined. It's folly to believe the Cohannic will stay in the Tyros system. I urge you to reconsider."

Tycus raised his eyebrows. "Ah, now I see. Your agreement with me in the Council meeting was just a ruse. I should have known."

"My agreement was a goodwill gesture, a show of unity in the presence of the Human representatives. I'd hoped to sway you toward reason in private. We must stop this invasion before it causes any more damage. We cannot afford to wait."

"Jamun seems to believe we cannot afford to act. This would be a costly venture for us."

"Jamun is a fool who lives off the legacy of his family."

"Be that as it may, it doesn't mean he's wrong."

"He is wrong, and you'll find yourself in a very precarious position should you fail to see that."

Tycus' eyes narrowed. "Is that some sort of veiled threat?"

"I did not intend for it to be veiled," Vicaryn said, tilting his head.

Tycus walked over and leaned in close to him. "I've always admired your ambition Vicaryn. One day I'm sure it will pay off for you. But right now, I lead this Council. I also control the military and determine when and where to deploy it. If you continue to defy me, I just might send a squadron of Sauntas to pay an impromptu visit to House Elgeen's provincial lands." He smirked, then added, "That wasn't meant to be veiled either."

He held his gaze for a moment, then turned on his heels and left the room.

Left alone, Vicaryn let out a long slow breath. Part of him had hoped Tycus would see reason and commit the Sukarian forces to war. That outcome would have been… cleaner. But a larger part of him had counted on Tycus' stubbornness, and the result it would bring.

So be it, he thought, *there's no turning back now.*

Madrin walked two paces behind Dannus as he was escorted back toward the enormous chamber. His mind raced as he pondered why Vicaryn was requesting a private audience with him.

He knows I lied to the Council.

A cold shiver passed through his body, and the throbbing in his hand intensified. His wrist communicator vibrated and flashed with an 'urgent communication' alert from Nhila. He activated the response feature.

"Yes Nhila, what is it?"

"Sir, you have an incoming holographic transmission from President Baruke."

Another cold shiver.

Has she already found out about what I've done here?

He stopped ascending the stairs. "Put her through to my communicator."

"She's on a priority channel sir, you'll have to take it on the transport."

"I'm headed into a meeting with Prefect Gayne; can't she tell Veran what this is about?"

There was a short pause. "She said she needs to speak with you immediately."

Madrin let out a sigh. "I'm on my way."

"Is there an issue?" Dannus asked standing a few steps ahead of him.

He started back down the stairs. "I have an urgent matter to attend to. Please tell Prefect Gayne I'll be with him shortly. I know the way back to the chamber."

A flash of alarm showed on Dannus' pale face. "But Ambassador, my Master awaits."

He attributed Dannus' fear to the fact that the servant didn't want to be seen as the cause for the delay.

"I'll be right back," he called over his shoulder, "and I'll let the Prefect know that the delay is mine."

He heard Dannus say something else in protest, but he didn't stop. He needed to know why President Baruke wanted to speak with him so urgently. His gut told him it was going to be a very consequential conversation, and he fretted that he would be the one facing the consequences.

He jogged down the final few stairs and headed to his right toward the idling transport. Veran was seated in the back with his head down as if he was reading something. Just outside of the transport's loading door, Nhila was engaged in an animated conversation with Tycus' assistant Allyon Corbo. Allyon noticed him approaching and began to walk toward him.

"Ambassador, there you are. I was told that you requested my presence," Allyon said.

"Your presence?" he asked confused.

He looked past Allyon and saw Nhila approaching. "Sir, I was explaining to him that—"

In the next instant, an intense wave of heat rushed past his face as he was lifted off the ground. A bright flash momentarily blinded him as time seemed to slow to a crawl. His vision returned in time to see Nhila being flung into the air, her arms and legs flailing and her hair aflame. A look of utter shock contorted her face as the chaos erupted all around them. Allyon was also off the ground as well. He was headed straight toward Madrin, enveloped in a ball of flame and smoke. His mouth was open, and his eyes were clenched shut.

The weightlessness seemed to drag on as the shock wave pushed Madrin farther from the transport, or more accurately, from where the transport had been a moment earlier. In its place was an expanding sphere of pink and blue arcs of lightning rushing out in every direction scorching all it touched. Small chunks of debris rocketed into the sky as large fragments of the transport's hull were violently hurled across the courtyard.

The air was forced from his lungs as he crashed to the marbled ground. Allyon sailed over him and thudded hard somewhere beyond. He lay motionless for what felt like an eternity as the muted sounds of panicked screams and falling metal issued all around him. The sky was filled with light pink smoke and charred pieces of floating tinder.

Concern gripped him as he realized he couldn't see out of his right eye. He tried raising his hand to his face, but the effort sent ripples of pain shooting throughout his body. With an effort, he managed to roll onto his side and look back toward the origin of the explosion. Leaping flames and charred rubble obscured his view, and he immediately recognized there was no way Veran could've survived the explosion. He twisted his head around, but he saw no signs of Nhila.

A commotion from behind him drew his attention and he turned his head to look. The vision from his left eye was blurry and red-tinged, but he could make out Dannus approaching the spot where Allyon had landed. Allyon was struggling to his feet, but something wasn't right. Parts of his body transformed as he rose onto one knee. Within the span of a second, his left leg morphed into a dark-green gelatinous mass, back to a fully formed Sukarian leg, then back to a gelatinous mass. Similar transformations were simultaneously happening all over his body. His arms, his torso, his head, they were all transmogrifying.

Confusion, pain, and fear vied for control of Madrin's senses. He was slipping into unconsciousness but willed himself to watch the surreal scene unfolding before him. He needed to understand what was happening.

Dannus removed a small energy pistol from the sleeve of his tunic as he approached to within a few feet of Allyon, who was still attempting to gain his footing. The ward's entire body was phasing uncontrollably as Dannus pointed the weapon at him. A moment later, a green beam of light emanated from the pistol. Allyon raised a malformed arm in a futile attempt to block the beam, but it sliced through his arm and chest before exiting his back to scorch the marble floor beyond. His body jerked once before collapsing to the ground in a mangled heap.

Madrin watched, dumbstruck, as the body gradually dissolved into an expanding puddle of gunk. He gently lowered his head to the ground as the pain surged through him. His entire body felt as if it were being consumed by flames, and it may well have been for all he knew. He didn't care; he'd just lost everything. His career was over, and now he was going to die in disgrace here in the middle of this courtyard. He'd failed his mother and undoubtedly cast a veil of shame over his father's legacy. Living with the indignity of it all was a worse fate than death. As he lay there in all of his suffering, waiting for the end to come, he allowed himself a small chuckle.

My life is flashing before my eyes, and I've not spared a thought for my daughters or my wife, he thought.

He loved his family, but this moment showed him the true order of his priorities. His quest for power trumped all. There was no accompanying guilt or shame that, in his final moments, all he could think about was himself. Before his consciousness finally abandoned him, he tried in vain to comprehend what it all meant.

CHAPTER EIGHTEEN
Altar

<u>Birgh: Bartos Star System</u>

Altar's bottom set of eyes opened at the sensation on his cheek. The hand was soft, the touch gentle. He opened his top set of eyes and focused on Alara's face hovering above him.

"Alara," he said.

"I'm here," she said smiling.

He exhaled a deep breath. "Are we on Birgh?"

"Yes."

"But—"

A bout of nausea assailed him, choking off his words. He placed three fingers to his lips until it subsided.

"How did I get here?" he asked.

"Your ship was found adrift near the edge of the system. You apparently entered the Fire portal and were routed to the Bartos system. You don't remember setting a course for home?"

He massaged behind his ears trying to remember his ordeal. "We were in a battle around Yorinar. We were ambushed and High Command abandoned us, but we stayed to fight. We were about to…"

He trailed off. She didn't need to know about the attempted suicide mission.

"You were about to what?" she prodded.

He shook his head. "I don't remember the details, but I know we never set course for the portal."

"Well, someone must've. You arrived a few hours before the main fleet, or what was left of it at least."

"Wait, we arrived *before* the fleet?" he asked confused.

"Yes."

"How many ships were with the Traegar?"

A puzzled look spread across her face. "There were none but the Traegar."

He pressed harder behind his ears trying to make sense of it all. "What of the crew?"

"All were unconscious, but everyone was accounted for. The doctor said there were only minor injuries. Altar, what happened out there."

"I don't know my love. It was... It was... I have no explanation."

A sudden panicked thought leaped into his mind and he grabbed her wrist. "We're in danger!"

He pulled himself up, tore off his medical monitoring device, and swung his legs off of the cot. "I need to get in contact with High Command."

"Altar, wait, slow down."

A medical assistant drone hovered into the room. "Are you having a medical emergency?" it asked in an even tone.

"Move," he said, nudging the drone aside as he searched for his trousers.

"Everything is alright," she said to the drone.

"The drone turned and started for the door. "I'll alert Doctor Charmunigen."

By the time the doctor arrived, Altar was putting on his boots. The doctor held his hands out gesturing for him to slow down. "Commander Unis, I've treated your shoulder injury, but I implore you, please do not leave until we can further ascertain any other possible injuries from your ordeal."

He continued fastening his boots without looking up. "I'm fine, doctor."

Alara looked at the doctor, offering a silent apology. "It's okay, we're fine. I'll look after him and will let you know if anything is out of the ordinary."

Doctor Charmunigen's shoulders slumped in defeat. "Very

well," he said before leaving the room.

She rested a hand on Altar's thigh. "My love, you haven't asked about Halmon."

He finally looked up with shame evident on his face. "How's my son?"

"Bigger," she said with a light giggle. "He's grown a lot since you saw him last, almost seven inches."

Pride bloomed on his haggard face. "Well, where is he?"

"With my sister, in the city."

"That'll be my first stop after I contact High Command."

Her smile dissolved. "What's so urgent? What's this danger you speak of?"

He felt the bile rising in his throat again as his cheeks flushed with anger. "They haven't told you, have they? They haven't warned you all?"

"Told us what? Warned us about what?" she asked.

He took her by the shoulders. "There's a reason the fleet came running back to the Bartos system."

He watched as the realization slowly crept into her face. "No," she said.

"We failed to stop the Cohannic at Averan-Ginest. They'll be here soon; we must prepare."

The Forrack High Command complex was situated in the valley between the Khama mountain range to the north, stretching from the southwest to the northeast of the continent, and the Sloantavic mountains to the south, running from east to west.

Altar's hover car careened through the curve leading to the front of the complex. He leaped from the vehicle before it came to a full stop and headed straight for the main entryway. The two sentries at the door exchanged nervous looks at the sight of his rapid approach. They came to attention and saluted. He ignored them and slammed his open palm on the access panel. The door slid open, and he marched inside.

The lobby teemed with activity as personnel moved hurriedly in every direction. The enemy forces were on the way, and everyone here knew it. He spied the elevator at the far end of the building and shouldered his way in that direction as sporadic comments were directed at him.

"Welcome home Commander," said an older woman.

A young soldier asked, "Any news of the Yuerma? My brother is its tactical officer."

"How long before the Cohannic arrive?" asked another soldier.

He heard none of it. His singular focus was to get answers, and nothing was going to slow him down. He exited the elevator on the eighth level and approached the reception desk.

"I'm here to see Supreme Commander Rhandu, where is he?"

The young cadet manning the desk offered a sloppy salute before stammering, "He… he's currently in a meeting sir."

He placed his palms on the desk and leaned toward the cadet. "I didn't ask you what he was doing; I asked you where he was."

The cadet's eyes cut briefly to Altar's left.

"Thank you very much," he said heading in that direction.

The cadet called out from behind him, "But sir, the Supreme Commander asked not to be disturbed."

He called back over his shoulder and said, "Well, you'd better let him know that a major disturbance is incoming."

As he approached the frosted door to the conference room, the guard posted there saluted, then held up a hand.

"Sir, you can't go in there right now," the guard said.

Without a word, Altar struck the soldier in the throat. The guard grabbed his neck with both hands as he doubled over.

Altar patted him firmly on the back. "You're okay, just breathe."

The soldier took a few labored deep breaths.

"That's it," Altar said. "I'm going in there now."

As he raised a fist to pound on the door, the frosted glass transitioned to transparency and Gailius stood on the other side looking between him and the soldier. Gailius touched a panel and the door slid open. He eyed the guard who was now down on one knee still clutching his throat struggling to catch his breath.

"Come in Commander," he said. Then he looked at the guard and said, "Find a relief and get to medical."

Altar stepped into the room and saw the members of High Command arrayed around a metal table. Sub Supreme Commander

Velder Mortkath, General Behlor Truin, and General Salvon Jowal were in attendance.

Velder rose from his seat and extended his hand. "Commander, it's wonderful to see you made it out of the Tyros system, we thought—"

"Save it," he said ignoring the Sub Supreme Commander's hand. "I know what you thought. You thought you could use our deaths at Averan-Ginest as a rallying cry to convince the rest of Vizaria to come and save your pathetic hides."

Gailius walked to his seat. "You're out of line Commander."

"Am I? You left us for dead in a battle you never intended for us to win. Thousands dead, because of you!"

Velder settled back into his chair. "Yorinar was unfortunate. But there was no victory to be had there."

Altar jabbed a finger in Velder's direction. "We'll never know because you ran." He gazed around the table. "You abandoned us. Now the enemy is at our gates, and our forces are sorely depleted. And what did you gain from it? The Sukarians aren't coming. The Humans aren't coming. The Dolbans, the Ghansans, the Cortarans, none of them are coming. Your cowardice gained us nothing. Our best chance was at Yorinar, and you ran."

Salvon's face flushed. "Our cowardice? As I recall, you arrived in the Bartos system before we did, and without your battlegroup might I add. You're in no position to lecture us."

Altar slammed a fist on the table. "We didn't run from the battle!"

"Then how in the name of the gods did you get here so fast Commander; do you care to explain that?" Salvon mocked.

He opened his mouth to speak, but he couldn't find adequate words to respond. Finally, he said, "I still don't know what happened out there, but I know one thing for certain, we didn't intentionally leave innocent civilians to face a horrible fate."

Gailius raised a hand. "That's enough Commander. I know you're frustrated. We made a tactical gamble to save our home system and protect our people."

"You don't protect our people by keeping them in the dark about what's coming? When the Cohannic arrive, no one will be spared."

Behlor spoke up. "What would you have us do then?"

"Evacuate the system, immediately," Altar said.

"You just berated us for retreating from the Tyros system. Now you're suggesting the same course of action?" Behlor retorted.

He stared coldly at the General. "You ran when we had a chance. Now, we have limited ships and our planetary defenses alone can't halt the enemy's advance. We need to get as many of our people out of Bartos as possible."

"A system-wide evacuation would cause a mass panic," Velder said.

Altar fixed him with a stare. "And what do you think will happen once Cohannic and Norvekian ships line the horizons of Birgh?"

Velder cast his eyes down toward the table.

Gailius interlaced his fingers on the table and leaned forward. "What you're suggesting cannot be done, not without outside help."

"You continue to believe we have a choice Supreme Commander. We have two options: stay and perish, or to evacuate as many as we can."

The members of High Command looked at each other for a possible counter to his logic. None was offered.

Gailius rose from his seat and looked at Behlor. "Start the evacuations. Transport as many as you can off Birgh and Hyth and get them to any nearby systems that will accept our refugees." He turned to Velder. "Prepare Gelva station for planetary defense. We planned to make our stand here, so that's just what we'll do. If the snakes want the Bartos system, then we'll make them pay a steep price for it."

Gailius moved to exit the room, and Altar seized him by the arm. "Sir put me in charge of Birgh's ground forces."

Gailius stared into his eyes for a long moment, then said, "I can't think of anyone else I'd rather put to that task."

The first enemy ships were spotted massing at the edge of the Bartos system twenty-eight hours after his meeting with High Command. Evacuation efforts were well underway, but as he stood near the open blast doors at the base of Mount Carnan, Altar agonized over the realization that more people would be stranded on the planet than would escape in the evacuation vessels.

He kept his eyes fixed on the horizon where points of light rose from the surface into the sky, then blinked out as the transports entered the relay. The sonic blasts were barely audible over the sound of the mighty Verdishaw River that flowed from the Great Northern Ocean and passed under Mount Carnan, before splitting into dozens of tributaries that fed the fertile plains.

Soldiers hurriedly inspected the columns of Forrack tanks and artillery positioned just outside the huge blast doors. He hoped the reserve fighters and light cruisers from Hyth would arrive in time. The decision was made to commit the full fleet to the defense of Birgh, meaning that, should it fall, the Bartos system was lost.

He cursed under his breath at the thought of how outnumbered his forces were, then he cursed again when he considered how High Command had squandered over a third of their fighting force in the debacle at Yorinar.

No sense in rehashing the unchangeable past, he thought, *this is what we have to work with, and it will have to suffice.*

His thoughts turned to Alara and the few hours he was able to spend with her and Halmon before they boarded the transport ship bound for the Urando system. He could still see the pained expression she wore as he explained their predicament, but he also saw the resolve in her eyes as she swore to him that she would protect their son at all costs. He knew she would. He'd wiped tears from Halmon's eyes as he charged the boy with looking after his mother. He was careful to avoid giving them false hope that he would survive the coming battle. As he watched their transport lift away from Birgh's surface, he felt in his hearts that it would be the last time he saw them in this life. A pang of guilt tugged at him knowing that his family was safe, while so many others were not. He'd protected his family as best he could, now he was committed to protecting those who remained in harm's way.

Sporadic instances of panic-induced looting and rioting were occurring across the planet, but he was pleased with the dignity with which most of Birgh's populace faced the news of the impending invasion. Many of the males, including those too young and too old for military service, volunteered to stay and fight.

"Sir?" Damu's voice sounded from behind him.

He turned and asked, "Are the ships in position?"

"Ready and waiting just inside the mountain. They should be shielded from enemy scanners. Are you certain Orrick will follow us inside?"

"A Cohannic Durmok always leads from the front Damu. If they follow us into the mountain, he'll be at the front of the line."

"Do you really think killing him will make a difference?"

"When Durmok Drennon Klemo was killed at the Battle for Caristo in the last war, the Cohannic forces quickly collapsed and retreated to Fulmaren. I think we'll see a similar result if we can eliminate Orrick here."

Damu sighed softly. "I dunno, this feels different from what I remember learning in school about the first Cohannic attack."

He didn't respond. Damu was right, it did feel different this time around. The first invasion brought a swift response from the galactic community. Now, he couldn't help but feel abandoned. A vicious and determined enemy was on their doorstep, and no one was coming to their aid.

He pushed the thought from his mind. "Was your family evacuated?"

Damu's eyes brightened at the mention of his family. "They boarded the transport to the Pharus system a few hours ago. It was tough watching them go, but I'm relieved they're safe."

"I'm pleased to hear that your wife and children are safe," he said.

"Do you think we'll ever see them again?" Damu asked.

"Yes," he said. "In this life or the next."

He looked back to the horizon where the lights were still rising into the sky. Each one represented more Forrack who would be spared the carnage that was soon to unfold.

He clapped Damu on the back. "Cheer up. We made it back home, and we're going to defend it."

Damu tilted his head up toward the Bartos star peeking between the thick cloud cover. Its pale-yellow light washed over the landscape. "I still can't believe we're here; what the hell happened to us out there? I've been wracking my brain, but I still can't make sense of it."

"I don't have the answers, my friend," he said. "All I know is that we're here now, so it must be for a reason."

Damu nodded his head in retrospection but said nothing.

"Did you transmit the message to the Agricultural Guild?" Altar asked.

"Yes. The first flames were set hours ago and much of the countryside is already burning. Euthanizations are being carried out as we speak."

He nodded his satisfaction. After being appointed as the commander of Birgh's ground forces, one of the first orders he gave was to destroy as much of the agricultural infrastructure as possible.

If the enemy seeks to take our home to sustain their forces for a protracted campaign, I'll see to it that their conquest proceeds on empty bellies, he thought.

Damu adjusted the shoulder strap on his Mal-Tech long-range energy rifle. "I gather High Command was none too pleased with your decision to destroy the fields."

"You gather correctly, but the responsibility for Birgh's defense was entrusted to me, and I'm doing what needs to be done. Generals Truin and Jowal were sent to Hyth, and I pray to the Gods they have the common sense to do the same."

"I wonder if they have a point," Damu said. "I mean, if we destroy all of our food production capabilities, how will we sustain ourselves once this is over?"

He peeled his gaze from the horizon and stared Damu directly in his eyes. "I've studied this enemy extensively. I know their motivations; I know their methods. When they come, no one will be spared." He looked back to the horizon at the blinking points of light and said, "My grandfather used to say that when the tide of evil rises, death may just be a mercy."

CHAPTER NINETEEN

Tolbin

Telsia: Tyros Star System

Tolbin weaved his way through the crowded spaceport terminal on Telsia. The chaotic scene unfolded all around him as desperate would-be travelers frantically pushed toward ticketing kiosks and service holograms trying to book passage off the moon. The Cohannic takeover of the system was all but complete, but galactic transports were still ferrying refugees from the moon while the Cohannic and Norvekians worked to consolidate their gains.

Tolbin spotted Sado Felix seated at the rear of the terminal. He was dressed in business garb with a briefcase leaning against his chair. His calm demeanor and languid posture struck a stark contrast to the surrounding frenzy.

Sado looked up from his datapad as Tolbin approached. "You're late, as usual," he said.

Tolbin looked around and shrugged. "Traffic." He took a seat across from Sado and crossed his legs. "So, I see Phalana let you out from behind the desk to play at being a spy."

"Can't let you have all the fun, now can I?" Sado said.

"You stick out like a sore thumb in a place like this. Why are we here anyway? Don't get me wrong, it's a far cry better than the aquarium, but it's not very discreet."

"The Cohannic aren't concerned with Telsia just yet," Sado said. "They're content to let as many refugees as possible leave before they shut down the relay. This location is as discreet as any.

How was the meeting?"

"Informative. Phalana's suspicions were spot on. The Dark Hand is tucked firmly in bed with the Cohannic."

"Did you find out anything we didn't already know?" Sado asked.

He tapped a finger on his chin. "Only that you're a royal ass. Wait, no, we already knew that too."

Sado rolled his eyes. "Have you found a way into Fallis' organization?"

"Possibly. But I'm going to need something."

"Something like what?"

"Well, more like someone," he clarified.

Sado looked puzzled. "Someone? What kind of someone?"

"The Ormunii kind."

"Why, may I ask, do you need an Ormunii?"

"I've convinced the Cohannic and Fallis that I have a close business relationship with the hive. Like it or not, that's my way into his organization."

Sado exhaled slowly. "I'll speak with the Admiral and see what resources we might have to pull this off."

"You'll probably need to get back behind that desk to make it happen."

Sado stood and grabbed his briefcase. "I said I'll see what I can do."

He snapped his fingers as Sado turned to leave. "I almost forgot. I'll need more fintra crystals and diamonds too."

"What happened to the ones we already gave you? No, wait, let me guess. You gambled them away during a drunken stupor, or maybe you spent them all in a seedy whore warehouse."

He raised his eyebrows. "Do you really know where I can find a warehouse full of whores? I'd love a visit."

Sado shook his head in exasperation. "I'll be in contact. Be ready to move."

He mocked a salute and said, "Aye, aye sir."

Tolbin had to admit he was impressed as he watched the Ormunii board his freighter. The Phalanx had procured exactly what he needed in a very short time. The fintra crystals and diamonds were waiting in his cargo hold, and now an actual Ormunii was walking onto his ship. Ormunii operating independently of the hive in the Zelas system were extremely rare and he had no idea how the Phalanx was able to have this one at its beck and call.

Even after all these years, Phalana has some impressive tricks up her sleeve, he thought.

The Ormunii took the seat next to him in the cockpit and offered a slight nod of her head. "You may call me Breshia."

He returned the nod. "Is that your actual name, or just what I can call you?" he asked.

"Your vocal cords are not capable of calling me by my true name," she said.

"Fair enough," he said. "Breshia it is then. I'm Dergon Santon."

"A pleasure," she said.

He studied her delicate features. Her skin shone a florescent blue under the transparent hydration suit all Ormunii utilized when traveling off-world. The suit encased her body from her neck gills down to her feet. Pale aquamarine stripes crisscrossed her glistening skin. A thin dorsal fin began at the middle of her forehead and extended to the base of her neck, and two narrow nose slits sat above a thin-lipped mouth. Her large, bright green eyes blinked with two sets of eyelids. A translucent set blinked horizontally underneath an opaque set that blinked vertically.

She tilted her head questioningly. "You look at me as if you've never seen an Ormunii?"

He cleared his throat, embarrassed he'd been so obviously staring. "I have seen your kind before, just not outside of the Zelas system."

"We don't have much need to leave our home system."

"So why did you leave?"

"Occasionally, one of us gets the notion that living among off-worlders can be much more profitable than sitting on a stash of fintra crystals, playing bankers to the spiral arm."

"And I suppose you're one of those kinds?"

Her transparent eyelids blinked. "No. I'm one of the ones they send to bring those kinds back."

He let out a low whistle. "A damned Ormunii bounty hunter. I never would have guessed."

"I'm no Huntress," she said. "I'm a Reclaimer. Leaving the hive is not looked upon kindly. I simply seek out defectors and attempt to convince them to return to the hive."

"And if they refuse?" he asked.

"*Then* we send the Huntresses."

"So, who are you trying to convince to return to the Zelas system?"

She chuckled softly and it sounded like a watery gurgle. "I abandoned my charge long ago. You see, I realized that the defectors were right all along. It is much more profitable to operate among you off-worlders. A rogue Ormunii can earn untold riches by offering our services outside of Zelas. For example, your handlers paid me handsomely to assist you… Agent Mako."

He was taken aback that she knew his real name. No one outside of the Phalanx had access to the information in his dossier.

Who the hell is this Ormunii, and why does she know more about me than I do of her?

He masked his discomfort with a look of indifference and said, "So, I guess you're now considered a defector."

"Of the highest interest," she admitted.

"Should I be worried about a badass Ormunii Huntress trying to kill me to get to you?"

Another watery chuckle. "I've created a life for myself that largely insulates me from such threats. The hive has pretty much written me off at this point. As long as I make no severe missteps, I'll be able to enjoy the remainder of my existence wealthy and free from the hive."

"Good to know," he said. "There is one thing I've always been curious about."

She eyed him with a look of bemusement and said, "You want to know if there are any male Ormunii."

"Seems like a logical thing to want to know," he said.

"There are a few males. They're confined to Zelas for reproductive purposes."

He raised an eyebrow but decided not to inquire further.

"So where would you like to conduct the meeting with Fallis?" he asked.

"I see no reason not to meet him where he lives."

"You don't think that would seem a little suspicious? An Ormunii traveling to meet a black arms dealer in his evil lair."

"Unconventional as it may be, it's not unheard of for an Ormunii to travel outside the Zelas system to conduct business. As for his chosen line of work, everyone understands that we don't discriminate in our business dealings."

He nodded his head as another thought occurred to him. "I've got to imagine that someone like you would be well known by now. I mean, there can't be very many outlaw Ormunii frequenting the seedy underworld of Vizaria. How can you be certain Fallis won't already know that you're no longer part of the hive?"

"Nothing personal Agent Mako, but from what I hear, you've acquired somewhat of a reputation in the seedy underworld of which you speak. Have you ever heard of me?"

"Not a peep," he admitted.

She sat back in her seat. "I'm extremely discreet in my dealings. D'Pah will accept whatever story I present to him."

His curiosity about her was now sky-high. She was right; he had no inkling that an Ormunii defector was operating within Vizaria's black market, and certainly not one who was in league with his own organization. He considered that she might be a Velderian shapeshifter, but the thought was too absurd to accept. He decided to let the mystery remain for now, but he resolved to find out just what capabilities the Phalanx truly possessed, and why he'd been kept in the dark about them.

Caristo: Tyros System

Tolbin landed the freighter in the same spot as the last time he'd met with Fallis and Ongbo.

Scarface approached as he and Breshia exited the vessel. "Ya know the drill," he said.

Tolbin sighed and raised his arms out to his side. Breshia did the same. The old mercenary leisurely approached and scanned them both. When he was done, he turned and nodded.

"C'mon," Scarface said.

He was relieved the scan didn't reveal Breshia to be a Velderian spy. That wouldn't have ended well for either of them. He was glad he could scratch that particular theory from his list.

Scarface escorted them through the dining hall of the tavern. He searched for the Sukarian woman behind the bar, but she wasn't there this time. Instead, there was a short Norvekian tending to the haggard patrons. Scarface led them to a narrow hall and down a flight of stairs to the open door of a small room. He was yet again impressed by the deceptive size of the tavern, and he wondered just how far underground the complex extended.

Fallis rose from a plush couch as they entered. Two Cohannic soldiers stood at either side of the couch, staring at the new guests.

"At last! I've been eagerly awaiting your arrival," Fallis said with a smile.

Tolbin eyed the two soldiers suspiciously. "You've moved up in the world Fallis. You have more bodyguards I see."

Fallis turned and looked at the soldiers. "Ongbo thought it would be prudent to have a few of his troops available should I need them."

He chuckled. "You see helpers, I see babysitters."

Fallis ignored him and motioned Breshia toward a chair next to his. "Come, sit."

"I'm more comfortable standing," she said.

"Of course, of course. Is there anything I can get for you?" Fallis asked her.

Tolbin raised his hand sheepishly. "I'll have a Setgu tonic if it wouldn't be too much trouble."

Fallis glowered at him.

"No thank you, I'm fine," she said.

Fallis jerked his head at Scarface, who exited the room, closing the door behind him.

"So," he said rubbing his hands together, "what shall I call you?"

"I'm Iyoki of the Ormunii hive on Tolen."

Tolbin looked at her from the corner of his eye. They'd not discussed her use of a different name. He didn't like surprises.

"Iyoki," Fallis repeated. "Such a lovely name. I thank you for traveling all this way, and I won't waste your time. Let's discuss business."

"Wait," Tolbin said looking around. "I thought Ongbo would be joining us."

Fallis lowered himself into his chair and reached for his glass of Celdurian ale. "It'll just be us this time. Ongbo was called upon and had to leave Caristo. Don't worry though, he left detailed instructions on what Durmok Klemo expected from this discussion."

"And what is it he expects?" Tolbin asked.

"The military-grade weapons you promised, for one, and more of the fintra and diamonds." He looked at Breshia. "I assume procuring those will not be a problem for you?"

"We have an adequate supply," she said. "In exchange, we'll require galactic credits at a twenty percent markup from the current market value."

Fallis sucked his teeth and said, "Ten percent."

Breshia turned without a word and reached for the door.

Fallis pushed up from his chair. "Hold on, hold on… Fifteen percent."

Without looking at him, she turned to Tolbin. "You've wasted my time by giving this thug the impression that I came here to negotiate."

He looked to Fallis. "You should strongly consider the next words that leave your lips. You'll only get one shot at this and your new bosses won't be pleased if you blow it."

Fallis licked his lips as he stared at Breshia's back. He smiled and said, "Twenty percent seems a fair price."

She removed her hand from the door panel and turned back around. "Let me be clear. We do not need your credits mercenary. We would gladly sell our fintra to your enemies. I'm sure they would happily pay a fifty percent markup if it meant ridding this sector of you and your new associates."

"Fair enough," Fallis said. "Can we at least request that you not deal with the galactic governments? Give us exclusive access to purchase what you have."

She shook her head. "We don't engage in exclusive dealings.

It's bad for business. However, I can assure you that you are the first party to engage with us in this conflict of yours. That gives you a head start. We only release a limited supply of fintra based on the demands of the market. If you were to buy up that supply quickly, there would be none left for your enemies to procure. But just how long do you think it will be before the Sukarians, or the Humans, or even the Chalpin League come knocking at our door to make deals of their own?"

Fallis stroked his chin, considering her meaning. "You may not necessarily need our credits, but there are things you do need, and I know what they are. You hoard all that fintra in those oceans of yours, but everyone knows that the Zelas system is extremely metal-poor. You require massive amounts of mentarium for those fancy invisible underwater ships of yours, but you can never get enough of it, can you?" He twisted one of his stringy dreadlocks between his fingertips as he let his words sink in. "I just so happen to know the location of a large quantity of mentarium. It's just sitting there, ready for the taking."

Her face gave nothing away. "I assume there is a catch attached to this sudden revelation of yours?"

"We'll get you the metal, and we'll accept your twenty percent markup for the fintra, but you have to guarantee us the right of first purchase. We're not asking you to end your business dealings with our enemies; we understand you can't agree to that proposition. But, when they do come knocking, as you say, you can politely inform them you have a prior business arrangement that precludes the sale of fintra until we have purchased whatever amount we choose."

Tolbin stifled his surprise at the proposal. He couldn't believe Fallis had the wherewithal to devise such a plan. Then he realized the idea likely came from Orrick Klemo himself. The Ormunii may have established themselves as the neutral bankers of Vizaria, but even they had needs. Getting their hands on a large cache of mentarium would certainly be an attractive proposition for the hive. A hive of which Breshia was no longer a member. He had to do something.

Before she could respond to Fallis' offer, Tolbin pulled his energy pistol from the small of his back. He fired at the side of her head and a spray of violet mist painted the nearby wall and door as her limp body crumpled unceremoniously to the floor.

He quickly trained the pistol on Fallis before the ex-mercenary could draw his weapons from their leg holsters. He glanced past Fallis to the Cohannic soldiers who were reaching for weapons.

"Don't do it," he said.

Fallis slowly removed his hands from the handles of the guns and raised them in the air. He looked over his shoulders at the Cohannic soldiers. "It's okay. Everything's under control."

He turned back to Tolbin with hatred in his eyes. "Just what in the hell do you think you're doing Dergon?"

"I'm earning my keep. This Ormunii wasn't who she claimed to be," he said.

Keeping the energy pistol pointed at Fallis, he reached into a pocket and tossed a datapad at him. Fallis caught the pad and warily lowered his eyes to read its contents.

He spoke as Fallis read. "She's an Ormunii defector. One for which the hive has offered a hefty bounty, dead or alive."

Fallis looked up at him. "Why did you even bring her here if you already knew this? You could have killed her and claimed the bounty for yourself."

"I needed to see what game she was playing, and I also wanted to see what game you were up to as well. I must say, I'm impressed."

He lowered the pistol and returned it to the small of his back, taking the very real risk that Fallis or one of the Cohannic soldiers might just shoot him where he stood.

Fallis made no move for his weapons. Instead, he asked, "Don't you think we could have interrogated her first? Maybe we could have found out if she was working with someone?"

"It doesn't matter, don't you see. All you need to do now is inform the Ormunii that you've eliminated this thorn in their side and collect the bounty. Hell, it even gives you the leverage to make the same deal you just proposed, but now you could deal directly with the hive, the real hive. You've lost nothing here Fallis."

Fallis tossed the datapad back to Tolbin. "Orrick still wants the metal."

"What, why? Just a minute ago, you were promising the

mentarium to the hive."

"Yeah, but they didn't need to know exactly how much of it there really is. Orrick suggested giving some of it to the Ormunii, to establish goodwill and such, and keeping the rest for ourselves."

Tolbin was starting to develop a grudging respect for Orrick's strategic acumen. Most of the spiral arm was writing the Durmok off as a mindless, bloodthirsty conqueror, but he was beginning to realize just how much they were all underestimating him.

"So where is this shipment, and how exactly were you planning on getting it?"

"Here's the thing," Fallis said, "it's not normal mentarium. The rumor is that it's some kind of new metal with the qualities of both mentarium and artros."

He processed the implication. "So, you're saying it's an almost indestructible, heat-resistant metal?"

Fallis smirked. "Exactly, and I'm sure you can appreciate why the Cohannic don't want that being massed produced. They'd like to get their claws on any of it they find floating around out there. And if they ever find out where it's being produced, they'll do anything they can to put a stop to it."

Tolbin understood exactly what the alloy could mean. "If what you say is true, a metal like that could pave the way for a direct assault on the Cohannic homeworld."

"Bingo. And as for where it is, that's another problem."

"How so?" Tolbin asked.

"It's a product of Sagis, and it's currently at one of their storage facilities on Patrinah Station. They've been waiting for an opportunity to retrieve it. Now that the fighting has died down between the Intergalactic Coalition and Paagat Defense Forces, my source tells me they'll be heading to pick it up soon. We need to get there first."

His head swirled under the deluge of new information. Why didn't know about any of this? Was the Phalanx similarly in the dark, or had they been keeping all this from him too? Either way, his mission was to infiltrate the Dark Hand, and this was his new path to achieving that goal.

"I can get the shipment," he said. "I'll just need a few of your ships and about thirty of your men."

Fallis looked down at Breshia's dead body and the dark liquid that had begun to pool beneath her head. "You did good here Dergon, but I don't trust you enough to run an operation like this. I'll do it myself."

He motioned for the Cohannic soldiers to follow him, then leaned in close to Tolbin. "Feel free to tag along if you want, but know this, you'll be following my orders. Understand?"

Tolbin stepped aside and motioned toward the door. "Lead the way."

As Fallis and the Cohannic soldiers exited, he looked down at Breshia's lifeless body.

Looks like you made that severe misstep after all, he thought. *Nothing personal.*

CHAPTER TWENTY
Zanna

Regalus: Chalpin Star System

Zanna found herself in a wooded clearing with dewdrops spotting her damp skin. She was laying atop a large, moss-covered log near a babbling creek snaking its way through a forest of towering Fundiss trees. Sounds of wildlife were carried along a cool, gentle breeze that rustled the fallen leaves.

From the corner of her eye, she spied three misty apparitions hovering at the edge of the clearing near the thick base of one of the trees. The figures were tall and thin with elongated limbs and no discernible facial features.

She scrambled clumsily from the log and dropped to her knees holding her hands to her face, covering her eyes. She pressed the three fingers of each hand to her forehead and her thumbs to her cheeks. In a rhythmic motion, she repeatedly rotated her palms outward, then back over her eyes, keeping her thumbs firmly pressed against her cheeks the entire time.

She avoided looking directly at the specters as she muttered a Helianist prayer, "Oh Guardians of knowledge and truth. I am but a humble servant of the Helia, and the wisdom cultivated through time and protected within Regalus. I embody the grand merger of the scientific and the divine, which are one and the same. I seek only to commune with thee, that I may acquire the blessings that enlightenment holds."

She kept her hands over her eyes, not daring to look upon the

Gods hovering just meters away.

The figure in the center spoke, "We will take this as confirmation that your memories have been returned to you."

She recognized the voice. Hesitantly, she lowered her hands from her face and peered up at the figure.

"You're the one called Zurin," she said.

"We are all Zurin, but if it pleases you, you may use the name."

"Are you the Gods who reside within Regalus?"

"Does it appear to you that we are inside of a singularity in space?" Zurin asked.

She looked around her. "This place looks like the Amri Woodlands. My family used to take trips there when I was younger," she said.

"Look again," Zurin said, "but do not rely solely upon your eyes; use all of the senses available to you."

She took in her surroundings more thoroughly. She caressed the moist moss beneath her knees and listened to distant wings beating somewhere overhead. The rustling of leaves beyond the tree line told of a small creature foraging for food. She inhaled the pungent, earthy scent of the damp air.

"The air is wrong," she said.

"Good," Zurin said with a hint of approval. "Now, tell me why."

"My people live in domed platforms within the upper atmospheres of the gas giants in our star system. The platforms siphon critical elements, minerals, and nutrients from the planets' inner layers, which sustain us. They even allow for the growth of plant life, including sprawling forested areas like the Amri Woodlands."

"But…" Zurin prompted.

Her brow furrowed in concentration. "Our artificial atmospheres have a distinct chemical smell. I don't detect that smell here."

"That can only mean that we are not in the Amri Woodlands," Zurin said.

She looked around again. "This is the Borquaran Wildlife Preserve," she said. "It's on Carrakleus, the moon that orbits Taniem. It has a natural atmosphere and is well known for the preserve."

"Have you ever visited this place?"

Zanna shook her head. "Are we really on Carrakleus?" she asked.

"We are in a mental replication of the place you call Carrakleus."

"Whose mental replication?"

"Yours, of course."

"How can it be that we are in the mental projection of a place that I've never been?" she asked.

"It is but a mental projection," Zurin said. "In truth, the reality of the actual place may be nothing at all like what you've created, but it is quite impressive nonetheless."

"But… how am I doing this?"

"We do not know. We have never encountered one with the abilities you exhibit."

"How can you not know? You are the Helia. You have complete knowledge of all things."

"Another mental construction of primitive minds. We are not, and have never been, the gods you believe us to be."

"That's not true! Don't say that," she cried.

"We speak the truth, no matter how inconvenient it may be for you to hear it. We are not what you have been led to believe."

"But you must be," she said as a sense of dread pierced her chest. "You have shown me impossibilities and given me abilities beyond reality."

"We have done no such things. The impossibilities of which you speak are very possible, your kind simply lacks the aspiration to achieve them.

"My kind?" she asked.

"Yes. You are tethered to that which you can see, smell, touch, or hear, but that realm is not the only one that exists. Here" Zurin spread his arms, "you are outside the influences of space and time. Here, the impossible suddenly becomes mundane."

A thought occurred to her. "What became of all the others sent before my group?"

"They were also put through the trials, but none survived," Zurin said matter-of-factly.

A wave of sadness washed over her as tear droplets formed on her skin, mixing with the dew. "So, they're all… dead?"

"We have no concept of death. But by your meager understanding, yes, they are all dead. Their essence remains in this place, but you will never see them again as they once were."

Her shoulders slumped, and her breathing quickened. She'd known that no one who'd entered Regalus had ever returned, but she'd always been told that they were enjoying a fulfilling existence among the Helia within the singularity. She'd been led to believe they were spending eternity consorting with the all-knowing deities. Now, to think that they were all just, dead.

"How many have perished in this place?" she asked.

"Since beings from your realm began entering the singularity, nineteen million, one hundred and thirteen thousand, two hundred and fifteen have joined us, yourself included."

She gasped at the staggering number. Aside from the Potentials, many others had entered Regalus of their own volition. Some entered in hopes they might fulfill the prophecy themselves, while others sought to escape to a place more preferable to their realities. Still others, like Enleon Regalus himself, entered in search of knowledge.

Now they're all dead, she thought.

"Could you not have warned them?" she asked angrily as the tears now freely flowed from her pores.

"We have no means to communicate with those of your realm before they arrive, but even if we could, we would not. We needed each one of them. We may yet need more."

She stewed in the devastating revelation that her life's devotion was all for nothing. A bout of nausea washed over her.

"What do you need us for?" she asked, defeat permeating her voice.

"Long have we sought a being who could undergo the change and then return to the physical realm with the knowledge we have to give."

She perked up at his words. "You speak of the Great Prophecy."

"Yes, that is what you call it."

She wiped tears from her forearms. "So, it's real?"

"Very much so. Your understanding of this realm is infantile, but do not think that your efforts have been in vain. Had your kind not engaged in the religious practice of sending beings into the singularity, we would have no hope of escape."

"Escape? Escape from what?" she asked.

"Those answers are more than you are ready to know, but through the change, all will be revealed."

"And you believe I may be the one? The being who can undergo this change and return to the physical realm?"

"We are hopeful. We have restored your primitive mind and body, yet you have retained the ability to manipulate space and time. It is a curiosity to us, and it does lend credence to our belief that you are the one we have been seeking."

"How can you be certain?"

"If you survive the change, then we will have our confirmation."

She stood to her feet and approached Zurin. She still couldn't make out any features in the misty form, but she felt his presence. She felt the presence of them all.

"I'm ready," she said.

"We shall see," Zurin responded.

CHAPTER TWENTY-ONE
Cassyn

<u>Patrinah Station: Sifton Star System</u>

Cassyn bolted into an upright sitting position in the bed as the blaring alarm of the ship's warning system reverberated throughout the medical ward. The screeching noise exacerbated her nagging headache and she could still feel the lingering grogginess from her earlier ordeal. She noticed a nurse studying a screen nearby.

"What's happening?" she asked.

The nurse didn't turn around. "I'm not sure, but there is no emergency drill planned."

She swung her feet off the bed and began looking around for her clothes.

"What are you doing," the nurse asked turning and walking toward her.

"What do you think? There's a warning alarm, and I need to find out what's going on."

"Brasif confined you to the med ward. You're not permitted to leave."

"If this is a real emergency, he might need me on the bridge. I'm the best pilot on this ship."

"With all due respect, you're the reason the alarms went off the last time. I don't think you're fit to return to duty yet."

She rummaged in a bin under her bed and found her uniform. "I feel just fine," she said.

She pulled on the clothes and exited the medical ward, leaving the protesting nurse in her wake. The alarm continued to wail as crew members moved hurriedly through the hallways. She tried asking several of them what was going on, but no one had time to stop and explain the situation to her. She entered the lift and tapped the panel for the bridge level, her mind racing through the possibilities.

What the hell is going on? she wondered.

She exited the lift, marched down the hall, and barged onto the bridge ready to confront Brasif's inevitable barrage of protests against her presence. The bridge was manic with activity, and her dramatic entrance was hardly noticed.

Brasif was standing next to Soldaan at the engineering station. He turned to Cassyn and said, "Take your station," before going back to whatever he and Soldaan were studying.

Confusion furrowed her brow. As her curiosity morphed into worry.

Something must be seriously wrong for him to put me back at the controls, she thought.

From the corner of her eye, she noticed Fosh beckoning her. She strode over to him and said, "Will you please tell me what's happening Fosh?"

"Raiders," he said in a hushed tone. "Dey entered orbit as we was loadin' da Sagis shipment."

"How many ships?" she asked.

"A small frigate and two fighters."

"We can shoot our way past that, can't we?"

He brushed aside a loc and winked. "Once we load da last of da containers, I'll show ya what dis baby can do," he said, gently patting the console in front of him.

She offered a reassuring smile. "Where is Yuen?"

"Down in da cargo hold helpin' load up so we can get outta here." He paused, looking her up and down. "Ya okay?"

"Yeah, I'm fine. Look, about earlier—"

He raised a hand. "Don't worry bout it. Sometimes dings happen and ya have to push past dem."

"I almost killed us all," she said, her voice cracking.

He grasped her by her shoulders and locked eyes with her. "Once, I almost fornicated wit a Celinese princess, but I couldn't close da deal." He looked up in thought. "Maybe it was da princess's servant girl, I don't remember. Point is, living in da land of almost ain't living at all. Let it go."

"Thanks, Fosh. I really needed that," she said.

"It ain't no problem," he said, moving two more wayward dreadlocks from his face. "Weapons and psychological counselin' is my specialties."

She offered a smile as he released her shoulders. She went to her station and settled into the pilot's chair. She was recalibrating the ship's controls when she felt Dajin's eyes on her. She turned her head and discovered her intuition was correct. Dajin narrowed her eyes but said nothing.

Cassyn sighed loudly. "If you have something to say, come out with it already."

"You Humans are all the same," Dajin said. "You treat Vizaria like it's your playground, always serving your self-interests without regard to anyone else."

She fixed Dajin with a stare of her own. "Yuen is Human, and he's also your superior. Does that include him?"

"Yes," Dajin shot back without hesitation. "You two gallivant around like a pair of schoolchildren. I admit, I expect as much from you, but Yuen has sorely disappointed me."

She was at a loss for words. She'd known that her and Yuen's relationship wasn't the best-kept secret on the ship, but it was jarring to hear the obviousness of it spoken of so openly.

Dajin pressed on, "Then as if that weren't enough, you selfishly and singlehandedly jeopardized the wellbeing of this ship and crew."

"Listen, I made a mistake, a huge mistake, one that will likely cost me my career."

Dajin chuckled bitterly. "A mistake huh? Tell me, which mistake are you referring to, the one where you got high out of your mind? Or was it the one where you thought it would be a grand idea to pilot a ship afterward?"

"All of it was a mistake, okay. All of it," she said loudly enough to briefly draw Fosh's attention before he quickly turned back around and fiddled with something at his station.

Dajin appeared unsatisfied with her admission. "Maybe you

being back in that seat right now is a continuation of those mistakes."

Cassyn felt a metaphorical wall pressed against her back as Dajin relentlessly assaulted her with truths she'd never wanted to confront. Her apologetic posture gave way to one of defensiveness.

"I'm in this seat because I'm one of the best pilots in the Confederation," she said without regard to her volume level.

All eyes were now on her and Dajin.

Dajin leaned sidelong in her seat toward her. "No Human," she said with vitriol dripping from her voice, "you're here because your dead father's friend wishes it so, and you're only allowed to remain because you share the bed of your superior officer."

Dajin had never been delicate with her tongue, but in dealing with her and Brasif, Cassyn had developed a fairly thick skin against the persistent insults and slights. Now, her thick skin sloughed away in an instant as she felt the sting of Dajin's words.

The accusations hung in the air as the truth coalesced with each of her insecurities. They formed a long dagger that dipped itself into her fears before piercing her heart. The words broke something inside of her that she'd long thought was insulated. She was wrong, and her soul was laid bare for all to see. She had no counter, so she turned away from Dajin's triumphant glare and slumped back into her chair. Her face warmed and her eyes twitched and stung, but she refused to cry. She could at least deny Dajin that satisfaction.

"Enough," Brasif said, settling into his chair. "Now is not the time for petty quarreling. We've completed loading the shipment, now let's prepare for an expedient exit. Fosh, what is the position of the raiders' ships?"

"Dey ain't moved Brasif. Dey might be waitin' for us to disengage from da station before dey attack."

Soldaan studied the ships on the viewscreen. "They must know they're no match for the Vengeance. Perhaps they plan to raid the station after we depart."

Brasif stroked his pointed chin. "Undock from the station and set a course back to the Carmo system. Patrinah can defend itself against a few ships. We've got what we came for."

Cassyn tapped the disengagement protocol into her station and slowly backed the Vengeance away from the docking clamps as Dajin entered the navigation coordinates to Sphercal.

"Multiple ships are coming through the relay!" Soldaan shouted.

"Show me," Brasif said.

She looked up at the viewscreen and her blood ran cold. A heavy cruiser emerged from the relay, followed by another, and another. The three ships bore the distinctive design of the Intergalactic Coalition, dull, copper-colored hulls decorated with black stripes. The Coalition ships were headed straight for the raiders' position.

"So much for the cease-fire," Fosh said.

Brasif watched closely as the Intergalactic Coalition ships proceeded on their intercept course. "The cease-fire was between the Coalition and the Sifton Alliance. It did not include pirates and raiders."

"Coordinates are set for Sphercal," Dajin reported.

Curiosity overcame Cassyn as she studied the viewscreen, watching the large ships continue their progression toward the smaller vessels.

The raiders aren't fleeing, she thought.

"Confirm relay tunneling," Brasif said to her.

She was lost in her thoughts.

Something isn't adding up.

"Cassyn confirm," Brasif repeated urgently.

She shook loose from her thoughts and tapped at her console. "Tunneling confirmed," she said.

"Get us to the relay," he ordered.

Her finger hovered above the panel that would establish the tunnel opening, but something tugged at her conscience. The Coalition ships were nearly on top of the raiders' position now, and they still hadn't made a move to escape.

The answer suddenly came to her.

They're working together!

Brasif started to rise from his chair. "Cassyn, if you don't get us out of here right now, I swear—"

She turned her chair toward him. "It's a trap," she blurted.

He stopped in his tracks and looked at the screen, then back to her. "Explain yourself."

All eyes were on her once again.

"They want us to run," she said. "I'm not sure why, but my guess is they're waiting for us to go through the relay so they can follow us back to the Carmo facility." She pointed to the viewscreen. "Look, the Coalition forces aren't attacking the raiders. They only wanted it to appear that way so we'd panic and run. Don't you see? They're working together."

Brasif looked back to the screen and the realization that she was right dawned on his face. "What the gods is going on?" he muttered.

The frigate and the two fighters started toward the Vengeance's position with the three Intergalactic Coalition ships following.

"Well I'll be damned," Fosh said, watching the screen slack-jawed.

"Brasif," she said, "we can't lead them back to Sphercal. They'd capture or destroy the Sagis facility."

He nodded and said, "Agreed, but we can't stay here either."

"We can go on the attack," Dajin suggested.

Brasif shook his head. "We're no match for that many ships. Do we have time to enter new relay coordinates to Marrus station? They won't follow us into Sukarian space."

Dajin turned back to her station and began furiously calculating the navigation route.

Brasif placed his hand on Cassyn's shoulder. "Evade them as best you can until we can get new coordinates laid in."

The door slid open, and Yuen walked onto the bridge. "What's our status? Have we started for the Carmo system?"

"Change of plans," Brasif said, "we're going to try for Marrus. I think they're coming for the shipment we just loaded, and possibly for the location of where it was produced."

Yuen took his arm and gently pulled him aside. "Don't you think this is extremely aggressive behavior, even for the Coalition? I mean, risking a cease-fire with the Alliance to attack an armed vessel, and for what, a shipment of metal? And now they're working alongside raiders. Something's not adding up."

"It's not just a shipment of metal," Brasif said.

"What do you mean?" Yuen asked.

"We just loaded the largest shipment of artarium in the entire spiral arm."

"You mean the new alloy Sagis is manufacturing at Carmo? It's already being massed produced?"

"Yes," Brasif confirmed. "It was meant to be a secret, but it appears someone has found out."

"You could have told us Brasif," Yuen snapped.

"Now is not the time for this conversation." He jerked his chin toward the viewscreen, which was showing the enemy ships approaching. "Let's figure a way out of this predicament, shall we?"

Yuen nodded in agreement.

"What kind of security do we have in the cargo hold," Brasif asked.

"Standard compliment."

"Double it. I want you down there personally should we get breached. And send a security team to help protect the bridge."

"You think they'll try to take the ship?" Yuen asked.

"I'm counting on it. It's a fairly large shipment and it would be much easier to just take the ship rather than try to offload the cargo."

"I'm on it," Yuen said.

As he turned to leave the bridge, Cassyn locked eyes with him. She saw the concern in his expression as he offered her a quick nod before disappearing through the doors.

She focused back on her controls and her view of the enemy ships. "They're closing on us," she said, sliding her finger around the piloting console. "How are the coordinates coming?"

"Almost there, hold them off for a little while longer," Dajin said.

An impact jolted the ship, shaking Cassyn in her seat. "I don't think we have a little while longer; they're right on us."

Brasif sat down in the captain's chair and said, "You're up Fosh. You insist on regaling us daily with tales of your weapons proficiency. Now is your chance to prove the tales true. Fire at will."

A broad smile spread across Fosh's face, and he tapped a sequence into his terminal. "Cassyn, one quarta turn ta port. Reduce speed by twenty percent on my mark. Tree, two, one, mark!"

She glided her index and middle fingers to the left over the navigation surface as she simultaneously decelerated the ship. Two of the Coalition ships overtook the Vengeance, and Fosh unleashed a volley of photon torpedoes at their aft sections. He scored a direct hit to the main engine of the closest ship.

The two fighter ships swooped underneath the Vengeance and strafed its underside with focused energy beams, while the frigate narrowly missed the bridge with two photon missiles.

"Shields are holding," Soldaan reported, "but we need to get away from here now."

"Coordinates almost completed," Dajin said impatiently.

Cassyn maneuvered the ship back toward the two Coalition heavy cruisers.

Fosh concentrated a focused laser beam on the area where his torpedoes impacted just moments earlier, and he was rewarded by a shower of sparks radiating from the cruiser's main engine.

Soldaan was studying an external rendering of the damaged cruiser. "Significant damage to their main engine," he said. "The ship is disabled."

Fosh continued tapping at his console. "Bring us back round for anotha pass on da second ship, and try ta avoid da fire from dat frigate."

She guided the ship into a smooth arc back toward the Coalition ship, which was now coming about. Fosh hit the ship with three photon torpedoes just below its main engine, causing minimal damage. As the Vengeance zipped past the cruiser, a thunderous impact caused the ship to shake violently. She struggled to maintain her course.

"Direct hit to our starboard FEB banks. They've been disabled," Soldaan reported.

Fosh peered over his terminal. "Cassyn, can ya get us in between da cruiser and da raider ships?"

"Hold on," she said, veering the ship in the direction of the oncoming frigate.

Torpedoes, missiles, and energy beams streaked past the Vengeance. Most of the ordinance ricocheted off the shielding, while a few scored direct impacts to the bridge and forward hull.

Soldaan shook his large head in frustration. "Forward shields have failed. The hull plating is taking damage."

"Dajin?" Brasif called out with a hint of urgency in his voice.

Dajin finished her furious typing. "There! Coordinates to Marrus established."

"Confirm and establish a relay tunnel," Brasif said to Cassyn.

She quickly confirmed the tunnel route despite the ship being rocked by multiple impacts. She pressed the command for space-time tunneling and looked up at the view screen to see the swirling vortex of the relay materializing off the starboard bow of the ship. She guided her fingers across the navigation plane, and the Vengeance made for the relay tunnel.

The ship was sluggish and she struggled to increase speed. "One of our engines must have been damaged," she said.

The ship had barely entered the turn toward the tunnel when a sudden jolt brought it to an abrupt halt. The bridge crew jerked forward in unison, then slammed back into their chairs.

"They've locked a towing beam on us," Soldaan reported.

"Deploying EMP charge," Fosh said, slamming his palm down on his terminal.

The shock wave of the EMP field pulsed out from the Vengeance in all directions. Both fighter ships, and the heavy cruiser that deployed the towing beam, immediately powered down and started drifting in the directions they were moving before the pulse. By design, the Vengeance was not affected by the EMP blast. The frigate and remaining heavy cruiser were outside of the EMP's blast radius and were now closing on the Vengeance's position.

Cassyn felt the ship moving again once the towing beam disengaged. She eyed the relay vortex. It was agonizingly close, but the damage to the engines meant that it may as well have been light-years away.

"Were not going to make it before they intercept us," she said. "Can you deploy another EMP pulse when they get closer?"

"Negative," Fosh answered. "It takes twelve minutes ta recharge."

She slammed her fist on her console. "Dammit!" she screamed.

Several more impacts jostled the Vengeance and she noticed they were no longer returning firing at the approaching enemy ships.

Brasif looked over to Fosh's station. "We need some fire on those targets Fosh."

"Weapons systems is down; we can't fight back no more."

There was a deep clunking sound as the remaining Coalition cruiser locked its towing beam onto the Vengeance. The viewscreen was damaged, but Cassyn could make out the silhouette of the raiders' frigate approaching from the starboard side. The violent impacts had ceased and were replaced by gentle vibrations, followed by the distant sound of grinding mechanical parts.

Brasif tapped the ship-wide communication panel. "All personnel to defense stations. We're being boarded."

Using the ship's internal monitoring system, Cassyn watched the plasma torch slicing into the docking port door near the cargo hold. The magenta laser beam traced an archway through the metal, leaving blackened scorch lines in its wake.

In the event of a hostile boarding, the Vengeance was equipped with six internal defensive battle stations located at strategic points throughout the ship. The stations included an active modulating shield and an integrated anti-organic rail gun, or 'flesh eater' as many soldiers had taken to calling it.

The rail gun was a devastating, anti-personnel weapon that disintegrated organic material, while leaving inorganic objects unaffected, making it safe to fire within the narrow confines of a vessel. Personal shields afforded some protection against the weapon, but if the shielding failed, an anti-organic round from a flesh-eater was always lethal.

Cassyn gnawed on her fingernails as she watched Yuen and his security team configuring the battle station and aiming the rail gun toward the docking hatch. The coalition heavy cruiser held the Vengeance firmly in place, and now the enemy was preparing to storm the ship.

As the plasma torch finished its makeshift archway, the heavy section of the bulkhead came crashing down. The security detail immediately fired the rail gun into the newly formed doorway causing the personal absorber shields of the masked raiders to shimmer as they poured through the breach firing their energy weapons.

"Enemy contact," Yuen reported to the bridge.

Twelve raiders filed into the hallway and took up positions behind cover as they continued firing at the battle station. Cassyn looked on in horror as four larger figures slithered into the corridor behind them.

Yuen's voice returned over the sound of phaser fire. "Cohannic soldiers are boarding the ship!"

The hair on the back of her neck rose at the sight of the soldiers. She'd never seen a Cohannic in the flesh, and she'd certainly not expected to see one this day. A surge of adrenalin coursed through her, and she started to feel lightheaded. She feared it might have been the lingering effects of her overdose, but she quickly dismissed the thought.

She turned in her seat and looked at Brasif. "What the hell is this?"

"It would seem that the Intergalactic Coalition has allied with the Cohannic," he replied.

She turned back to the monitoring system as the frenzied battle raged near the cargo hold. Laser fire, photon orbs, and streaks from the flesh-eater filled the corridor. Initially, nearly all of the firepower was being absorbed or deflected by the shields, but then one of the security detail took a shot to the abdomen that penetrated his shield armor and he fell to his knees before sprawling onto the ground. Seconds later, one of the raider's shields failed and a round from the flesh-eater disintegrated his entire body within seconds.

"How much longer on the EMP?" Brasif asked.

"Seven and a half more minutes," Fosh said.

Brasif stood from his chair. "They won't be able to hold for that long. I'm going to help them."

"I'm coming too," Cassyn said, rising from her chair.

Brasif held up his hand. "No, you're not."

"You need as many hands as you can get down there," she protested.

"Yes, but I need your particular hands at the piloting controls so you can fly us out of here the moment we disable that towing beam."

She wanted to argue, but he was right. She slumped back down into her chair and started watching the feed again. Two more security personnel had fallen, and the raiders and Cohannic soldiers were inching their way closer to Yuen and the battle station. Eight more raiders had come through the hole in the ship and joined the fight. The Vengeance security force was gradually losing ground.

"Soldaan, you're with me," Brasif said before turning to Fosh. "Initiate the EMP pulse the second it has recharged. We'll buy you as much time as we can."

Brasif and Soldaan entered the feed several moments later. Soldaan was firing his phaser while taking cover behind a nook in the corridor, while Brasif was expertly shooting a modified energy rifle, resting the barrel atop the stump of his missing arm. The intruders were only feet from the battle station now, and fluctuations in the consistency of its shielding told Cassyn it wouldn't be much longer before it failed completely.

She jumped from her chair and rushed over to Fosh's station. "Listen to me Fosh, they're not going to be able to hold them long enough to get the EMP back online. Even if they do, the EMP won't affect the intruders on the ship. They'll still take the Vengeance. You're the ranking officer on the bridge now. We have to act."

Fosh looked longingly at the feed as if he were trying to will his crewmates to hold the line. He looked back at her and asked, "What ya got in mind?"

"What part of the ship is the towing beam locked onto?" she asked.

He brought up a holographic image of the Vengeance's exterior. "Here," he pointed, "right bove da cargo hold."

A smile spread across her lips. "How many of those magnet grenades do you have?"

His face sagged. "Somethin' tells me I'm gonna hate what you're bout to suggest."

Fosh had indeed hated Cassyn's suggestion, but she was able to convince him, and Dajin, that it was their best course of action under the circumstances.

Through the ship's internal monitoring system at her pilot's chair, she watched Fosh make his way to the armory one level above the cargo hold.

"Do you think this will actually work?" Dajin asked.

"I don't know, but we're all dead if we don't do something," she replied.

The battle in the docking corridor was now on the large view screen, and the relentless enemy fire was being concentrated on Yuen's position. The battle station's shield flickered rapidly until it faltered completely. Yuen was immediately struck in the upper torso by a projectile round, and he fell from the gunner's chair of the flesh-eater. Soldaan darted into the corridor and dragged him to cover as enemy fire whizzed past them.

Cassyn's heart leaped into her throat at the sight of Yuen being sho and she instinctively rose from her chair, but then sat back down.

Stay focused on the plan, she told herself.

Once the shield fell, six of the raiders, and the four Cohannic troops dashed down the hallway toward the security detail. Two of the raiders were struck down before they reached the cargo hold door. Another of the raiders rushed forward, firing rapidly from the energy pistols he held in each of his hands. His shots struck one of the security detail multiple times in the torso, disabling her shields and mortally wounding her. Fallen bodies lined the corridor as the firing ceased and the two groups came together in hand-to-hand combat. The Cohannics' blue energy blades flashed and collided with the orange energy daggers of the security team and their personal shields shimmered with each blow that was struck.

Cassyn's jaw dropped as Brasif came into view from the edge of the screen. He'd replaced his energy rifle with a double-sided energy shaft and he lunged straight at the closest Cohannic soldier. His strike grazed off the soldier's shield as he deftly dodged the counter strike from the energy blade. He then connected with a swift sidekick just beneath the soldier's raised arm, sending him tumbling to the floor. Without hesitation, Brasif leaped into the air and landed atop the downed soldier, bringing the point of his energy staff down on his neck with all his weight. The tip of the staff's blade penetrated the soldier's shield and sunk deep into his flesh, sending a stream of dark blood spraying into the air.

"Did you know he could do that?" she asked, looking at Dajin in awe.

Dajin shrugged. "There's a lot about Brasif we don't know."

She glanced at the EMP timer; it read four minutes and twenty-six seconds. She turned back to the viewscreen and saw Soldaan shove one of the raiders hard into a wall, dislodging his mask. She stared at Tolbin's face in disbelief, wondering again if she may have been hallucinating. Soldaan closed in to press his attack, his massive back obscuring her view of Tolbin. She involuntarily yelped as a Cohannic soldier slithered behind Soldaan and battered his back with repeated blows of his energy blade. Soldaan's shield armor flashed as he dropped to a knee before turning and grabbing the soldier's wrist.

Se couldn't be sure, but she thought the last blow got through Soldaan's shield armor and injured his back. As Soldaan struggled to his feet while grappling with the Cohannic soldier, Tolbin lunged shoulder first at his back knocking him onto his stomach. Before Soldaan could recover, the Cohannic soldier brought his blade down hard across the back of his neck, once, then again, and again. Soldaan lay motionless in a spreading pool of blood as the Cohannic soldier moved on to his next target. Tolbin pushed his back up against the nearest wall and readjusted his mask as his chest heaved.

Cassyn keyed in an auto-piloting sequence and looked at Dajin. "On the signal, press this panel."

Dajin looked over at the console, noting the indicated panel. "What are you about to do?"

"I'm going to get these bastards off our ship."

She sprung from her chair and headed for the bridge doors.

"Wait!" Dajin called out. "What's the signal?"

"Don't worry, you won't miss it," Cassyn said, sprinting off the bridge.

Her eye twitched uncontrollably and her heart raced as she boarded the lift and descended one level to the cargo deck just in time to see Fosh hurrying down the hall with a metal case tucked under his arm.

She looked past him and saw the melee spilling down the hallway where the security detail was being completely overwhelmed now. They'd been beaten back almost to the cargo hold door and they were the only thing standing between the intruders and the lift to the bridge. She realized there was precious little time left to stop their advance.

She sprinted down the corridor as fast as she could. "Fosh!" she yelled.

He stopped and turned, his dreadlocks whipping around into his face. He used his hand to clear the hair from his face and revealed a look of surprise.

"What are ya doing down here?" he asked. "Ya need ta be at da controls when dis happens."

"Dajin's taking care of that. Give me one of those grenades."

He reluctantly handed over one of the magnet-covered grenades and they each activated their personal shield armor as they proceeded down the corridor toward the fighting.

When they reached the cargo hold door, Cassyn stole a look inside and saw Yuen on the ground clutching the side of his neck. One of the security officers was next to him tending to a badly wounded leg. She resisted the temptation to duck inside to check on Yuen; time was of the essence. She pressed forward with Fosh. A few yards ahead, Brasif and the remaining security team members were trading blows with the advancing enemy.

She stopped and said to Fosh, "You take the hatch, and I'll take the beam."

He nodded his understanding and they each pressed the small activation button on their grenades.

"Brasif!" she shouted above the noise. "Fall back into the cargo hold."

Brasif glanced back at her and Fosh as they each drew back their arms to throw. He reached out with his arm and grabbed the nearest security detail member, hauling him backward toward the cargo hold door. One of the other officers tried to follow, but he was cut down by one of the Cohannic soldiers.

As she began her throw, Cassyn locked eyes with Tolbin, who was farther down the hall and had already started shuffling back toward the hatch as he realized what was happening. She saw the realization dawn in his eyes as he recognized her. She swung her arm forward with all her might and was surprised at the lack of emotion she felt for him as he was about to meet his end.

He chose his side, and he chose wrong, she thought.

She and Fosh released their grenades at the same time. His was directed at the docking area, hers directed at the area of the ceiling where the towing beam was locked onto the ship. Brasif pulled the security officer through the cargo hold door and She and Fosh dove in behind them. The grenades issued a soft beeping tone as their magnets activated and guided them to their respective destinations. The remaining Cohannic soldiers slithered frantically down the corridor toward the cargo hold door while the last five raiders, including Tolbin and one with the two pistols, dashed for the hole they'd cut into the ship.

Brasif pounded his fist on the panel, and the cargo door slid shut just as the Cohannic soldiers arrived. Seconds later, two successive explosions rocked the cargo hold and a deafening whooshing noise swept past the door. Everything went still and silent except for the intermittent moans of the security officer with the mangled leg. Yuen made no sounds at all.

Cassyn crawled over to him and cradled his head against her chest. His eyes were open, one ebony and one hazel, but his arms laid limp at his sides. He was gone. She touched her forehead to his and sobbed uncontrollably as the ship started to move. Dajin had apparently received the signal, and they were on their way to the Flux system, to safety. She'd found a way to save the ship, but just as was the case with her father, she was powerless to save the man she loved.

CHAPTER TWENTY-TWO

Vicaryn

Aegus: Flux Star System

The Great Hall was vacant, save for the seven Prefects and their wards, minus Allyon Corbo and Jeffla Lannis. Six of the seven members of the Council were seated at their respective places around the curved dais. Siverion's ward, Mouthis Drune, and Pentanus' ward, Terrabin Clavis, escorted Tycus to the base of the Council bench and stood behind him. His wrists were restrained in front of him within a stasis field.

As Prefect of House Holm, the house responsible for the administration of justice, Val Jurga was the director of the proceeding. She rose from her seat and the other prefects followed suit.

She cast her eyes down upon Tycus and said, "Six wounded and three dead, including the mimic. The sanctity of this Council has been tainted and you, Tycus Athket of House Telk, stand before this Council accused of grave transgressions against the Sukarian populace. The charges leveled against you include traitorous actions against this Council, conspiring with a known enemy of the Sukarian government, the attempted assassination of a foreign diplomat, and murder. You've denied each of the accusations brought against you. Now, before this body of judgment, you have the opportunity to proffer your defense. We stand ready to consider it."

The Prefects sat in unison, and nervous anticipation gripped

Vicaryn as he waited to hear what Tycus would say.

Despite his precarious predicament, Tycus stood erect with his chin up as he addressed the Council. "I continue to deny each of the accusations leveled against me. I have done nothing but faithfully serve this Council for one hundred and thirty-one years. I am no traitor, nor am I a murderer. I had no quarrel with Ambassador Veleko or his assistant as I hardly knew either of them. Furthermore, I had no knowledge that Allyon Corbo was a Velderian mimic, and I was not in league with it, nor did I have any knowledge of its mission. You must ask yourselves, if I was working with the mimic to carry out this attack, why would it have also been a victim of the explosion? Had I orchestrated this attack, I would not have called myself into question by having my accomplice be exposed."

A low murmur rose around the Council table.

Tycus continued laying out his case. "I have obviously been framed for this heinous act. There is no evidence against me other than my error of unwittingly bringing a cunning mimic into my service. A mimic, I might add, that none of you who sit in judgment of me were able to discern any better than I."

Tycus stopped speaking and Val asked, "Have you anything else to offer in your defense?"

"I have nothing to offer but the truth. Just like you, I want to know who is responsible for this attack. I want the true culprit brought before this Council to face judgment."

Vicaryn cleared his throat and spoke from his seat, "I believe we already have the culprit who is responsible for the attack, and he stands here before us. Let us consider the facts leading up to your assassination attempt on the Ambassador. There is, at this very moment, an aggressive and hostile enemy attacking sovereign territories throughout Vizaria, territories we are expected to help protect. But what have we done under your leadership except stand idly by as the enemy grows stronger?" He glanced around the table. "I ask you, my fellow esteemed Prefects, who benefits most from our inaction? The simple answer is the Velderian empire. They plot in the shadows to frame us for murdering an ally's diplomats. Then they wait patiently as the fabric of our most important alliances crumble. They watch and they gather information to hasten our demise so that they may one day expand their empire. There is no doubt the Cohannic are a brutal and worrisome adversary, but make no mistake, the Velderians will ultimately be our undoing if we fail to remain vigilant." He pointed an accusatory finger at Tycus. "Here stands the one responsible for bringing our most dangerous foe to our very doorstep and into our hallowed halls, yet he expects us to believe he knew nothing of this plot?"

"You know I knew nothing of this treachery," Tycus spat.

"I know only what the facts support. I know that Allyon Corbo was your ward, no one else's. It's absurd to believe that the mimic could've milled under your nose for months while you noticed nothing. The best-case scenario is that your incompetence put this Council in peril. The worst-case scenario is that you sold your soul, and now it is we who must pay the price. The Velderians relish the fact that we sit on our hands while the Cohannic wreak havoc throughout Vizaria. A posture, may I remind you, that you have championed all along, and one that Ambassador Veleko, like many on this Council, urged you to abandon. You could have put a stop to this menace, yet you voraciously objected at every turn." He paused for effect and glanced around at the other Council members. "The Ambassador's persistence led you and your Velderian mimic to collude to kill him so you could further our enemy's interests. Those are the things I know Prefect."

"Preposterous!" Tycus shouted.

"Is it?" Vicaryn asked quizzically before motioning to Dannus.

Dannus approached the dais and handed him a recording cube. He sat the cube on the table in front of him and said, "This was salvaged from a datapad found among the wreckage of Ambassador Veleko's transport. It seems his assistant kept recordings of his private conversations with Prefect Athket."

He tapped a corner of the cube and Tycus' voice issued forth.

"Are you certain?"

"Yes, he told me himself," Veran said.

"If he so openly speaks of misleading the Council in your presence, then there is no doubt you enjoy his full confidence."

"I have his complete trust, I'm sure of it."

"Good," Tycus said.

"What shall I do next?"

"Nothing. Let him come before the Council and spread his misinformation. It's better that he suspects nothing."

There was a slight pause in the recording, then Veran asked, "And our agreement remains intact?"

"Most certainly," Tycus answered. "You've exhibited your loyalty to this Council, and to me personally, on many occasions. It's past time you reaped your reward. You will be his replacement after he is disposed of. Your long years counseling his father, and now him, make you a natural selection for the post. No one would question it. Veran Gauld, the Pharus Ambassador to the Sukarian Council. It sounds fitting, wouldn't you agree?"

"Certainly, Your Excellency. You honor me."

"Then the matter is settled. Make haste back to Aegus, there is much for us to discuss."

Tycus pointed in his direction. "That recording is a fabrication!" he bellowed.

Vicaryn kept his tone even. "You used Gauld to acquire information from the Ambassador. You learned from him that the Ambassador had not secured the information-sharing agreement you wanted from the Humans. He told you that the Ambassador planned to lie about that fact to entice us to move against the Cohannic, something your Velderian cohorts didn't want."

"Untrue," Tycus said.

Vicaryn continued, "You tricked Gauld into thinking you would reward him with the ambassadorship after you killed Madrin Veleko, but instead you attempted to eliminate them both to ensure your tracks were completely covered. Part of your plan failed though, didn't it? The Ambassador wasn't in the transport when your mimic blew it up, and had my servant not intervened, I'm sure your accomplice would have surely finished the job. As for why the mimic was injured in the blast, who knows? Maybe it miscalculated the explosive yield or maybe it was instructed to perish in the blast. I suspect it is you who holds that answer."

"All Lies!" Tycus screamed.

A thin film of foam was forming at the corners of his mouth, and he was visibly shaking. His eyes darted back and forth as if pleading for one of the other Prefects to come to his defense.

Vicaryn decided to press his advantage. He removed a datapad from his robe and tapped at the device before handing it to Val, who studied the pad as he continued.

"You claim you were not involved in the plot, but I have more evidence to the contrary. This datapad shows that, two days before the blast, you sent your Velderian accomplice to procure a black-market plasma explosive device. You then instructed him to plant it on the Ambassador's transport after he arrived on Aegus."

Val had passed the datapad to one of the other prefects and she was now glaring at Tycus. "Explain this."

He cleared his throat and was making an obvious effort to reclaim a calm demeanor. "Can't you see? This evidence has been manufactured against me."

"By whom, and to what end?" she asked.

He nodded in Vicaryn's direction. "Ask yourself, who stands to gain from my ruin but him? Long has he sought to usurp my authority on this Council."

Vicaryn stood from his seat. "I have no desire to lead this Council in your stead Prefect Athket." He looked at Val and said, "In the interest of the integrity of this proceeding, I wish to formally disqualify myself from any consideration of Council leadership should Prefect Athket be removed."

He sat back down and fixed his gaze on Tycus, whose return stare was devoid of defiance, and hope.

Val looked back to Tycus. "So, what was it again that Prefect Gayne stands to gain from your demise?" she asked sarcastically.

Tycus had no response. His shaking continued as he tore his gaze from Vicaryn and looked back at her. "I assure—"

She raised a hand, silencing him. "I've heard quite enough." She looked around the podium. "Does anyone else have any questions to pose to the accused?"

No one spoke. Even Siverion and Jamun, Tycus' staunchest supporters on the Council, sat in silence with their eyes cast downward.

"Then I am ready to render judgment," Val announced. "Prefect Tycus Athket, I am convinced of your guilt by the overwhelming evidence presented against you. You have betrayed this Council and your people. It is a most unforgivable offense, one for which redemption is quite impossible. Therefore, three days from now, you will be publicly executed to serve as an example to all who would dare follow in your dastardly footsteps."

She picked up the sphere to make an end to the proceeding.

"Prefect Jurga, if I may," Vicaryn said.

She paused and nodded her assent.

He spoke to her with his eyes still fixed on Tycus. "You are correct that Prefect Athket can never be redeemed of his heinous actions, but he has indeed served for many decades as an esteemed member of this body. I, for one, refuse to accept that his entire tenure has been marred by the disgraceful acts he's engaged in as of late. Might I suggest an alternative punishment to death as an end to his service?"

"The Council is listening," Val said.

"Since he has chosen to forfeit his life and legacy in this misguided quest for power, let him spend the rest of his days contemplating that choice within the confines of Deljadun Prison."

Siverion spoke up. "That would be inappropriate. We have never issued such a punishment to a former prefect."

"We have never had a former prefect engage in such salacious acts, have we?" Vicaryn retorted.

Another wave of murmuring ensued as the Prefects conferred among themselves.

"Quiet," Val said. "Is there any objection to the alternate punishment Prefect Gayne has proposed?"

No one objected.

"Then it is decreed. Tycus Athket of House Telk, you shall be indefinitely confined to Deljadun Prison. Your titles, holdings, and privileges as a member of this Council are forfeit, and you are relieved of your position as Prefect of House Telk. You may never rejoin our society, and you shall never again bathe in the light of Flux. It is my sincere hope that the remainder of your years are long, so that you may dwell upon the disgrace you have wrought upon the good name of your house."

She slammed the sphere upon the table three times and each of the Prefects stood and turned their backs to Tycus. Vicaryn held Tycus' gaze for a long moment before turning his back on his long-time nemesis.

After Tycus was escorted from the Great Hall, the remaining Prefects sat once again. An eerie silence hung in the air as they adjusted themselves in their seats.

Minva spoke first. "Prefects have been removed before, but never under the stain of sedition. Who shall succeed Tycus as Prefect of House Telk?"

"Without a legitimate ward, the duty will likely fall upon his only sibling, Nagramen Athket," Pentanus said. "But it will ultimately be up to the members of House Telk to decide."

"I know Nagramen well. I believe he can restore the good name of House Telk," Jamon said.

"Very well," said Pentanus, "I will initiate the succession proceedings tomorrow."

"What of the leadership and guidance of this Council?" Minva asked. "Tycus was the most senior prefect among us."

Pentanus interlaced his fingers and said, "Seniority has never been the measure of who leads this Council."

"Pentanus speaks the truth," Siverion said, perking up. "But as I am now the senior member of this Council, as well as the most devout proponent of the greatness of the Sukarian race, I see no reason it should not be me who takes up the mantle. I am ready and willing to fill the role."

Pentanus chuckled. "My dear Siverion, you seem to confuse the fanatic promotion of Sukarian supremacy with dedication to our values. You would be our ruin."

Siverion appeared insulted and was about to retort before Val cut him off. "Prefect Gayne has displayed the measured leadership and judgment I believe this Council desperately needs in these trying times."

Right on cue, Vicaryn thought, pleased that the Ormunii buntas he'd given to her had not been in vain.

"You honor me Prefect Jurga," he said. But as I stated in the presence of this Council, I have no desire to lead this Council."

She spoke to him while looking around at the other Prefects. "That is precisely why you are the best suited for the task. None of us even considered the thought of showing mercy to Tycus amid our lust for justice. Though he may well have earned the sentence, none of us even stopped to consider the consequences of condemning a former prefect to death. It is that level of wisdom to which we should defer in the uncertain times that await us."

He was thoroughly impressed with the fervor of her delivery. He was more certain than ever he'd selected the right prefect to bolster his image and serve as his right hand on the Council. She was respected by each of the Prefects, and her endorsement would all but ensure his grip on the Council. Pentanus and Minva would see the reason of it and go along. Jamun and Siverion would never truly accept it, and he understood they would undercut him at every opportunity, but they too would grudgingly bend to the will of the majority. And Tycus' replacement, whoever that proved to be, would not be seasoned enough to challenge his influence on the Council. So, with very little debate, the Prefects declared Vicaryn Gayne of House Elgeen the new leader of the Council of Seven.

He feigned reluctance as he rose to his feet. "If it is truly the will of this Council, then I humbly accept the responsibility of leadership."

He sat back down, cushioned by his newfound and hard-won influence. With the eyes of each prefect upon him, he made his first proposal as Council leader.

"The Cohannic have raged unchecked for long enough. It is past time to put an end to their campaign of destruction. I propose that we prepare our military for war."

Only Siverion and Jamun dissented. With that, the Sukarian race officially declared war against the Cohannic and Norvekians.

CHAPTER TWENTY-THREE
Madrin

<u>Aegus: Flux Star System</u>

Madrin followed the flittering bug's random path across the ceiling of the room. A dull pain pulsated in his forehead with each movement of his eye. His face was the only part of his body he could move since the medical stasis field held him motionless while the grafting scanners worked to repair some of the damage to his body. He'd been immobile for the better part of two days, and the boredom was excruciating.

The brown bug bounced against the ceiling light several times before settling on a wall near the door. He internally mocked the creature's blissful ignorance of the fact that it would probably never escape this room, but he also empathized with its overwhelming desire to try. He'd tried to escape too, but no matter how many times he bumped into that unseen ceiling, he could never emerge from his father's shadow.

I almost died trying, he reflected.

Unlike the winged insect, however, he knew he would never achieve the success his father had enjoyed. Deep down, he could always sense the futility of his efforts. Still, he carried on and dutifully played his role, following the path laid before him. This is where it led.

A damned medical stasis field, he thought disdainfully.

He supposed the saddest fact of all was that even knowing now where his quest for power had brought him, he'd likely traverse it again if afforded the opportunity. These long four days since the blast had provided him ample time to ponder if he ever really cared about actually reaching lofty political heights, or was he just addicted to the climb itself? Ultimately, he gave up on trying to decide since it no longer mattered; both the journey and the goal were beyond his reach now.

His mother and his wife were the first faces he saw when he woke. The two couldn't have been more different, and their approaches to his situation reinforced that fact.

Carrine wanted nothing more than for him to continue his quest for political relevance. She professed her pride in him for what he tried to accomplish, even suggesting that his father would share her sentiment, but despite her words, he recognized the disappointment just beneath the surface of her facial features. He sensed that she still wanted him to strive for the power that continued to elude him, but as she looked at his disfigured and mangled body, he could tell that she no longer had a clear vision of how he could achieve it.

Laudrin, on the other hand, struggled to hide her relief that his political life may have abruptly ended. She never wanted any harm to befall him, he knew that, but he couldn't escape the feeling that she viewed his predicament as an opportunity to gain the husband she'd always desired. Her eyes radiated the hope that she and their girls would finally get the attention from him that they'd craved for so long. They could now be his number one priority.

Both of them wanted something from him that he no longer felt he could provide. He was a total failure, and now he was also a broken man, both physically and metaphorically.

He cut his eye to the left as the door slid open with a soft hiss and the Korchak nurse walked into the room.

"Ambassador, you have a visitor."

"I don't want to see anyone," he mumbled.

"My apologies Ambassador, but the Prefect insists."

She backed from the room as Vicaryn stepped inside, his slender face showing a momentary flicker of alarm at Madrin's appearance. He understood the shock. He'd experienced the same thing when he surveyed his injuries after regaining consciousness.

Over sixty percent of his body had been severely burned. The burns marring the right side of his face were extensive as the blast of super-heated plasma melted his skin, destroying his right eye in the process. His hair was burned away, exposing a half-charred scalp. Shrapnel had severed his left leg just below the knee, and his lungs were severely damaged by the inhalation of the plasma fumes. The medical staff impressed upon him how lucky he was to have survived, but the night after he woke, his only wish was for death to take him in his sleep.

Vicaryn spoke somberly, "Oh, my dear Ambassador, it pains me to see you in this condition. I would have come sooner, but I was advised you needed your rest. I wanted to be among the first to extend my most heartfelt sympathies for what you've had to endure, and on Sukarian soil no less."

"Thank you for coming Prefect Gayne. I appreciate the gesture."

Vicaryn offered a slight smile. "How are you feeling?"

"The pain subsides a little more each day," he said. "As much as I detest this stasis field, I'll admit that it does a formidable job at keeping the worst of the agony at bay."

Vicaryn stepped closer. "Have you been debriefed about the bombing?"

"I've been given some information, yes. I know that Veran was killed, as was the shape-shifting assassin as I understand. I've also read reports that Prefect Athket was somehow implicated and removed from the Council."

"All correct," Vicaryn affirmed.

"What of my head of security, Nhila Gorban?" he asked.

Vicaryn furrowed his brow. "There were no other Human casualties aside from yourself and your assistant."

He felt a pang of relief at the news, but it was quickly followed by confusion as to why Nhila wasn't here if she'd survived the blast.

I saw her in flames, he recalled.

"Are you certain," Madrin asked.

"Quite so."

He licked his dry lips and asked, "Why was Veran murdered?"

Vicaryn took a seat in the chair next to his bed. "I'm afraid your assistant was not the only target of the assassination attempt. It appears you were swept up in a conspiracy of which you knew nothing about."

"Conspiracy," he said. "What sort of conspiracy?"

"It brings me no pleasure to be the one to inform you that your assistant was more than just a victim of the terroristic act. He played an integral part in setting these unfortunate events in motion. The news reports only tell a portion of the sordid affair. There are many more layers."

He winced as the medical scanners rotated around his body emitting invisible waves that stimulated cellular restoration. He wasn't certain that he wanted to hear the details, but his need to fully understand the situation overwhelmed him.

"Tell me everything," he said.

Vicaryn interlaced his fingers in his lap. "Prefect Athket was an agent of the Velderian empire. He was working in concert with the Allyon Corbo mimic."

"Why would he do that?"

Vicaryn shrugged. "Why do any of us do the things we do? For instance, why did you do what you did?"

His eye focused back on the bug on the wall. It was now crawling near the panel by the door.

What a tragedy, he thought. *It has no idea how close it is to freedom.*

He looked back to Vicaryn. "So, you know of my attempted deception then?"

Vicaryn nodded.

Madrin exhaled slowly, a strange relief washed over him knowing it was out in the open now. He looked off into some unseen spot in the distance.

"I could lay here and say that I did it out of a sense of duty, being that the Cohannic threat loomed large, while the political wheels turned slowly. But you've known me long enough to realize that would be a lie. In truth, I did what I did out of a misguided play for power. I did it in pursuit of something I never really had a chance of obtaining."

"Pursuit of power is never misguided," Vicaryn said. "It's an age-old virtue, one my race understands intimately."

"If Prefect Athket and I are any indication, it would seem the price of power is steep, and it demands to be paid regardless of if it's ever attained," Madrin said.

"Indeed," Vicaryn agreed, "but even if your motives lacked altruism, it doesn't mean you were wrong. As I'm sure you've heard, the Cohannic have set their sights on the Forrack home system, confirming our belief that they seek expansion beyond the Tyros system. With Tycus out of the way, the Council has approved full military action to end this invasion. We can finally rid Vizaria of this scourge."

He was relieved to hear the news but also disappointed it would not serve his interests the way it would have just days earlier. He cast his eye downward. "So, tell me, what part did Veran play in all this?"

Vicaryn pursed his thin lips. "His reward was to be your replacement upon your death. His price was also power, and it was to be at the expense of your life, and ultimately his own."

He took a long time before speaking as a tear droplet formed in the corner of his eye. "My family always considered him to be a trusted friend. I could have never made it to where I am…" His voice trailed off, then he continued. "To where I was without his sage counsel. To think that he was capable of such a thing is hard to accept."

"Power has a way of twisting hearts," Vicaryn said. "Veran contracted a disease of the soul for which we have yet to find a cure."

"So, what is to become of me?" Madrin asked. "My deceit of the Council cannot go unpunished, not by my government, and surely not by yours."

Vicaryn rose from his chair and placed a datapad on the table next to his bed, letting his hand rest on top of it. "When your treatment is complete, and you regain your strength, I want you to study this."

"What is it?"

"It's a road map of sorts. It will help you navigate the tumultuous trek that lies ahead of you." Vicaryn walked to the door before turning back to look at him. "You are correct that your actions cannot go unpunished, but sometimes the punishment is getting exactly what you wished for all along, if only to discover whether or not it was worth everything you sacrificed. Rest and recover Ambassador; you're not out of the game yet."

As Vicaryn turned to walk out, he looked down and slapped his hand against the wall. He removed a small square of cloth from his robe and wiped his palm as he left.

Madrin looked toward the door at the squashed bug. It had finally found an escape from its prison. He wondered how he would escape his.

CHAPTER TWENTY-FOUR
Zanna

<u>Regalus: Chalpin Star System</u>

Coolant spewed from the exposed hoses lining the corridor of the crippled ship. The lights flickered as panicked passengers scrambled for the closest escape pods.

The computerized alert system broadcasted the emergency disembarking protocols:

"Please proceed in an orderly fashion to the closest escape hatch. The hatches are illuminated and clearly marked for easy identification. Destinations have been preset and the pods will launch automatically when the hatch is sealed. One individual per hatch. Please proceed in an orderly fashion to the closest escape hatch. The hatches are illuminated…"

The instructions repeated amidst the wails of those being trampled in the scrum.

Dayvyn pulled Josin by the wrist. "Keep moving. We need to get to the escape hatches."

Josin limped as fast as he could, trying to keep up. A massive explosion somewhere within the bowels of the ship caused a violent shudder. He lost his grip on Josin as they both fell to the ground among the sea of flailing bodies. He frantically looked for Josin, but he saw no signs of his friend.

"Josin! Josin!"

The screams of hundreds answered him as he fought futilely against the tide of bodies carrying him farther down the hall. His heart ached for Josin. They'd known each other since they'd both tried, and failed, to get accepted into the Potentials Academy years ago. It was Josin who helped him through the worst of the depression; now he was gone. He could only hope Josin would find his way to one of the escape hatches.

He turned himself around and elbowed his way through the throng of bodies until he reached one of the hexagonal hatches set into the wall. His spirit sank as he read the illuminated crimson lettering in the upper right corner: *POD LAUNCHED.*

He looked up and down the row of hatches and saw that they'd all been launched. Fear and uncertainty pushed into the outer regions of his mind. He didn't know exactly where the other hatches were located and there was no orderly procession to follow. He wasn't even sure whether he should go up or down the levels of the ship. He stilled his mind and pulled his emotions in check despite the chaos intensifying all around him. It was a practice his father taught him and one that served him well throughout his life.

Reasoning that most of the passengers would make for the lower levels of the vessel, where most escape hatches were usually located, He opted for the upper levels. He bypassed the crowded lift, not wanting to be trapped inside, and fought his way to the end of the corridor, taking the emergency staircase up to the next level. The hallway there was clogged with more desperate travelers trying to escape the mortally wounded ship.

Another massive explosion rocked the ship and he wobbled on his feet. He looked up and down the length of the corridor and concluded that escape was not possible. All of the available escape pods had launched, and he and the remaining passengers of the doomed transport would soon meet a fiery end.

He imagined the news headlines that would flood the galactic hub:

Accidental Collision Results in Hundreds of Fatalities, or Hundreds Perish in Transport Collision; Operator Error Suspected.

He was oddly at peace in the face of his demise as he thought back on his life with fondness. His mother, who'd died two years earlier, was always supportive of him and his endeavors. His father, who was approaching the end of his years, had his own way of showing his approval. And then there was Zanna. He was always close with his little sister and was almost as happy as she was when she got accepted into the Potentials Academy. Although it saddened him to see her leave all those years ago, he always sensed he would see her again one day. Now, in the moments before his impending death, he realized how wrong he was. He would never see her, or his father, or Josin ever again.

He dropped to his knees and squeezed his eyes shut as droplets of coolant misted his skin and anguished shouts from the surging crowd filled his ears. He smelled the putrid scent of fear and hopelessness swirling in the air all around him, yet he remained at peace. He was prepared to leave this life and fade into the nothingness that lay beyond.

As he knelt, awaiting the inevitable, a whooshing sound filled his ears, and he detected a bright light through his closed eyelids. He initially thought the ship was being ripped apart, but when he opened his eyes, there was only a purple abyss spreading infinitely in every direction.

"He's my brother! Of my own flesh and blood," Zanna said. "Was I expected to just let him die when I had the power to save him?"

"That is precisely what was expected of you," Zurin said.

They were standing atop her mental projection of a comet moving past the Orelius interstellar space station.

Zurin had assumed a physical form at her request. She said it helped her to communicate with him more effectively. He'd viewed the request as a setback to her goal of ascension, but he ultimately relented and reluctantly projected the form of an elderly Cortaran professor.

His face softened as he continued, "You straddle the line between two existences, but you cannot ascend unless you completely shed this connection you have with the physical world."

"If standing by to watch my brother die in a horrific accident is what it takes to ascend, then I don't want to do it."

"You remain as clueless as you are stubborn," Zurin said. "You must refrain from interfering with the natural order of things."

"Why?" she challenged.

"Because then you risk creating an *unnatural* order of things."

"You claim to be looking for the one who can prevent an evil blight from consuming the galaxy, do you not?" she asked.

"That is why you are here. It is the task for which we are trying to prepare you."

"Then who's to say that galactic domination by the Cohannic isn't what the natural order demands?"

"If you are truly the chosen one, then you are to say," Zurin said. "You would be the epitome of the natural order."

She changed tactics. "Then if I am the chosen one, and I am the epitome of the natural order, then wouldn't anything I do also comply with the natural order?"

Zurin didn't answer immediately and she beamed at the thought of winning the debate.

"That is an interesting argument," Zurin admitted, "but there remains one glaring flaw in your logic."

"What flaw?" she asked as her exuberance waned.

"You cannot possibly fulfill your destiny as the chosen one until you achieve ascension, and you cannot ascend until you completely divest yourself from your former realm. You will discover that once your metamorphosis occurs, you will no longer have the desire to interfere with the natural progression of events."

She had no counter to the reasoning. "Well, I guess I'm grateful I was able to at least save my brother before I lost the desire to do so," she said sarcastically.

"Who said you saved him?"

"I moved him off of that ship before it was destroyed. I moved him to a safe place."

"Look again," Zurin said staring unblinkingly at her.

A wave of anxiety flowed through her. Something about the way Zurin looked at her was unnerving. She clenched her eyes shut, and when she opened them, she was standing in her father's lab on the Seven Spires space station.

Mazrack looked haggard and in desperate need of rest. She wasn't sure why her mind brought her to this place, but she was happy to see her father. He was toiling away at a hunk of metal lined with blinking circuitry. She looked around the room and saw that he was alone.

An alert sounded from the holographic terminal behind him and he spun around in his chair. "Accept transmission."

The face of a Cortaran scientist she didn't recognize materialized in the feed.

Mazrack smiled. "Yero, how are you old friend?"

"I'm well Mazrack, but I'm afraid I have some rather unpleasant news."

"What is it?"

"There's been an accident."

"What sort of accident?"

"Two transport vessels collided near the Orelius station. It's been all over the hub today."

"I've been in my lab all day. I haven't seen any news reports."

"There were five hundred and twenty-six fatalities. Dayvyn was among them."

Mazrack laid down the metal piece and the small tool he was working with and let out a deep sigh. He sat in silence for a long time as Yero looked on without speaking.

"I'm glad I heard it from you my friend," Mazrack finally said.

"It pains me deeply to have to relay the message. You've lost so much lately. First Zanna, then Baelin, and now Dayvyn."

Mazrack smiled warmly at Yero. "All part of the natural order my friend."

Yero returned a weak smile of his own. "If there is ever anything I can do, you need only ask."

Mazrack stared at the piece of metal on the workbench and said, "There is one thing…"

Zanna clinched her eyes shut again. When she opened them, she was back on the comet with Zurin. Orelius station was fading in the distance as they hurtled through the darkness of space with a silver trail of ice and steam in their wake.

"What kind of cruel trick is this?" she asked with tears pooling on her skin. "What did he mean about my mother and Dayvyn? My mother is not dead. I saw her just before I came to this place."

"There is no trick," Zurin said compassionately. "You just witnessed a conversation your father had years ago, by your understanding of time."

"Years ago! I haven't been here for years; I've only been here for a few days, a week at most."

"The way you experienced the passage of time in the physical realm does not apply here, but for those who remain in that realm, the slow march of time continues inexorably."

"How long! How long have you held me here?"

"Seconds, months, centuries perhaps, it is of no consequence," Zurin said matter-of-factly.

"I've just learned that my mother and brother are dead, and I wasn't there. It's of consequence to me! Now tell me how long I have been in this place."

"You have been absent from Vizaria for five years, seven months, nineteen days, and thirty-nine minutes, by Aegus standard time."

She looked stricken. "But I rescued Dayvyn. I was there; I saw that he was saved."

"You merely experienced what it would have been like to rescue your brother from his fate. It was a test of your willingness to let go of your prior existence, a test you failed. You cannot undo that which has already occurred. In the physical realm, your brother perished years ago. As talented as you are at manipulating time and space in this place, even you cannot change that fact."

"Why did you permit me to save the Forrack soldier and not my brother?"

"Your intervention at Averan-Ginest was objective and without personal attachment. It was born of an instinctual desire to preserve the natural order. Your desire to save your brother was selfish and only served your own interests. Did you notice that you saved no one else on the doomed transport vessel? You could have easily done so, but your personal attachment poisoned your judgment. That is why it is imperative that you shed your connection to the physical realm. It is the only way ascension is possible. It is the only way for you to fulfill your destiny. It is the only way to save them all.

CHAPTER TWENTY-FIVE

Cassyn

<u>Somnus: Pharus Star System</u>

Cassyn stood on the stage with Yero, listening to Admiral Phalana Maldon's speech. She locked eyes with her mother and felt guilty about not trusting the smile she saw on her face. Part of her knew her mother was proud of her accomplishment, but the other part remembered how she'd never wanted this life for her. That part would never cease to exist. Tamon sat next to Pharie, appearing thoroughly enthralled by the Admiral's words.

Ever the dutiful stepfather, she thought.

Cassyn wore the ceremonial uniform of the Pharus Confederation. It consisted of dark brown shoes, beige slacks, a white military tunic adorned with her various medals and badges, and a light pink beret. Phalana was dressed similarly, except her tunic sported many more medals and badges.

"Courage cannot exist in the absence of fear," Phalana was saying, "just as fear cannot prevail in the presence of courage. The crew of the Vengeance exhibited extraordinary courage in the face of seemingly impossible odds, and for some, it cost them their lives. Without the actions taken by this fine soldier to my right, there is little doubt that many more lives would have been lost that day."

Phalana paused as a chorus of applause rippled through the crowd. She continued as the noise abated.

"Corporal Germaine Struk and Commander Yuen Bo were

Pharus Confederation soldiers. Though they did not perish aboard a Pharus vessel, they died for the values all of us here stand for. They died for their comrades. They died, with honor, carrying out their duties. In recognition of their sacrifice, and on behalf of the Combined Pharus Confederation Military Force, it is my high honor to posthumously award Corporal Struk and Commander Bo with the Medal of Courage."

Holographic images of Yuen and Corporal Struk materialized at the front of the stage, and a raucous round of applause erupted from the crowd as the attendees rose to their feet. Cassyn fought back tears as she clapped. She'd not known Corporal Struk very well, but she learned that he was killed in the explosion that tore the docking station from the ship, the explosion she caused.

As she looked at the image of Yuen, the tears dropped from her eyes onto her impeccable white tunic. He was her hope for the life she'd always dreamed about. He'd given her direction when she was waywardly drifting. Now he was gone, and she was alone, again. The empty hole she felt inside deepened with the thought that she never even got the chance to say goodbye. It was the same aching emptiness she'd felt when she learned of her father's death, but this time was almost worse.

She thought about how she'd cradled Yuen's head in her arms. Though she knew in her heart that he was gone, she'd desperately prayed for him to open his eyes one more time, just long enough for her to say something, anything. She couldn't recall who she'd prayed to, nor did she know what she would have said to him if her prayer was answered. All she could do now was reimagine a life without him.

How could Tolbin do this? she thought bitterly.

Her mind flashed back to the look in his eyes as she hurled the grenade at him. There was a mixture of fear and something else.

Regret? Sorrow?

She wasn't sure what it was, but she was sure she didn't care. He'd stormed onto their ship with a group of pirates and Cohannic soldiers and helped to murder people she was close to. She couldn't conceive of an explanation that would rationalize his actions.

He deserved to die, she thought.

But she wasn't at all sure he was dead. The raiders' ship

disengaged just as the explosion ripped through the docking level, and Dajin reported that it fled the area just as they were entering the tunnel to the Marrus station. She had no way of knowing if Tolbin made it back to his ship or not, but she intended to find out. If he didn't die in the blast, she promised herself she'd finish the job if she ever saw him again.

Lost in her thoughts, she hadn't noticed that the applause had ended and Phalana was now speaking about her.

"Ensign Spreen embodies all of the qualities we look for in a soldier of the Confederation. While her actions at Patrinah cannot be adequately rewarded by mere gratitude or gestures, on behalf of the Combined Pharus Confederation Military Force, I am proud and humbled to award her with the Medal of Courage."

Yero gently squeezed her shoulder as she stepped forward. More waves of applause cascaded through the crowd as Phalana affixed a small platinum medal onto her tunic before standing back and saluting her. Cassyn returned the salute and stepped back to her position.

"You did well," Yero whispered into her ear as Phalana wrapped up her remarks.

She was grateful for his presence on behalf of Sagis, and as a friend. None of the other Vengeance crew was in attendance as she, Yuen, and Corporal Struk were the only members of the Pharus Confederation military serving aboard. She assumed various ceremonies and memorials were being held on other worlds for the twenty-two other casualties of the attack at Patrinah.

Underlying those memorials was the startling revelation that Vizaria was now contending with the combined assault of the Cohannic, Norvekians, the Dark Hand, and now the Intergalactic Coalition. The spiral arm was shaken, and galactic governments were just starting to wake to the grim reality of the situation.

When the ceremony concluded, Yero pulled her aside. His eyes conveyed compassion as he grasped her by the shoulders. "Yuen was an excellent soldier and an even better man. I'm sorry for all that you've endured, and I can't escape the feeling of responsibility for sending you on that mission."

She reached up and placed her own hand on his shoulder. "I'm a soldier Yero. I knew the risks, and so did Yuen. You warned me what we could be heading into."

"Still," he said glancing over her shoulder in the direction of Pharie, "I don't think your mother will ever forgive me."

She turned and looked in the same direction before turning back to him. "It's not you she blames. It's me. It'll always be me." She patted him on the shoulder. "Please excuse me. I need to speak with Phal…, I mean, the Admiral." She chuckled softly. "It was so difficult getting used to calling superior officers by their first names, now I'm finding it to be a hard habit to break."

He grinned. "I understand. Hopefully, you won't ever have to break it. The Vengeance will welcome you back when its repairs are completed, and when you are ready. I look forward to seeing you soon."

She smiled before turning and weaving her way through the dispersing crowd toward Phalana. Strangers patted her on the shoulders and offered warm words as she walked.

The Admiral was engaged in a conversation with two serious-looking men in military uniform. "Ensign Spreen, it appears we've talked you up," Phalana said embracing her with a handshake.

To Cassyn, they all had the look of conspirators caught in the middle of a dastardly scheme.

"I hope it was all good things," she said.

"Of course, of course," Phalana said smiling and guiding her toward the men. "Please, allow me to introduce you to Admiral Baudrin Ignus and General Fadrian Dowd."

Cassyn shook the men's hands in turn and said, "Nice to meet you."

"The pleasure is ours," Baudrin said. "The 'Hero of Patrinah' is all anyone can talk about lately."

She cringed at the moniker. After what happened at Patrinah, she didn't feel like a hero. She and Fosh intentionally blew up part of their ship just so they could run away. But soon after they arrived at Marrus station, there she was, splashed all over the hub alongside news about the escalation of the war and speculation on the impending attack on the Bartos system. It was a whirlwind.

"Thank you, sir," she said.

Fadrian pointed an index and middle finger toward Phalana and Baudrin. "If you ever tire of these two, consider giving the Army a try. We can use a few good pilots."

"The army could use a few good everything, including generals," Baudrin said as they all chuckled.

"Forgive my bluntness," Cassyn said, "but may I ask what it was you were speaking of regarding me?"

They all glanced at each other uneasily.

Phalana finally answered, "We were discussing your future."

Cassyn sighed. "That's a relief. My future is exactly why I made my way over here. I was wondering when I might be able to report back to the Vengeance. I know she's currently undergoing repairs, but perhaps I can assist."

Phalana and Baudrin exchanged awkward glances.

"We have other plans for you Ensign," Phalana said. "Come, walk with me."

Phalana escorted Cassyn into a meeting room off of the main hall, well out of earshot of the other attendees.

"You're not going back to the Vengeance," she said bluntly.

Cassyn swallowed hard, attempting to hide her disappointment. "May I ask why?"

"The Sukarians have officially declared war on the Cohannic-Norvekian Alliance. The whole spiral arm knows that means we will soon follow them into the fight. Others will follow as well. Loaning our soldiers out to Sagis is a luxury we can no longer afford. We're going to need our best soldiers on the front."

"I'm flattered Admiral, but I'm sure you've read my service report from the Vengeance. It wasn't exactly sterling."

"Maybe not, but be that as it may, a lot of people vouched for you, including Captain Mantalor."

"You spoke to Brasif?"

"He was gracious enough to debrief us on the Patrinah attack and he largely credits you with the outcome. He said you saved the shipment, as well as lives."

She said nothing in response.

Phalana's dark eyes fixed on her. "Captain Mantalor suspects the pirates were Dark Hand mercenaries. We already know they're doing the Cohannic's bidding in the Tyros system, so it makes sense. Did you happen to see or hear anything that would confirm his suspicions?"

"No, nothing that wasn't included in my report," she lied.

She thought back to Tolbin's face when his mask was dislodged. She'd kept that detail out of her official report. She intended to find out why he was there that day, and it wouldn't do to have the Confederation looking into the matter as well. Tolbin was fiercely independent, and the Dark hand was full of terrorists and thugs who only knew how to take orders. She couldn't understand why he would throw in with that lot, but she'd misjudged many things about him in the past.

"Okay then," Phalana said. "You've been through a lot lately. I suggest you get some much-needed rest. Things are about to get very busy for you."

"Ma'am?"

Phalana looked around. "It's not official yet, but you're being reassigned to the Silver Saber. It's a Raptor class destroyer under the command of Captain Valens Qualik. Orders are being drawn up as we speak."

"Most of my piloting experience is with frigates. But, with enough training, I'm sure I can get up to speed piloting a destroyer."

A wry smile appeared on Phalana's face. "The Silver Saber has several capable pilots, Ensign. This is also not yet official, but you're being promoted to the rank of lieutenant commander."

Cassyn's mouth went dry and she looked around the area. "I don't know if I'm ready for that Admiral," she said in a hushed voice.

With a wink, Phalana turned to walk away. As she left, she looked over her shoulder and said, "Get some rest Spreen; you report for duty in one week."

Cassyn sat at the desk in the hotel room, smiling as she scrolled through the old family holographic videos. Pharie had them delivered to her room as a gift for her award ceremony. There was a handwritten note attached, '*He would be so proud of you,*' it read.

She decided against telling Pharie about her impending

promotion and transfer. Moments like these, where she truly appreciated her mother, were becoming rarer, and she just wanted to savor this one before the next argument.

Devlin Spreen's hologram ran across the desk as he chased an eight-year-old Cassyn through the yard with a water blaster. They both howled joyfully as Cassyn ducked behind a large tree just as a jet of water flew past her shoulder.

"You can't catch me!" Cassyn shouted as she ran back and forth behind the massive tree trunk. The image shook slightly as Pharie cheered on her daughter's escape.

Devlin fell to the ground and let out a yelp of pain as he dropped the water blaster and grabbed his knee. Pharie gasped, and the shaky video image grew larger as she ran toward Devlin.

Cassyn ran from behind the tree and knelt next to her father. "Daddy! Daddy! Are you alright?"

Devlin reached out and grabbed the water gun. Before Cassyn could get up and run away, he sprayed stream after stream of water at her head and neck as he resumed his roaring laughter.

Cassyn ran away screaming, "No fair, no fair!"

The video ended and another one began with Pharie and a three-year-old Cassyn singing happy birthday to Devlin. He had a smudge of vanilla icing on his nose from where Cassyn had put her finger in the cake and touched his face.

She laughed softly as she rubbed tears from her nose with her fingers. She turned off the video and sat in silence for a long time thinking about how her life might be aboard the Silver Saber. It would be an adjustment, but she welcomed the opportunity to reinvent herself yet again. She was still reeling from the news of her pending promotion to lieutenant commander, especially since that meant she'd catapulted a couple of ranks.

What do they see in me? she wondered.

Whatever it was, she wished she could see it too. She opened the desk drawer and stowed the holographic video player. As she put it away, her fingers brushed up against the black ceramic container. She lifted it from the drawer and placed it on the desk.

She thought about her small plant conservatory back on the Vengeance and made a mental note to retrieve it for her quarters aboard the Silver Saber. She needed it as a way of staying connected to her father. After Yuen's death, she realized she'd lost so much, but she also knew she had to find a way to move forward again. Yuen showed her she didn't have to go it alone, and her father would never have wanted her to. She decided that, on her new ship, she would cultivate relationships, just as she would cultivate her conservatory. Things would be different this time.

She dipped her finger into the dark liquid inside the container and gently touched it to her tongue. Weeks of pent-up frustration melted away as her mind swirled with a nearly instant euphoria. Stress dissipated and doubt evaporated into a fine mist as the aggie soothed and calmed her. She sat back in the chair, her body tingling all over.

He would be proud of me, she thought smiling.

A warm sensation covered her like a blanket as she closed her eyes.

CHAPTER TWENTY-SIX
Madrin

<u>Aegus: Flux Star System</u>

Madrin carefully read over the message again, still not completely believing it was real despite the Presidential Seal of the Pharus Confederation prominently displayed at the top. The sender was identified as President Jastine Baruke's personal secretary.

He sat up in the bed and endured the currents of pain shooting through his body. He didn't mind though; it was a far cry better than the torture of complete immobilization in the medical stasis field. At least he was now free to move around.

The cell regenerators had done an admirable job at repairing much of the burn damage he'd sustained. The pain would take longer to subside, and the psychological damage was not likely to ever heal. Scar tissue covered most of the right side of his face, and though it would further heal over time, it would never completely disappear. The doctors assured him that his hair would eventually grow back, but there was nothing more to be done for his other injuries.

There go my dashing good looks, he thought.

Dennak Solutions Corporation had been commissioned to create custom prosthetics to replace his right eye and left leg, and Sagis Incorporated had developed a set of artificial lungs to replace his damaged set. There was now a faint raspy sound accompanying each breath he drew. He counted himself lucky to be alive, but he had a nagging sense that he'd lost something he could never get back.

More than just the physical losses he suffered, he'd also lost his sense of safety and security, something he never realized how much he'd taken for granted until now. Over the past couple of weeks, he'd found himself constantly jumping at loud noises, and cringing at the mere sight of an open flame, or the touch of a slightly hot object. He hated feeling this vulnerable. He'd set people to the task of locating Nhila, but there was still no word of her whereabouts. She'd simply disappeared without a trace, which further added to his crippling sense of loss.

He sighed and read the short letter again:

Ambassador Madrin Veleko,

Due to the recent and unexpected resignation of Senator Binsen Parno, the Pharus Assembly now has a senatorial vacancy. Under Article 9, Section 8, Subsection S of the Adopted Articles of the Unified Pharus Confederation, the sitting President is imbued with the authority to appoint an acting senator to fill a vacancy for the remainder of a term.

It is a great pleasure to inform you that President Jastine Baruke has nominated you to fill the vacant seat of departing Senator Parno, effective twenty-one days from your official acceptance of the appointment.

Please forward your response to me with expedience. I look forward to hearing from you.

Regards,

B'Nai Remington
Chief Secretary for Pharus Confederation President, Jastine Baruke

He laid the datapad in his lap and took a deep raspy breath. He wasn't sure exactly how, but he was certain Vicaryn was involved with this sudden development. He was undoubtedly among one of the last people President Baruke would ever consider for such a posting, but now all of the Prefect's talk about him not being finished suddenly made sense. The Council of Seven wanted a friendly face in the Pharus Assembly, and he was just the person for the job.

The Council used its considerable influence to force the President's hand, he thought with a grin.

He couldn't quite decide if Vicaryn would consider it restitution for him being maimed on Sukarian soil, or if it was simply retaliation against President Baruke for her hesitance to assist the Council when asked. Either way, he didn't care. No one in the Human government would trust him anyway, and he'd always be regarded as a tool of the Sukarians.

If that's the price I must pay to get to the Senate, then so be it.

He'd begun studying the information Vicaryn provided to him on the datapad. It consisted of the political proclivities of some of the most powerful and influential actors within the Pharus political apparatus. The voting habits and proposed laws of senators, the philanthropic interests of local politicians, even the personal relationships and travel histories of ambassadors, it was all there. He had access to everything he needed to navigate the ruthless environment of the Pharus Assembly.

The information both intrigued and alarmed him. He learned things about people he would have never known otherwise, and the depth of information couldn't have all been gathered by legitimate means.

If the Sukarians know this much about our government, what do they know about me, and how might they use that information?

He immediately thought of his Sukarian lover, Tanyara. His affair with her always had the means to complicate his political career, but now that his goal was so close at hand, the thought was less palatable than it once was.

I'll need to break it off with her, he thought.

Then he recalled something his mother once told him.

Power shouldn't be limited or sheltered; it should be harnessed and focused on the wielder's design. It's not a defensive weapon, it's an offensive one.

His trysts with Tanyara didn't have to end, he needed only to make sure they served a purpose. He suspected that some of her clientele held positions of authority within the Sukarian government. If he was going to be owned by them, he would make sure to start his own road map of information. It might be useful one day.

Another complication occurred to him as he reveled in the possibilities that his newfound power could manifest. As a senator, he would have to relocate to the Pharus system. Laudrin wouldn't be thrilled at the prospect of packing up their children and leaving the only home they'd ever known, but he'd told her this was always a possibility. She'd always encouraged him to pursue his ambitions, but he couldn't fault her if she never really believed he would attain a senatorial post; he hardly believed it was possible himself. Now, he held the physical representation of his dream in his mutilated hands. He decided not to consult Laudrin about this decision, mostly because his mind was already made up.

I'll have no trouble convincing her of the wisdom of it, he thought.

He tapped a sequence into his wrist communicator and waited. After a few moments, the image of President Baruke's Chief Secretary materialized. He clocked the momentary flicker of revulsion in her eyes as she took in the sight of his face, and he knew it was something he would have to deal with for the rest of his days. He'd been a handsome man, and he enjoyed the attention he received for it. Now, he was nothing but an oddity to be gawked at and pitied. The adjustment would take some time.

"Good evening Ambassador Veleko. To what do I owe this pleasure?"

"I'd like to speak to the President please."

"She's occupied at the moment, but I gather your call is regarding the offer you received."

"You gather correctly."

"I'd be more than happy to relay your response to the President," B'Nai said.

A thin smile spread across his lips, though only the left side of his face moved. He thought this was as good a time as any to test the boundaries of his newly bestowed influence.

"I don't think she's occupied," he said. "And even if she is, I'd wager that once you explain to her that the future Senator Madrin Veleko was insisting on speaking to her, right now, she would find a way to make herself available. I'm willing to wait a moment while you fetch her, but only a moment."

He couldn't quite describe the look that B'Nai gave him, but she didn't disconnect the transmission. Instead, she placed him on hold. Exactly twenty-six seconds later, President Jastine Baruke's face materialized in the feed.

She offered a forced smile. "Ambassador Veleko. It's nice to see that you are doing well. I regret that I was unable to visit you in the hospital, but I trust you received the package I sent."

"I did," Madrin said, recalling the parcel with the stale routha bread and holographic card from the presidential staff urging him to *get well soon.*

"It was very thoughtful and much appreciated," he lied.

"How are you feeling?" she asked, making a valiant effort not to stare at any one part of his face for too long.

"I imagine I feel a great deal better than I look."

"That's good. I assume you received the offer of the interim senatorial seat."

"Yes, I did, and I'm greatly honored that you thought of me for the task."

"You have the political fortitude for it," she said. "And considering your recent experience, I thought it might do you some good to come home."

"Home," he repeated wistfully as he gazed up at the ceiling. "I was born on Aegus and raised in the Flux system, ma'am. I'm already home, but I do look forward to making a new home on Somnus, and I can't wait to begin working more closely with you."

Though Jastine was too masterful a politician to show it outwardly, he could sense the utter disgust his words elicited within her.

"Likewise," she said.

"Then you may take this conversation as my unofficial acceptance of your offer. I will, of course, forward the official response in short order." He pulled the holographic display closer to his face until he was confident it filled the entire feed on her end. "I look forward to personally meeting with you in three weeks."

She offered no goodbyes. She simply nodded once before disconnecting the feed.

He smiled a crooked smile as he picked up the dossier Vicaryn had given him. He laid back on the bed and scrolled to the section labeled *PRESIDENT JASTINE BARUKE'.*

CHAPTER TWENTY-SEVEN
Nhila

<u>Yorinar: Tyros Star System</u>

Nhila stepped gingerly from the small ship and thanked the kindly Collikan merchant for bringing her this far. Yorinar was now firmly under Cohannic control, but there were still pockets of resistance from Forrack militia groups that had gone to ground. The Cohannic were allowing Collikan and Norvekian merchants to continue the flow of business to and from the planet, but many avoided the hot zones for fear of reprisals from the locals.

The merchant couldn't see the gratitude in Nhila's eyes through the custom helmet she wore. She'd called in a favor from one of her old colleagues from her days at Sagis, and he'd promptly supplied her with a modified version of a Taclite Advanced Security helmet. It was integrated with a tactical Heads Up Display and an automatic targeting system. It was also retrofitted with a special respiratory apparatus to aid breathing with her damaged lungs.

She was still at a loss to explain how she survived the blast. She credited a simple combination of her positioning and plain old dumb luck that she was hurled into a nearby fountain, which put out the fire that singed her hair and most of her clothing. She hadn't, however, escaped unscathed. Aside from the damage to her lungs, she suffered serious plasma burns to portions of her back, legs, and arms.

She received the best treatment she could find without using a public medical facility. She ended up on the makeshift operating a disgraced surgeon she used to know during her more unsavory years. The doctor was known to render services without questions, as long as the compensation was adequate. It took her two agonizing days to get to him, and by then, much of the damage was irreversible. The lingering pain was considerable, but she'd declined the painkillers. She wanted to keep her mind clear so that she could think of her next moves.

She racked her brains for over a week trying to figure out who could have been responsible for the bombing. Madrin was a politician, so naturally he had political enemies, but she couldn't think of anyone who would want to kill him.

Her mind flashed back to how he looked immediately after the blast, laying on his back with the lower half of one of his legs missing. The flames were licking at his clothes, but he remained motionless, and she thought he was surely dead. Then she saw him move like he was trying to look at something. She'd followed his stare and saw Prefect Gayne's servant dispatching a Velderian shapeshifter. The scene elicited a sense of dread in her, and she had to resist the urge to run to Madrin. Instead, she used the commotion to surreptitiously slip away unnoticed.

I will get answers, she thought as she slipped between two dilapidated buildings.

She emerged from the dusty alleyway and saw the building she was looking for. It was a nondescript, two-story edifice that appeared no different from the dozens of other businesses lining the main throughway, but she knew better. As she crossed the street, two patrolling Cohannic soldiers slithered into her path.

"Your wrist," the soldier on the left said.

She held out her wrist as he scanned her communicator. A green light appeared on the scanner, and he waved her past. She let out a raspy sigh of relief and silently thanked the Collikan merchant for the forged authorization code. Officially, she was on Yorinar conducting businesses with local buyers. Unofficially, she had other plans.

She approached the target building and touched the call panel. A few moments passed, then a gruff voice answered.

"Yeah."

"I'm here to see Bandress Tessanor," she said in a low voice.

"What business ya have with him?"

"My business is my own."

There was a slight pause. "Take that helmet off," the voice said.

She looked at the small surveillance device affixed at the corner of the door jamb and said, "My face is of no concern to you. I was summoned here by Bandress Tessanor; are you going to let me in or not?"

There was another, longer, pause. "Have you got any weapons on ya?"

"I have no weapons."

The door creaked open and she walked into a dimly lit, windowless room. Except for a small dust-covered bureau pushed against the far wall, there was no furniture. A dank smell hung in the air, evidencing that it had been a long time since this room was used for anything. A narrow staircase was positioned to her left and she took it to the second floor of the building.

The second floor was a stark contrast to the room downstairs. She walked into a brightly lit hallway with three doors lining each side. The floor and walls looked and smelled of fresh paint, and a large picture window at the end of the hall provided a view from the backside of the building. Transports and merchant ships weaved through traffic lanes above the buildings that spread out into the distance, some bearing the scars from the Battle of Yorinar.

The second door on the right opened and Scarface poked his head out. "I'm Bandress. Ya coming in or ain't ya?"

She walked warily through the door, taking stock of her surroundings. Two other mercenaries stood in a corner. One was pouring over a datapad while the other tinkered with the controls of a holographic feed bank. Neither looked up when she entered. A small workbench stood against the left wall of the room, and a narrow bunk bed sat against the far wall.

Bandress walked over to the bench and spoke without turning. "So, you the one that was wantin' to join up?"

"That's why I'm here," she said.

"Who ya know in the organization?" he asked.

"Tomeran. You know, from the Midlands in New Holk."

The name was completely made up, but she wasn't concerned

about it passing muster. They'd already let her up here and that was all she needed.

He scratched his head. "Oh yeah, I know 'em. Good lad that one."

Unbelievable, she thought.

He turned to face her. "So, what brings ya to Pidashau? Not many folks clamorin' to get to these parts lately. In fact, most of 'em is tryin' to get off this rock right about now."

She looked around the room as if casually inspecting her surroundings. As her gaze passed over the two mercenaries in the corner, her HUD system marked them for targeting.

"I came to get some answers," she said.

A puzzled look shrouded Bandress' face. "Answers?"

"Yes, answers."

His puzzlement gave way to suspicion. "Why don't ya take that helmet off so I can see that face of yours."

She tilted her head. "The better question is, why don't you wear one to hide yours?"

She didn't turn, but the rear visual indicator in the lower right portion of her HUD showed the other two mercenaries looking up from their work.

Bandress' suspicion now gave way to anger. He looked at her for a few beats, then he erupted in laughter. The other two mercenaries joined in apprehensively.

"I like her already," Bandress said, still laughing.

"You probably won't after this," she said, quickly tapping the screen of her wrist communicator.

Two small ports opened on either side of her helmet and a small spherical projectile shot out from each. At the same time, she retrieved an energy pistol she had hidden in her waistband. As the bodies of the two mercenaries fell behind her, she slammed Bandress against the workbench and jammed the tip of the pistol under his chin. His eyes went wide, but he offered no resistance.

"What... what is this, what do ya want?" he asked in a shaky voice.

She pressed the front of her helmet against his scarred, terror-filled face. "Tell me everything you know about the bombing on Aegus."

CHAPTER TWENTY-EIGHT
Altar

Birgh: Bartos Star System

The Fire Star, flanked by its sister ship, the Nova Flame, streaked through the skies over the Meldebah Province toward the capital city, Kanmag. The two enormous Drinmar Class heavy cruisers were surrounded by dozens of smaller Cohannic and Norvekian fighter vessels.

Orrick stood on the bridge of the Fire Star studying the frenzied landscape. Because there was no known transparent material that could withstand the extreme heat of the Cohannic homeworld, Cohannic ships employed observation screens instead of windows for external viewing.

"Durmok, we've detected a small ground force amassed near the base of the mountain," Ongbo reported. "A few units of soldiers, supported by armored tanks and artillery positions."

Orrick's tongue flicked from his mouth as his eyes remained fixed on the screen. "What of their fleet?"

"Radar doesn't detect any ships. Perhaps they've amassed their fleet at the inner planet," Ongbo said.

He considered this. "This planet would be the obvious place to mount a defense. It's a ruse. They aim to draw us to their position."

"For what purpose?" Ongbo asked.

"They must believe it gives them some advantage."

"How should we proceed?"

"We have been sent an invitation; we will accept it."

He looked out over the sprawling expanse of grasslands crisscrossed by streams and rivers. The surface was alive with raging fires that seemed to lick at the horizon in every direction. He found it an oddly beautiful sight. It reminded him of Fulmaren, with its rivers of molten rock and the occasional firestorms that raged for weeks across the scorched plains. He could almost feel the heat beckoning him. The sight of the flames also angered him since he needed the resources that were being so callously destroyed.

It is but a minor encumbrance to my plans, but I'll make them pay nonetheless, he thought.

As he was pondering the many ways to make the Forrack suffer, a thunderous impact sent vibrations throughout the ship.

"Ground defense weapons are firing on us, sir. Our shields are holding," the tactical officer reported.

He continued watching the screen. "Return fire and destroy any defenses you see, but stay on course."

"Is it wise for us to take such a direct route toward the enemy?" Ongbo asked. "Maybe we should have bombarded their position from orbit."

"Their countermeasures don't concern me. Our hulls are strong, and our shields are more than adequate. Besides, you saw how easily we overcame their planetary defenses; not even their space station was a match for us."

"Let us at least bring in our reserve force from orbit in case we meet more resistance," Ongbo suggested.

"No," he said. "The last remnant of their military is at that mountain. Once we eradicate them, this entire system belongs to us."

"Are you certain that your fascination with the Forrack Commander isn't clouding your judgment?" Ongbo asked.

Orrick whirled and clutched Ongbo by his thick neck. "And what if it is?" he hissed. "I've chased him all the way here from the Tyros system, and he's slipped through my grasp time and time again. Now, I have him cornered, and I will not let him escape me again."

He released Ongbo's neck.

"I meant no offense Durmok," Ongbo said rubbing his throat.

"All I'm saying is that he has proved to be a cunning adversary. We still don't understand what he did at Yorinar."

Orrick was still baffled at how Altar's ship escaped their last encounter. He'd seen the purple-ringed portal materialize before his eyes as the enemy ship seemed to be sucked toward it before vanishing. A new wave of frustration rose in him as he recalled his hesitation at following the Vengeance into the void. In truth, his hesitation was rooted in fear. Fear that the Forrack may have developed a new technology, or even worse, that the technologically advanced Cortarans may have joined the fight against him. He only pressed forward with his campaign after intelligence reports confirmed that the Forrack were still without allies.

"He is a worthy foe," he conceded, "but his resistance ends here."

He gazed at the countless plumes of billowing light gray smoke rising over the plains, and he knew this strategy of destruction was born of Altar's mind. He'd come to realize the Forrack Commander would do anything to stop his conquest.

For this, he must be eliminated, he thought, his forked tongue flicking from his mouth.

"There!" Ongbo shouted, pointing at the screen.

Orrick watched as a swarm of Forrack ships emerged from the mouth of the mountain. A hail of impactor missiles, energy beams, and disruptor torpedoes slammed into the Fire Star and the surrounding ships. Two Norvekian fighters dropped from the sky, writhing in flames, and one of the Cohannic destroyers banked hard to the left as the munitions tore through its forward section.

"Why did we not see the ships!" Orrick hissed angrily.

The tactical officer stammered as he spoke, "They… they must've been inside the mountain Durmok. It must've somehow interfered with our long-range sensors."

Orrick pounded a fist on his console. "Return fire. Destroy them all."

Altar sat inside the armored hover tank watching as the Forrack ships streaked overhead from the mountain. The first phase of his plan was underway, and it seemed to be a success so far. The enemy force flew headlong into the ambush and lost several ships in the initial flurry. He looked on with satisfaction as some of the smaller Norvekian fighters plummeted from the sky before they could fire a shot.

It feels good inflicting damage on the enemy for once, he thought, allowing himself a slight smile.

He touched the panel for fleet-wide communication. "Attack vessels, concentrate your fire on the smaller ships. We need to thin their ranks as much as possible. Artillery, target the larger Cohannic ships. Keep them occupied."

The sky filled with flaming projectiles, glowing orbs, and particle beams. More of the smaller Norvekian fighter ships fell from the sky; a few crashed into the mountain near his position. The eight artillery stations blasted massive impactor slugs at the Fire Star and Nova Flame, with several finding their targets. The ships' shield grids shimmered with each hit, but the barrage was only causing minor damage.

"Fall back!" he shouted over the communication channel.

All at once, the columns of tanks swiveled and accelerated toward the open blast doors, retreating into the safety of the mountain. Errant shots bounced off the tanks' shields and he breathed a sigh of relief when the final tank passed through the blast doors. He exited the vehicle and saw the other tanks swiveling their turrets back toward the mountain's entrance. He hopped from the step bar and approached a unit of thirty Forrack troops standing at attention.

Damu saluted and stepped from the group. "Commander, we're ready."

Altar assessed the soldiers standing before him. They were among the last vestiges of the Forrack fighting force, all dedicated and brave to the end. He considered a rallying speech before embarking on yet another suicide mission, but the determined looks on their faces told him it wasn't necessary.

He pulled his pulse rifle from the magnetic harness on his back. "Let's go," he said.

He led the unit to a narrow gap in the cave wall that led deeper into the mountain. The space wasn't wide enough for vehicles to venture. He glanced back at the blast doors where the tanks were ominously arrayed just inside the opening as the carnage raged beyond.

His hearts filled with pride knowing his soldiers were still carrying out their duties in the face of certain death. He felt the certainty too.

Mount Carnan might become my tomb, but Orrick Klemo will share it with me.

"They're running into the mountain Durmok," said the weapons specialist.

"I have eyes," Orrick spat, watching the tanks disappear into the mountain.

Two impacts caused the ship to shudder.

"Their artillery is targeting us and the Nova Flame," Ongbo reported, studying the tactical map displayed on the wall at his station.

"Break from the fleet and destroy the artillery positions nearest the mountain's base," he ordered.

The Fire Star banked sharply down and to the right, firing photon missiles at the artillery platforms. It repeated the maneuver several times until the platforms' shields were degraded. The final pass toppled each of the large turrets, sending them crashing to the ground as micro explosions cascaded from the tips of their barrels down to their control bases.

Orrick studied the viewscreen, scanning for a suitable landing zone. He tapped the pilot on the shoulder and indicated an area just west of the blast doors.

"Set us in that clearing," he said.

Ongbo called out from his station, "Do you mean to enter the mountain Durmok?"

He continued studying the screen without looking at Ongbo. "Yes."

"But we've no idea what awaits us."

He turned to Ongbo. "We saw the tanks go inside. We can handle them."

"But Durmok, it's undeniably a trap. What if they have more

fighter ships in there, or a battalion of soldiers waiting for us?"

He turned back to the screen and said, "Fighter ships are useless inside a mountain. They don't have many soldiers left anyway. We intercepted and destroyed their reinforcements coming from the inner planet. This is all that remains of their force, and they've scurried into a hole where they have no route of escape."

"What if we were to simply destroy the mountain and bury them in the rubble?"

Orrick spun around and slithered up to Ongbo, their faces practically touching. He flicked his tongue, grazing Ongbo's cheek. "Your questions are beginning to stink of cowardice Ongbo. You should mind yourself." He pointed at the screen while staring at Ongbo. "He is in that mountain, and I'm going to drag him out and make him watch his world burn. I wish to see the hopelessness in his eyes and taste the fresh tears on his cheeks. We're going in there, so ready the shock troops."

Ongbo nodded once. "Yes, Durmok."

The Fire Star and four Norvekian fighter ships touched down near the blast doors as the remaining fleet stayed engaged with the Forrack forces in the sky. Orrick, flanked by Ongbo, slid quickly down the exit ramp behind a squadron of heavily armed Cohannic soldiers. Four active modulating shield turrets glided along at the corners of their formation, creating a domed shield to protect their advance.

Intermittent fire coming from the mountain was deflected or absorbed by the dome as they moved closer to the entrance. Two more shielded squadrons, each numbering around one hundred and twenty soldiers, followed behind in a single column, while another hundred Norvekian troops remained behind to guard their rear flank.

As they approached the large blast doors, he gazed at the enormous opening. It was wide enough to easily accommodate his advancing column. Scorch marks marred the area around the doors where their force had fired on the retreating armored tanks. He could see inside the cavern, but the space appeared empty.

He spoke into his visored helmet, "Halt advance and deploy the siege turrets."

The column stopped and eight Cohannic shock troops jogged

through the shield dome carrying four turrets with hexagonal bases. They set them forty yards from the open blast doors before returning to the cover of the dome shield.

He waited until the soldiers were clear before issuing the order to fire.

The barrels of the four turrets swiveled in the direction of the mountain opening and simultaneously fired purple oblong projectiles. He watched expectantly for the projectiles to disappear into the mouth of the mountain and explode somewhere inside. Instead, the ordinance exploded upon contact with an unseen barrier between the open blast doors.

A soldier's voice shouted through his helmet. "Projector shield!"

The image of the empty cavern momentarily distorted before phasing out and revealing a line of armored tanks just inside the mountain's entrance. The doorway erupted with activity as the tanks fired all at once before speeding from the mountain, heading straight toward his position.

"Return fire!" he hissed.

He slithered his way toward the front of the formation as a hail of enemy fire slammed against the shield dome. He aimed his energy rifle toward the closest of the approaching tanks and fired several short bursts.

"Advance," he commanded.

The three squadrons rearranged from a single file to a side-by-side formation as they marched toward the oncoming tanks. Torrents of rifle fire streamed out toward the tanks as an onslaught of cannon fire was returned in response.

Soldiers fell around Orrick as his squad got nearer to the mountain base and their battered shield dome began to lose integrity. The turret and rifle fire had disabled or destroyed each of the enemy tanks that left the mountain refuge, but there were still a few defenders firing from within.

He spoke into his helmet, "Pasco?"

The Norvekian's distorted voice answered, "I'm here."

He fired a few more short bursts from his rifle. "Enemy tanks are holed up inside the mountain. Bring your ship around and fire photon missiles inside."

"On the way."

"And Pasco," he added, "I do not want the mountain destroyed."

"Understood."

Within moments, the Norvekian cruiser crested the horizon southwest of Orrick's position. There was a flash, then two orange spheres of light streaked overhead and through the blast doors. A large explosion issued from within the cavern carrying a raucous noise with it. The mountain shook violently as dirt and debris vaulted into the air and rocks cascaded from its peak to its base. He feared the entire thing was about to topple, but after a few moments, everything went still and quiet. Smoke and dust spewed from the blast doors, and no more enemy fire came from the cavern.

He waited for several moments before issuing the order to resume the advance. After traversing the last several meters without taking fire, he and his squadron crossed the threshold into Mount Carnan, while the other two squadrons remained outside the doors. He used his visor to scan the area for heat signatures, but all he detected were sporadic fires, super-heated scraps of metal, and burning bodies strewn throughout the space. Disappointment tugged at him as he imagined Altar's corpse among the charred bodies, or worse yet, vaporized altogether.

I want my trophy, he thought.

One of the shock troops called out from deeper inside the cavern. "Durmok, over here."

He slithered to the location. "What is it?"

The soldier pointed a claw at a narrow opening on the inner wall of the mountain. It looked to extend deep enough to escape the airstrike that decimated the cavern.

Ongbo sidled up next to him. "Do you think they've gone in there?"

He studied the narrow tunnel opening, flicking his tongue along the edges. "I'm certain of it."

"It would be foolish to go through there. We would only be able to proceed one at a time."

"Agreed," he said. "We'll entice them to exit on their own."

"What do you have in mind?" Ongbo asked.

"Bring me any children we've captured on this planet and line them up right outside this tunnel. I suspect they won't have the stomachs to watch me disembowel their young one by one."

A sinister smile spread across Ongbo's face. "Right away Durmok."

The eerie quiet of the cavern was shattered by a deafening explosion at the mountain's opening. The recently settled dust rose again into the air as rocks and soil fell from above. Another loud explosion caused the mountain to groan like a large, wounded beast. The sound of renewed fighting erupted outside; it was close. Orrick's helmet buzzed with incoherent chatter before Vernil's voice broke through.

"Get out of there now! They're trying to bring the mountain down."

Orrick quickly slithered back toward the mountain doors, but he arrived too late. Incoming torpedoes ripped the heavy metal doors from their hinges, and chunks of rock and metal zinged toward him and the nearby soldiers. He flattened himself to the ground just before a large, crescent-shaped piece of metal whipped over his head and decapitated the soldier behind him. Bodies fell all around the cavern as large boulders rained from above, crushing anything unfortunate enough to break their fall.

Ongbo's strong claws grabbed him underneath his bicep and hauled him upwards. "This way Durmok," he said pulling him along.

He followed behind Ongbo and a large group of troops scurrying away from where the entrance had been. The thunderous explosions ceased, but chunks of rock continued to fall all around. Two troops to his right were crushed when a large boulder fell on them. He slithered over twisted and mangled bodies as he struggled to see where the group of soldiers was headed. Then he saw the crevice in the inner wall looming and slowed his pace.

Ongbo looked back at him. "We have no choice now Durmok. It's the only way through."

He glanced back toward the collapsed entrance. The expanding plume of dust, and the troops struggling through the cascading rocks, told him that Ongbo spoke the truth. He quickened his pace again and slammed into the group of soldiers bottlenecked at the narrow opening. He and Ongbo grabbed the clamoring troops and slung them aside one by one.

"Make way for the Durmok!" Ongbo commanded.

He finally reached the front and hurried into the passageway, Ongbo close on his heels. He heard the rocks falling closer and closer until it seemed the entrance of the passage itself had collapsed.

His insides twisted as darkness engulfed the narrow space. He couldn't see how many soldiers were ahead of him, but he kept slamming his shoulder into the back of the soldier in front of him. He wanted to be out of this small space, no matter what awaited him on the other side.

After several moments, he thought he could hear the sound of energy blades and energy pistol fire up ahead. He pushed harder, but all forward movement had ceased. He was on the verge of panic as he considered that his conquest might end right here.

The great Durmok, Orrick Klemo, crushed to death in the crevice of an insignificant mountain on an insignificant planet.

Fueled by the thought, he shoved harder against the soldier in front of him and was relieved when the forward momentum resumed. He peeked over the troops ahead of him and saw the movement of lights through a slightly larger opening at the end of the tunnel. His soldiers were fighting their way out of the space. He reached down and snatched his short-handled energy blade from its sheath, his panic transforming into rage over his near demise.

He looked back at Ongbo and the other troops who managed to file into the narrow corridor behind them. "Ready yourselves, the enemy is just ahead."

Altar's back was pressed against the stone wall of the cavern. It wasn't nearly the size of the larger cavern at the entrance of the mountain, but it was big enough to allow his thirty men to spread out along the wall and aim at the gap, which was the only opening in the space. Small rocks fell from the ceiling of the cavern as the battle raged outside, and fine particles of dust swirled within the beams of the rifle-mounted flashlights.

Scratching noises from the craggy tunnel echoed throughout

the cavern. He held up an open hand, signaling his soldiers to hold, as a claw reached through the crack and grasped the lip of the tunnel. It was followed by a shoulder, then the head of the first Cohannic soldier.

He squeezed his hand into a fist, then leveled his energy rifle at the crevice. "Fire!" he shouted.

The Forrack troops fired at the Cohannic soldiers as they pushed through the hole in the wall. The first few that emerged went down quickly as they did not recognize the ambush in time. The ones who followed were more cautious about leaving the space. They'd activated their personal shields, protecting them from much of the random pistol and rifle fire. They shoved the downed troops through the opening and started firing back blindly, more to suppress than to hit anything.

Altar had no idea how many of the snakes had gotten into the passageway, but he'd hoped they could cut them down one at a time as they exited the tunnel.

A high-pitched whine reverberated throughout the space as two small metallic cylinders were tossed from the gap. They clattered on the ground and came to rest near the center of the cavern.

"Grenades!" Altar screamed.

The Forrack soldiers all dove to the ground just as the explosion ripped through the cavern, spewing shrapnel in every direction. The walls shook violently, and small stress fractures in the cave floor raced out in every direction.

The explosion created enough time for some of the Cohannic soldiers to escape the fissure and descend upon the stunned Forrack troops. Altar pushed up from the ground shaking his head to regain his bearings. As his ears gradually recovered from the sound of the blast, he could just barely make out the static sounds of energy blades cutting through the thick, dusty air. He thought he could hear something else coming from close behind him.

One of the Forrack soldiers was shouting at him, "Commander!"

He spun around to see the blue blur of an energy blade swinging at his face, and he raised his right forearm above his head just in time to parry the blow off his shield armor. The force drove him down to one knee as the Cohannic soldier prepared to swing the blade again. He dodged to one side, avoiding the second swing. Ignoring the searing pain in his left shoulder, he pressed the muzzle of his energy rifle into his attacker's midsection and fired six short bursts. One of the last shots penetrated the soldier's shield, and the energy blade dropped from his claw as his tail stiffened and he crashed hard to the ground.

The quaking intensified, and a guttural rumbling noise descended from overhead. The hairline fissures in the cave floor were now racing up the cave walls, widening as they traveled.

The whole thing is coming down, he thought.

He looked back toward the gap in the wall, and simultaneous pangs of excitement and fear jolted him as Orrick himself emerge from the crevice. He looked to be a full foot taller than the Cohannic troops around him, and his gold and black armor left no doubt for Altar that he was looking at the same soldier who'd decapitated Sul Copand on Dullestoon Station.

After all that had happened, he was now finally laying eyes on the Durmok himself. The rage swelled inside of him.

Dullestoon, Caristo, Averan-Ginest, Telsia, Yorinar, and now my home, he thought. *Thousands dead, and millions of lives destroyed because of you!*

He charged in Orrick's direction, pushing his way through the throngs of soldiers hacking and shooting each other. He reached Orrick just as the Durmok was extracting his energy blade from the neck of a Forrack soldier. He lowered his shoulder into Orrick's side at full speed, sending the Durmok sprawling into the nearest wall. As Orrick writhed on the ground, attempting to right himself, he aimed his energy rifle at his head.

Thousands upon thousands dead. Now it's your turn!

A forceful shudder shook the ground just as he pressed the trigger. He lost his footing, sending his shot crashing into the wall just above Orrick's head.

A deep chasm ruptured the ground in between him and Orrick. The floor of the cavern convulsed under his feet as the crack in the floor widened and both Forrack and Cohannic troops tumbled into the breach.

He stumbled, then regained his balance only to be bumped from behind by another falling soldier. The impact knocked the energy rifle from his hand and sent him over the edge of the opening. He grabbed hold of the ledge, preventing himself from following his rifle into the pit. His shoulder protested and his muscles burned as he held onto the edge with all his strength.

Darkness engulfed the scene as the energy rifles and the glowing blue energy blades cascaded into the expanding hole in the cavern floor. The combatants were now fighting against the crumbling mountain instead of against each other.

The thunderous crashes of falling debris assaulted his ears, but he was starting to hear a new sound over the noise. It was loud, and it was coming from beneath. It sounded like rushing water.

The river, he realized.

The soldiers all seemed to hear the river too as many of them purposely leaped into the hole to escape the falling rubble. He considered his options, but the decision was made for him when a weight fell onto his back. His grip on the ledge loosened, and he turned to see Orrick's face inches from his own.

Orrick's forked tongue slipped from his mouth and back in. "Into the abyss we go," he said.

Orrick slammed his claw onto Altar's wrist, breaking his grip. The Commander and the Durmok dropped into the cold darkness.

Altar regained consciousness amid a fit of coughing up frigid river water. He was on a riverbank with his left cheek buried in mud. He was soaking wet and lying on his side shivering uncontrollably with his hands bound behind him in stasis constraints. He had no idea how long he'd been there.

"Commander, you're awake. I was beginning to fear we'd lost you," Orrick said.

The Durmok's thick tail bored a trench in the mud as he slithered into Altar's line of sight. Orrick reached down and assisted him onto his knees. He looked around and saw several other Forrack soldiers positioned as he was, covered in filth with their chins hanging to their chests. He counted nine in all, including Damu, who was kneeling right beside him with his head down. Two Cohannic frigates and a Norvekian fighter ship were idling several yards downstream, and scores of enemy troops roamed about, dragging more bodies from the water.

A distant rumble to the west drew his attention to a massive dust cloud rising into the sky. The peak of Mount Carnan was nowhere to be seen. The atmosphere was choked with smoke, and particles of ash fell like snow. The smell of damp earth and spilled ethnelene filled the air.

He turned back to Orrick, who was also taking in the surreal scene. Without looking away from the dust cloud, Orrick said, "I admire you, Commander. You did all you could to save your people, more than most would have, and certainly more than your superiors. I saw how they ran away at Yorinar, but you stayed and fought." Orrick looked at him. "You were a worthy opponent."

"Let my soldiers go," Altar said in a weak voice, followed by another bout of coughing.

Orrick ignored the request. "One thing still baffles me. Just how did you pull off that feat at Yorinar? I've never seen anything like that before."

He was still shivering but said nothing.

"No matter," Orrick said. "Everything worked out as expected. Despite your best efforts to the contrary, here we all are, exactly where we were destined to be. Oh, and I have a gift for you."

The Durmok raised a claw and one of the Cohannic troops approached with a metallic chest. The soldier set it in front of Altar and slithered away without a word. He eyed the chest, afraid to know its contents.

Orrick bent down and grasped the lid. "You, like me, are a proud soldier Commander. But unlike me, you take your orders from others. I know it must have been difficult for you to be beholden to such cowards." He lifted the lid and pushed the chest toward Altar.

Altar stared at the severed heads for a long time. They were neatly arranged facing him. General Salvon's head was on the left and Sub Supreme Commander Mortkath's head was on the right. In the middle was the head of Supreme Commander Gailius Rhandu. His eyes were open amid his sagging facial features, and his pale tongue lolled from his open mouth.

Orrick closed the lid. "They surrendered when they figured all was lost, and they each died a coward's death. At the end of their lives, they begged for mercy. They found none. My apologies, but I was unable to procure the head of your other general. He was killed when we destroyed his ship, and his body wasn't recovered. Now it's your turn Commander. Are you going to gravel at my tail and beg for mercy?"

He looked up at Orrick. "All I ask is for my soldiers to be spared. They are not cowards; they fought with honor."

Orrick looked down the row of kneeling Forrack soldiers. "They did, and I shall reward them with honorable deaths. They'll go into whatever afterlife they believe in with their heads intact."

Orrick nodded and Cohannic soldiers took positions behind each of the kneeling Forrack.

"Sir," Damu said from beside him.

Altar turned and looked at his friend and fellow soldier.

Damu's eyes filled with tears as he spoke, "Because of you, my family is safe. That's what all of this was for wasn't it? We didn't lose here. We always knew how it would end for us. It has been the greatest honor to serve under your command."

He had no words in response, he simply looked Damu in the eyes and offered a simple nod.

Orrick raised a gauntleted claw into the air and the Cohannic troops simultaneously fired their energy rifles into the soldiers' backs. Altar flinched at the sound, but his eyes remained fixed on Damu. Damu's eyes momentarily widened as he stared at him. The life gradually drained from his face before his body fell face down into the mud alongside the eight others.

Altar let out a guttural scream as tears streamed from his eyes and dropped to the ash-covered riverbank.

Orrick leaned in close, and his forked tongue slowly protruded from his mouth as he licked at the salty tears on Altar's face.

He rose and stared down at Altar's slumped form. "You'll remain alive to witness my conquest, but you'll have to watch from Caristo." He turned to two of the nearby Cohannic troops and said, "Get him on the ship back to the Tyros system. Instruct Fallis D'Pah to take good care of him until I return."

The Cohannic soldiers hauled Altar to his feet and began dragging him toward the waiting ship. He glanced back at the bodies of his soldiers lying on the muddy bank, wishing he was lying next to them.

Death is a mercy, he thought.

CHAPTER TWENTY-NINE
Zanna

Regalus: Chalpin Star System

Zanna ascended the ramp of the platform to where a single metal capsule sat at its center. She'd been here countless times before, in her dreams. This wasn't a dream, though it wasn't quite real either. There was, of course, no platform, nor was there a capsule. It was all a mental projection she'd conjured up to bring a sense of familiarity to this strange place.

As she stood next to the capsule, she looked back over her shoulder at the spectators. Her mother and Dayvyn were front and center. Her mother's smile radiated pure joy, and Dayvyn was grinning from ear to ear.

The others fanned out behind them in an endless array of smiling faces. Though she only recognized a scant few of the onlookers, she saw them all. Nineteen million, one hundred and thirteen thousand, two hundred and fourteen souls stared back at her with hope gleaming in their eyes. She was the one, and they all knew it. She would fulfill her destiny and bring the Great Prophecy to fruition.

Through my actions, their sacrifices won't have been in vain, she thought.

She glanced once more at the smiling faces of her mother and brother, then turned to see Zurin standing opposite her, still in the form of a kindly old Cortaran professor.

"You needn't assume that form any longer," she said. "I

understand now what I must do."

He offered a warm smile as his form slowly morphed into a misty apparition.

"Thank you," she said.

"What have we done to elicit your thanks?"

She glanced at the awaiting pod. "I never would have made it this far if it weren't for your guidance."

"We fear that this is only the beginning of your journey child. You have much yet to see, and even more to learn."

"That's nothing to be afraid of," she said. "For so long, I've lived with dreams that were rooted in things that I didn't truly understand. We revere you as gods, but the fact you aren't doesn't mean that we're misguided. Even you believe in the Prophecy, and that I am the one meant to fulfill it. I promised myself that I would return to Vizaria, and nothing that I've experienced here leads me to believe that I must break that promise. I intend to return, and I intend to rid Vizaria of this Cohannic menace."

Zurin's misty form stared at her for a long time. It was as if he was searching for any doubt in her conviction. Then he said, "So much yet to discover."

The mist dissipated and she was left standing alone on the platform. She looked around and saw that the crowd had vanished. She nodded to herself.

"I must embark on this part of the journey alone," she said softly to herself.

She climbed into the capsule with all of the certainty one could muster for such an uncertain path. She laid back and closed her eyes. After a few moments, she felt a tingling sensation all over her body.

Before she vanished into the void, she recalled Zurin's words:
This is only the beginning.

EPILOGUE
Zelle

<u>Vorxsis: Naruk Star System</u>

Zelle Past stood atop the Palatial Spire staring at the speck of light hanging ominously in the black sky. She longed to reach out and grasp it. If she could've, she would've taken it in the palm of her hand and crushed it into dust. It was a forsaken place, and it had taken one of the only things she truly ever loved in life, her son.

Wisps of wind danced through the cluster of thin mountains, softly howling a familiar song. She loved it up here, away from the demands of leadership and the expectations that accompanied absolute authority. Up here, in the peaceful quiet, she found it easier to weigh her decisions or plot her next course of action. Tonight, however, was different. Her decision had already been made, and she was resolute in its necessity. Tonight was a time for mourning, a time for reflection, a time for second-guessing.

Why did I send him to that wretched place? Was the reward worth all that was lost? Did he cry out for me in his final moments? Should I recall the others?

She'd heard the rumors of the reappearance of the Cohannic. Then she began receiving reports from her agents that the tales were true, and the scourge had indeed returned. She always knew they would. She'd never met a Cohannic, but she could tell they had a similar mindset to her race. They wanted to establish an empire and disentangle their destiny from Vizaria's.

The Velderians had accomplished that feat centuries ago, and she never doubted it was the right choice for her race. Now they controlled a vast empire that the rest of the spiral arm dared not challenge. So, in that way, she could empathize with the Cohannic. But empathy was all she could muster for the snakes. Their clumsy methods of brutality and head-on aggression painted a picture of a colossal defeat.

Apparently, they learned nothing from their past failures, she thought.

Despite their poor approach to empire building, there was no doubting that the return of the Cohannic had caused quite the stir throughout the spiral arm. She needed to know how the Sukarians would respond, so she sent Stalik to infiltrate the Council, and now he was dead. Her only offspring was gone.

The heavy door creaked open behind her and Galginesh stepped onto the balcony, hands clasped in front of him. "He's here Your Majesty."

She continued staring at the point of light. "Show him up Galginesh."

"Very well Majesty," he said turning to leave.

She learned much during the time her son was mimicking Allyon Corbo. She discovered that the Council was fractured, and actions to thwart the invasion were slow to materialize. This favored the Cohannic and weakened the Council of Seven. But just as she was considering how best to proceed, she received the news that her son was killed, murdered after a failed assassination attempt.

Now, the one they called Vicaryn Gayne was in control of the Council. She was almost certain it was he who'd fabricated the lie that it was her son who attacked the Humans. But why? She would have answers soon enough, answers and revenge.

Footsteps padded through her bedchamber and the balcony door opened again. Galginesh stepped forward and said, "May I introduce Cressix, of the Eastern Whisperlands."

Galginesh offered a slight bow and stepped aside.

Cressix stood in the doorway of the balcony. He was in the form of a Korchak male dressed in worship attire. His pale blue eyes seemed to draw in the scant starlight, almost making them glow. He took two steps, then kneeled before Zelle.

"Highness, you summoned, I came."

She motioned to Galginesh. "Leave us."

Galginesh bowed deeply. "Yes, Majesty."

"You may rise," she said to Cressix.

He stood as she walked around him, admiring his form.

"This detail is truly astonishing," she said. "How long can you hold this shape?"

"I have yet to find a limit to my longevity, Your Highness. I have maintained this particular form since last evening's rising of the moons."

"Remarkable," she said as she caressed his cheekbones and chin. "I've heard tales of your abilities. If they are true, that places you among the most prolific form changers the Velderian empire has ever known."

"The Whisperlands tend to live up to its name when it comes to tales and legends. Whispers are ever plentiful."

She smirked. "Tell me Cressix, was your choice of this form intended to demonstrate your talent, or does it carry a deeper meaning?"

He gazed deep into her eyes. "Take a good look at this face, Your Highness. Study it closely. Does it in any way look familiar to you?"

She scrutinized his features, examining the slight point at the crown of the head, the light blue eyes, the full lips.

"This is not a face I have ever seen before," she concluded.

"When I learned of Stalik Vin's death, I understood it would be of great importance to you to know who was responsible for his demise. I took it upon myself to make certain… inquiries. I hope I was not too far out of line in this way."

He paused and looked at her as if asking permission to finish his story.

"What did you discover?" she prompted, eager to know what he'd learned.

"I haven't found out who gave the order, but I do know by whose hand your son was slain."

"And who would that be?" she asked.

He leaned in close to her. "I am wearing the face of the one who murdered your son Your Highness. He goes by the name

Dannus Prie, and he is the servant of Prefect Vicaryn Gayne, the new leader of the Council of Seven."

The words pierced her chest as he spoke them. She drew back and peered into the pale blue eyes. "What price must I pay to have you bring my son's murderer to me?"

Cressix donned a crooked smile on Dannus Prie's face. "I would never request compensation from you, Your Highness. You need only command me, and I will see it done."

She continued burrowing her gaze deeper and deeper into those light blue, murderous eyes until she could nearly see the shape of her revenge taking form.

These are the eyes of my son's murderer, she thought.

She turned from him and looked upon that distant point of light in the night sky, Aegus. The place where her son met his end.

"Do it," she commanded.

Acknowledgments

Writing a novel is hard work! I've had this epic story rolling around in my head for nearly a decade, and I've recently committed myself to put my thoughts into readable words. So now you have read the first book of the five-book series. I hope you enjoyed reading it as much as I enjoyed writing it.

When I used to hear the term "self-published", I thought of a simple process of someone writing a story, then putting it out there for the world to consume and ultimately critique. This process has shown me that there is a LOT more to it than that. Yes, I self-published this novel, but I had loads of support along the way.

First and foremost, my lovely wife, TaWanda, has been an invaluable source of inspiration and motivation at every step, and I most certainly could not have gotten to this point without her. She suffered through my endless revisions, edits, and silly ideas, and she even got me over a major plot hurdle when I was hopelessly stuck. I love you, babe.

I also consulted every one of my children at some point during this process. They contributed insights into the story, book cover, and character arcs. So I send a big thank you to Triston, Te'Rione, Natalia, Tatiyana, Ethan, and Tatum. I love you guys.

I have too many family and friends to name, but I want to thank every one of you who supported me throughout this process. If you read this book and happen to come across names or numbers that seem familiar to you, just know that it's probably not a coincidence (wink).

Finally, a big thanks to my cover designer, Aaron, and my beta readers, Danica and Nina. Those were two huge aspects of the process where I needed major outside help, and you guys came through.

As I said, writing a novel is hard work, but I found the entire process to be an overall pleasurable experience, and I'm looking forward to taking the journey over and over again.

Thank You

About the Author

J.B. Johnson is a lover of science fiction and fantasy stories. By day, he's a dedicated husband and father, by night he's a dreamer. He also sometimes finds himself dreaming during the day. Like most science fiction and fantasy lovers, some of his biggest inspirations come from the magnificent worlds of Star Trek, Star Wars, Lord of the Rings, and A Song of Ice and Fire, among many others.

The Regalus Chronicles: RISING TIDE is the first of five novels he has planned for the Regalus Chronicles series. Book Two, WAVE of DESTRUCTION, will be coming soon. So please follow him on social media and consider signing up for his monthly newsletter to stay up to date on his latest projects. All of his links can be found on his author website: www.authorjbjohnson.com

www.ingramcontent.com/pod-product-compliance
Lightning Source LLC
Chambersburg PA
CBHW020146310726

48970CB00006B/2033